I0552373

CHASING MAGIC

A CWPH Fantasy Anthology
Featuring 22 International Authors

ISBN-10: 1-946275-02-6
ISBN-13: 978-1-946275-02-8

DEDICATION

This book is dedicated to all writers who aspire to be published. Make connections, reach out to other writers, and dare to dream. This book contains 22 stories selected from over forty submissions. We have chosen works that best represent the theme of magic to highlight the imagination of each talented writer. Some of our contributors are very established writers, and some are newcomers. Keep writing, keep believing, and keep dreaming!

ABOUT CW PUBLISHING HOUSE

CWPH was founded in 2015, dedicated to publishing CWC novels. Due to numerous requests, we have opened our doors to submissions from completed collaborative novels and will work exclusively with collaborative novels written by two or more authors. CWPH has also arranged a number of anthologies, with more to come. To learn more about our books and our authors please visit:

www.cwpublishinghouse.com

A Note from the Editor

Chasing Magic is the fourth anthology by CW Publishing House and our first in the Fantasy genre. Our first three anthologies were holiday-themed horror stories, so naturally there were a lot of unexpected twists and combinations. The stories in this anthology offer the same quality of surprising, heart-wrenching, and fantastical tales.

Not surprisingly, most of the works in this collection also have a certain level of darkness to them, featuring the thin line between reality and fantasy. One of the beautiful things about this compilation is that, even through worlds, characters, and magical devices nonexistent in real life—and present only in dreams and the imagination—the heart of every piece rings true to what we as readers feel on a consistent basis. These stories strike the core of what it means to be alive, to care for something, to experience loss, love, and even joy. A few of these pieces have brought tears to my eyes even after the second, third, and fourth time visiting them. Some have given me chills, and others have made me smile for hours after reading them.

I hope you enjoy these beautiful, enticing, carefully crafted pieces as much as the authors enjoyed writing them. We did, and we're so honored to have this opportunity to share them with you.

Kathrin Hutson

CONTENTS

Morríghan
by Stacey Jaine McIntosh

The wind whipped through her hair, tossing the dark strands over her face and obscuring her vision. High above the sea on the rocky crag, the aerie was full.

Nemain settled on Morgan's shoulder, the bird's talons digging into the soft leather pauldron. She had become so used to it now, she didn't even wince as the bird took its time hopping about on her shoulder before settling down.

As she turned her head to look Nemain straight in the eye, the bird cocked its head to one side, its beady onyx eyes staring back at her. "Where are your sisters?" Morgan asked.

Nemain cawed once before raising one wing upwards, just as two more birds flew in. They circled once around Morgan's head, the beat of their wings echoing in her ears. Badb and Macha landed one after the other on the leather gauntlet covering her left arm from her fingertips up to her elbow.

Smiling, Morgan gave a brief nod to each bird in turn. As she picked up the reins, she nudged the dapple-grey gelding on with her thighs. Being careful to navigate her way down the steep path that had been worn into the cliff face after years of repetitive use, she headed across the field for home.

It was true; she could have spent all day up at the aerie, looking out at the sea below while observing the hatchlings, but Morgan knew if she did, she was only putting off the inevitable. Eventually, she would have to see Arthur, and while she quite enjoyed the solitude in having only the birds for company, she feared his wrath more.

Arthur, like most fey, was deathly afraid of birds, ravens in particular. It was said to see one was a bad omen; to lay eyes on three signified one's own death. So superstitious was Arthur that when he and Morgan had been presented the murder of ravens as a wedding gift, he'd threatened to spill their blood then and there in the reception hall.

What had been seen couldn't be unseen, however; Arthur was destined to die.

Had it been anyone else but the Queen of Camelot's kin who presented such a gift to the newlyweds, the lives of Badb, Macha, and Nemain wouldn't have been spared at all.

Pressing her thighs to the gelding's flanks, she worked him up to a trot before she gave the animal its head and allowed him to lengthen his stride until he paced at an even canter. Spying Arthur not far from the castle, she brought the horse under control, knowing full well what was in store for her should feathers wind up on his clothing.

Bringing the ravens out of the aerie at dusk was not entirely wise, but Morgan was never one to play by anybody else's rules but her own.

"Those *creatures* belong in the aerie, not out here by castle walls," Arthur said, facing her.

"And *fey* belong in children's storybooks," Morgan spat. "I'd hate to have to tell the bearer of such a generous gift that my *husband* doesn't appreciate their effort to find something so unique."

The Faerie Prince snorted indignantly at her stubbornness. "Just keep the damn things away from me!"

A smile crept over her face, and for the first time since she had been free of the crystal cave, she was happy. "We mustn't kill the messenger, Arthur."

As Morgan dismounted, Badb took flight, circling just above Arthur's head and getting dangerously close to touching him. Morgan looked up just as the bird plucked out one of its own feathers. It fell, landing on the shoulder of Arthur's grey coat.

Arthur turned his head to look at it, and Badb resettled herself on Morgan's forearm and began preening. Morgan kept completely still, watching Arthur pick up the feather by the quill and crush it in his fist.

"I won't tell you again, Morgan," he said, letting the damaged feather fall through his fingers. "The next time I see so much as a feather, I'll wring their bloody necks, wedding gift or not."

Badb cawed in alarm, and Nemain and Macha soon joined in on her song. Morgan could only glare at her husband in shock as he stormed off back towards the castle. "Hush, my pretties. It is not the Prince we want."

She bent down to pick up the feather, then turned her attention back to her gelding. Taking the reins and halter from him, she allowed her fingers to trail along the horse's muzzle. When she delivered a sharp slap to the gelding's rump, it startled forward, whickering a little, before running free of the castle.

"Arthur will have the stableboy's head for that horse being out, you know, Morgan," the Queen of Camelot said, stepping out of the shadows

Morgan jumped, cursing loudly as the Queen approached her. Their relationship was tenuous at the best of times. "I have it on good authority that neither the stableboy nor Arthur will even notice the horse is missing come morning."

"Oh?"

"There will be other things to worry about than runaway horses and errant stableboys."

"You've had a sending, haven't you?" There was panic in the Queen's voice that Morgan disliked.

"The sight has returned to me, yes."

"Why now?" the Queen blurted. "Forgive me, but I thought after all this time, it was no longer a burden to you."

"I don't know *why now*," Morgan snapped, "but it's certainly no burden. Of course you wouldn't see that. Would you, *mother*?" She brushed past the Queen and up the cobblestone steps of the castle. It wasn't until she was inside that she drew breath. *It will be done tonight*, she thought. *Uther Pendragon will be dead by morning.*

"Morgan!" the Queen called after her, but Morgan feigned deafness. There was nothing left to say. As far as Morgan was concerned, her mother had died the same day Uther Pendragon had stepped into their lives and taken a husband and father from those who had loved and cherished him the most.

***

Alone in her chambers, Morgan took the crushed black feather Arthur had discarded and laid it out on the altar before turning back to the leatherbound book before her.

She knew the page well enough by rote that she didn't have to look at it. The invocation of

Morríghan was fairly simple as far as such things went. All that was required was a raven's feather, raw meat, and wine.

Having not had the time nor the inclination to make any kind of animal sacrifice by her own hands, she had no choice but to take a small dagger to the flesh of her palm and make a cut. The blood welled to the surface; the ruby-red liquid trickled out and down her forearm. Using the wine goblet, she caught enough of her own blood to serve as a decent substitution for the raw animal flesh.

The rustling of wings broke her concentration, and her gaze shifted to the three ravens now perched on the large wooden stand by the window.

The candles—one red, one white, and one black—flickered in the early evening gloom that had settled over the castle and Camelot. It was an eerie calm and the only thing she found she'd grown to like since coming here. As she moved silently to stand before the altar, her mind filtered back to the last day she'd seen her father alive. She never did get to say goodbye.

Raising her arms wide above her head, her feet set shoulder-width apart, she began the invocation. She didn't need a book for what came next.

"I call to you Morríghan,
Goddess of Death, Giver of Rebirth and Purveyor of Strife!

I invoke thee.
Restore the Balance between Life and Death.
That is my will,
So mote it be!"

The candles flickered again, more violently than before, and the two oil lamps which had been lit were snuffed out. Morgan's chamber was now thrown into darkness, the sun having set as she'd prepared for the ritual.

"Such a slight young thing. Why, I'm surprised. Whatever possessed you to call on the likes of I, the Morríghan, Morgan of the Faeries?" the Goddess—in human form—asked, standing before her.

Morgan opened her mouth to speak, but no words came out.

Scanning the room, she felt oddly vulnerable. Something was missing. *Nemain? Macha? Badb?* She couldn't see them anywhere. There was no rustle of wings or cawing; actually, there was no sound at all, not even the sound of her own blood rushing through her ears as her heartrate accelerated.

"Did you think the bearer of such a gift completely naïve, Morgan? You may speak," the Goddess said. "I don't bite. I leave that up to the ravens."

"I d-didn't k-know what to think," Morgan stammered. "Arthur is afraid of ravens. Rumour has it they foretell when a person is to die."

"One of the fey taking stock in silly little superstitions? How awfully mundane."

"It's not true then?" Morgan eyed the Goddess with wary unease. It felt very much as if the Goddess was laughing at her.

"If it were, the fey would have ceased to exist long before now," the Goddess replied. "But you didn't invoke my presence merely to talk semantics of when and how Prince Arthur of Camelot is to die, did you? Or *did* you?"

Morgan shook her head vehemently. "I wish to seek revenge on the one who took my father from me when I was a girl. I wish to see Uther Pendragon dead!"

"And see yourself on the Throne of Camelot while at it, I suppose."

"My only goal is to see Uther Pendragon dead for taking my father from me!"

The Goddess laughed. "Well… it's good to see you've got spirit. I was beginning to think I was wasting my time." Morgan's eyes widened. A single candle flickered to life, making her jump. "Yes. I'll help you. Be sure to tell Arthur he's not going to die… or don't. Whichever you prefer. It is of no consequence to me. He will of course die one day, rest assured. Nothing lives forever, not even the fey."

"I've not seen his death," Morgan whispered.

"A good thing too, I suspect. For it is not a pretty one," the Goddess said. "You'll need Nightshade mixed with equal parts Yarrow and Rue.

14

Grind it up as fine as you can and slip it into his wine. It'll be a quick death."

Unlike my father's, Morgan thought bitterly, spinning around as she heard the familiar rustle of wings. Despite what she had heard, no ravens appeared.

Turning back towards the altar, Morgan pulled dried Yarrow, Rue, and Nightshade from the cupboard beneath. Placing them in the small stone mortar, she worked quickly with the pestle, grinding the herbs up small enough so they would be undetectable once slipped into Uther's wine. And when she was satisfied, she tipped the newly ground herbs into a small glass vial and corked it.

Somebody knocked at her closed door, startling her; quickly she gathered up the vial and slipped it into her shoe to hide it. Crossing the room, she opened the door to find Prince Arthur standing before her.

Peering inside, he noticed the distinct lack of birds. "What did you do? Turn them invisible?"

Morgan smirked. "No, the ravens are in the aerie." At least, she hoped they were. "Had I possessed the sort of magic necessary to turn *things* invisible, Arthur, I would have started with you."

Prince Arthur chuckled. "You certainly enjoy keeping a man on his toes, don't you?"

Morgan didn't respond, just stepped across the threshold, pulling the heavy door shut behind her.

Sidestepping Arthur, she walked in front of him all the way to the private banquet hall.

***

The long table had already been set by the kitchen staff and the wine poured. Morgan eyed Uther's place at the head of the table nervously. Checking to see if Arthur was coming up behind her, she walked towards it and quickly retrieved the glass vial from her shoe. Tipping the contents into the goblet, she tucked the empty vial back in her shoe, and just as she was about to stand, the sight came upon her.

She would have dropped to the floor if it hadn't been for Arthur, arriving just in time to catch her.

"Morgan, are you all right?"

"I'm fine," she said breathlessly, pulling herself out of his embrace to stand alone on unsteady feet.

"What did you see?"

"I don't…" Morgan paused upon hearing the voices of her mother Igraine and stepfather Uther as they entered the hall.

"I thought you two would have been seated by now. Is something wrong, Morgan?" Igraine asked.

"No, nothing," Morgan said quickly before Arthur had a chance to interject on her behalf.

"Morgan…" Arthur's tone was pleading. That he should care for her seemed strange, given how he'd treated her in the past.

"Leave it!" She snapped taking her seat.

Arthur huffed but otherwise remained silent as he walked to his place at the table. Seated next to Morgan, he made a point of looking at her, but she kept her gaze on the lit candelabra before them and ignored him.

***

When Morgan awoke, she was acutely aware that somebody was watching her from across the room. Standing in the doorway was Arthur, one arm leaning against the doorframe. It looked a little like he hadn't slept much, if at all, the night before.

Morgan rubbed the sleep from her eyes and sat up, the comforter falling to her waist, exposing the white of her long-sleeved nightgown.

"My father died in the night, you know. The physician is saying he was poisoned. Poisoned by whom, however, remains a mystery."

There was a hint of something—disdain, perhaps—that Morgan didn't like. "You think I had something to do with your father's death?"

"Did you?" Arthur accused without missing a beat

"Does it matter?" she asked, outraged.

"Of course it matters! He's my father and King! Do you think I wouldn't want justice carried out against whoever murdered my father?"

"So we do have something in common after all. I was beginning to think we'd never find any common ground," Morgan said.

"Now is not the time for games, Morgan. If you had any part in this—"

"You'll do what? Throw me into some other prison for another ten years?" she asked. "You could try, but I think you'll find that you'll fail."

Arthur sighed, his frustration mounting. They both knew he would get nowhere with his interrogation. "What did you see at dinner last night? In your vision, I mean?"

"Do you really want to know?"

"Yes," he whispered. His voice was so soft that Morgan wondered if somehow he already knew.

"I saw your death," she said, looking him directly in the eye. "Morríghan was right. It's not pretty."

Arthur swallowed stiffly upon hearing the words flying from Morgan's mouth. "You called on the Goddess of War just to see the back of my father?"

"Your father killed my father," Morgan stressed. "I'd say we're even."

"Even?" Arthur asked. "You waited ten long years to get your revenge. Why? I don't understand."

"You don't have to understand my motives, Arthur."

"Are you insane?" Arthur asked. "It's the only reason I can think of to explain your actions."

"Ten years shut away behind cave walls, one becomes many things," Morgan said. "Insane is not one of them."

"If you say so, Morgan," Arthur said, casting his gaze over her chamber. Despite having admitted to the crime, there was no visible sign that she had done anything in this room.

"Find what you were looking for, Arthur?" she asked sweetly, her gaze following his.

"I was wondering how you managed it."

"If I told you that, Arthur, I'd have to kill you," she said, leaning in close. "And as much as I'd like to, I simply don't have the heart for physical violence."

"I should have somebody cut out your heart for what you've done," Arthur hissed. "Killing the King is treason. I could have you locked up."

"As my King wishes." Morgan fell into a mock curtsey before him, eyes raised to meet his.

"I am not King yet, nor are you Queen," Arthur said. "And you won't be should anyone in Court get wind of what you've done."

Morgan smirked. "And why should I care about anybody at Court? What have the fair folk done for me, except wreak havoc on my life? I wish them no ill—"

Arthur interrupted her by kissing her, crushing his lips to hers. Morgan allowed herself, only for the briefest of moments, to be caught up in the feel of his lips before breaking the kiss.

"And once more, she rejects me," Arthur murmured.

"I reject you, *Arthur*, because you've been nothing but—"

"Kind and hospitable, given the circumstances. I was gentle, wasn't I? On our wedding night?"

Their wedding. It seemed so long ago now, but it had scarcely been two weeks. Of course he'd been gentle, but that wasn't what kept her from his bed, or from inviting him into hers. She'd been too busy planning how to kill Uther. She had never in her wildest dreams thought the Morríghan would have manifested in order to help her. It had been seamless; nobody suspected her, not even Arthur, until after the damage was done, and it was unlikely he would ever say anything given his desire for the throne and the threat of his own imminent death hanging over his head.

Morgan wondered what it felt like to know that death was close, but to not have any idea when it was coming. Did it consume Arthur just as revenge for her father's death had consumed her?

"Yes," she murmured.

"But?" Arthur prompted, eyebrow raised.

Morgan shook her head. She couldn't tell him.

Wouldn't tell him. "Nothing."

"Morgan," he growled.

"You don't scare me. You never have," she said, thinking back to the first time she'd met him. She'd only been a child then. They both had.

"Yes, I do," he said, his finger tracing her lower lip as it quivered. "You're trembling."

"I am not!" Morgan shrank away from his touch. Closing her eyes, she breathed in slowly. The fair folk had powerful magic at their disposal, and while she knew the inner workings of magic, her father had been mortal. Her mother too, despite the magic flowing through Igraine's blood, just as it did her own.

***

Camelot was burning.

Avalon was under attack ... from Dragons.

The very creatures who graced the banners flying high and proud on the many flagpoles were going to bring about its end. The symbol of Pendragon no longer stood for power, peace, and protection, but death and destruction. Their very existence in the skies above spelled ruin for all of Camelot, not just its King.

Was this what the Morríghan spoke of when she foresaw Arthur's death? Morgan couldn't be sure.

Laying a hand on her stomach, she felt the restless child within, as if it too sensed the calamity surrounding the world outside the womb.

She doubted the Morríghan would help her twice, and Arthur wouldn't suffer her insolence for long—not that she cared what Arthur thought of her. She'd sooner take up residence in a nunnery than carry his favour.

Even as she thought it, Morgan knew she was lying to herself. Arthur was King and Arthur was fey, and the fey did terrible things and weren't to be crossed, Morgan knew. Arthur's fears were few, and until a few months ago, his only fear was ravens. Now that he feared his own mortality, Morgan wondered if he—as she did—feared the Dragons.

She hadn't seen Badb, Nemain, or Macha for near on a fortnight now. It was unlike them to disappear, and she didn't think the Morríghan would have forsaken her so soon after announcing her presence. Unless the Morríghan, like Arthur, had fears of her own and those fears included Dragons. Did Gods have fears as mortals themselves had fears? Morgan didn't know, and she wasn't about to find out, sitting here holed up in the castle.

Outside, the sun faded in the sky. Arthur would be returning soon, and her heart filled with dread. Their relationship was strained. The prospect of war just made it real. As she stepped out into the courtyard and saw all the lamps were lit, her breath caught in her throat. Until now, she had only heard about the Dragon attacks. Seeing it for herself firsthand was far too intense. Directly above her in the sky, clearly outlined despite the fact that the sun was rapidly disappearing below the horizon, was a Dragon.

"What are you doing?" Arthur asked abruptly, appearing as if out of nowhere. Curse the darkness, she hadn't seen him, and now she was flustered. Perhaps he wouldn't notice. "You're supposed to be inside... locked up safe and sound. I won't have my *son* endangered. You *promised*, Morgan."

"I did no such thing!" she raged. She knew better than to make promises to anyone, especially Arthur. "And don't you see? Camelot burns. You need all the help you can get."

"But you're with child," he said. "*My* child!"

Morgan's gaze shifted up to meet his. He had yet to dismount from his horse. "I am no less capable, despite my condition, than you, Arthur," she snapped. "If I stay, the *child* and I both burn."

Arthur's mouth fell open at her outburst before closing. "Will you be calling upon anymore Gods to do your bidding, then, or will it just be you, wielding the killing blow this time?"

"I'll only be calling upon them if it pleases them to be called upon." Morgan plastered a fake smile across her face, one finger crooked, beckoning one of the stableboys closer. "Ready my horse. I ride with my husband and his entourage."

Her lips turned down at the word husband. It left a sour taste in her mouth, knowing their shared history, knowing that Arthur was capable of many things, but love wasn't one of them. War suited him. In war, he could be as ruthless as he liked and get away with it. It was everyday life where he lacked true compassion.

In the saddle, Morgan turned her horse out, heading for the gates surrounding the castle, and trailed behind Arthur for a while before forcing her horse on until they rode two abreast.

"I don't see your ravens." Arthur sounded smug.

Morgan scanned the sky, although he was right; she could see no hint of a bird, nor could she hear the beat of wings against the wind toying with her dark hair as they rode. "Oh, I'm sure they'll turn up in due course."

"You mean to say when I'm least expecting it," Arthur grumbled.

Morgan turned in her saddle, held both reigns in her right hand, and faced Arthur again. "I don't know the minds of my ravens, Arthur, as much as you like to think I do. Nor do the Gods come and go at my beck and call."

"But one did." He gave her a deadpan glare.

"It was an act of revenge. An eye for an eye. Your father for mine. I was a child when he was killed, just as I was a child when you tricked me into that blasted Crystal Cave—"

"A Crystal Cave from which you and Emrys managed to escape," Arthur pointed out. "Not an easy feat."

"Yes, we escaped, but at what cost? So I could be wedded to you…"

Arthur smirked. "Whatever happened to your cat? Merlin, wasn't it?"

Morgan sighed. "I don't know. I never saw him again," she muttered under her breath, nudging her horse on faster with her knees. Anything to get away from Arthur and his superiority complex.

***

The hill was the highest point in all of Avalon. It would give them an advantage for sure, Morgan thought. She watched the men rallying around, readying their bows and arrows as they looked to the sky for any sign of the Dragon. It didn't disappoint. As if on cue, it came swooping down low on the hill. The archers let fly a round of arrows, all aimed in the Dragon's general direction. It roared, blasting fire at the ground below. The men ran screaming like little girls, only to regroup and fire another round of arrows at the ungodly beast. But that didn't deter it, just made it angrier.

Morgan's eyes stayed glued to the skies, awaiting the ravens, but the only thing to grace her vision was one rather magnificent-looking Dragon. Where were the ravens? She could do with their comforting presence right about now, even if part of their allure was that they frightened Arthur so.

"Where are you?" she whispered. Silence

greeted her, along with a sinking feeling that the ravens wouldn't be making an appearance. She knew then with utmost certainty that she, along with the rest of Arthur's men, was on her own.

"Look out below!" one of the men roared, startling Morgan. "The beast's been hit. It's coming down!"

"Morgan!" Arthur's cry pierced through the rabble and noise of the men scrambling to safety.

"I'm right here," she said, placing her hands on her hips. "And I'm fine, thanks for asking."

"We need to get out of the way," Arthur said laying a hand on her arm. "The Dragon… it's…"

"Falling out of the sky," she replied for him. "Yes, I'm well aware. I have been paying attention to what's going on around me, you know."

Arthur sighed and ran a hand through his blonde hair. "I know."

"Good."

"I need your help, Morgan," he pleaded, eyes beseeching her. "*We* need your help!"

Morgan smiled. "As flattering as that sentiment is, Arthur, no. *You* don't. You have everything you need at your disposal. You trapped me in a Crystal Cave beneath the earth for a decade, and if you can do that to a mere child… Well, I'm sure outwitting such a dumb creature—even if that creature is a Dragon—won't be any trouble for you."

"But…"

"The ravens aren't here, Arthur," Morgan

shouted. "Morríghan isn't here! I cannot help you... even if I wanted to. I am nothing without them. I couldn't even get myself out of that damn Crystal Cave by myself."

"Then get them here!" he cried.

"Don't you think I have tried? They don't just come running at my beck and call. They are not servants I can command as you do yours!"

'Arthur Pendragon!' the Dragon roared. *'Why do you seek to destroy me and my brethren when it is our image that flies upon your banners?'*

"D-you hear th-that, Morgan?" Arthur asked. "The Dragon speaks!"

"You wounded it," Morgan said plainly. "Did you really think it would just sit back and allow you to rid the world of its presence without first questioning why you wished it gone?"

"You speak in riddles, wife," Arthur stated.

"As did you when we first met, if I recall correctly," she said, turning away from him.

'I find I grow weary of waiting, Arthur Pendragon. Do you have an answer for me or not?'

"I'll leave you to *your* Dragon, shall I?"

"Morgan," Arthur cried. "D-don't leave."

Morgan turned back to face him just as three ravens appeared in the sky. "Oh, you expect me to call on the Morríghan now that they have graced me with their presence, do you?" she asked. "See to the Dragon, before it decides you'd be better served as its next meal rather than a talking companion."

"But—"

"The Morríghan is not mine to make demands upon. She has her own agenda, and I doubt very much she would serve you when you seek to destroy those precious to her."

"The ravens?" Arthur asked confused.

"Yes." She nodded. "They are her vessels, under my protection. It was to be our protection, but you rebuked them. So now that burden falls to me, but if you threaten them, you threaten her."

***

The arrows had damaged the Dragon's wings to the point that they were just shreds, hanging like lace from the wing bones. Morgan couldn't look at the massive beast as one of Arthur's men lassoed it, securing a rope around its neck as if it were some animal to be paraded about. It wasn't, and it saddened Morgan to have had been witness to such a travesty. Dragons, as frightfully dangerous as she knew they could be, ought to be free, and here was Arthur shooting them out of the sky for the sake of glory and power. Winning wars, even wars against Dragons, didn't make a man—a King—powerful, and it certainly hadn't won Arthur her respect. Perhaps it had won him the people's respect, but the people of Camelot—of all of Avalon—were scared, Morgan knew. Scared because they didn't understand, but she understood because she knew the man that Arthur was—the man he would become if he kept on his current path. It was the same path which would lead to his death, as Morríghan had foretold.

I'm sorry, Morgan thought, feeling silly for apologising to a Dragon on behalf of the man she called her husband. She wondered if Dragons could hear the thoughts of humans, and if so, what did they think of them?

'*It is not your place to apologise, Morgan of the Faeries. The line of the Pendragon will end, though the end will be through us or the Goddess you call Morríghan. She is, as are we, protectors. Arthur seeks to throw off the balance. He does not understand the mysteries. The fey are blind to the changing natures of the outside world. Humans are forgetting us, forgetting the world of myth and magic in favour of technology and truths. If they do not remember, we will forever be forgotten. That is the way of all things borne of imagination,*' the Dragon said.

Morgan bowed her head as Arthur approached. His men now pulled on the rope, leading the Dragon to an unknown fate of fey design. Having dealt with the fey for much of her short life, Morgan already knew the trap the Dragon would endure. There would be no escape, not unless Arthur himself willed it, for Dragons didn't possess the same magic of fey or mages. Dragons only had fire and wings at their disposal … and a dragon without the use of its wings wasn't useful at all.

Guilt wracked her. The Dragons had never been anything to fear, and she had been stupid to think such a thing. It was nothing more than a misunderstood creature. Like the fey, she thought idly, they too were misunderstood. In silence, she also pondered the fall of Camelot. The Goddess had said Arthur would die, and Morgan had seen it; it was as grizzly as any death could be. But she'd never seen the face of the man behind the killing blow. Nothing but the cascade of black hair so like her own that it sent chills up and down her spine. She'd always suspected the child, even before she'd conceived. It was why the news of their marriage had always sat ill with her. A King expected heirs, heirs were expected to inherit, but without heirs, Camelot would falter.

A strangled sound, like that of a gasp, escaped her throat. It wasn't Arthur who would be at the epicentre of Camelot's fate. It was she. Morgan. It didn't matter that her own son was the weapon to cut Arthur down, for Morgan would be the one to birth him. His birth would mark the beginning of Camelot's fall.

Once again, a hand went to her belly, only the child was quiet, sleeping, Morgan thought. The destruction of Camelot lay within her. Heir to the throne and too innocent to know the depths of darkness and pain which now surrounded it outside the womb.

The child, surely, could not be allowed to live.

Stacey Jaine McIntosh

Stacey Jaine McIntosh was born in Perth, Western Australia, where she still resides with her husband and their four children. Although her first love has always been writing, she once toyed with being a Cartographer and subsequently holds a Diploma in Spatial Information Services.

In 2011, she had her first short story "Freya" published in an anthology. Eleven more have followed. The latest story "Morríghan" is included in the CW Publishing House Anthology, Chasing Magic. Stacey is also the author of a self-published novel Solstice, and she is currently working on several other novels simultaneously.

When not with her family or writing, she enjoys reading, photography, genealogy, history, Arthurian myths, and witchcraft. You can find her on social media here:

www.facebook.com/StaceyJaineMcIntosh

The Price of the Piper
by J. Anthony Gohier

Mathias gazed across the council chamber. The Governor stared back from the great stone chair at the other end. It was a throne, really, but no one in town would call it that. It would be admitting too much.

"What do you want now, vagabond?" the Governor sneered.

"I have come for payment," Matthias answered.

"Payment? For what?" The Governor coughed into his damp sleeve.

"The agreement was that I would be paid in full when the rats were gone."

"The agreement was that you would get rid of

the rats. You played a flute."

"It's a pipe, actually—and the rats *are* gone."

The Governor turned to the councilmen sitting around him in their wooden chairs. "There have been no sightings since yesterday," the nearest said. "It would seem the rats have left."

"And the cause?" the Governor demanded.

"A shift in the climate, perhaps," said another councilman, "migrating predators."

"Or a disease," added a third.

The Governor shifted in his seat as he eyed the third man. "Then it has nothing to do with this man and his pipe?"

"Our sciences give no indication that music would have any effect on the rodent population," the Chief Councilman said.

"Well, there you are," the Governor said, waving a hand in Mathias' direction. "Still, let it not be said that the men of Hamlin are not fair in their dealings. Council, pay the piper."

The Chief Councilman drew a single coin from his pouch and tossed it at Mathias. It clattered on the stone at Mathias' feet.

"This was not the agreement," Mathias said.

"The agreement was for you to get rid of the rats," the Governor said, "not to lie about amusing yourself until they went away."

"There must be payment," Mathias said, "or there will be consequences."

"You have no power to threaten here, Piedman, and you are no longer welcome in Hamlin."

The councilmen stood.

Mathias turned, leaving the coin on the floor, and left the chamber.

***

An hour's walk outside of town brought Mathias to a clearing at the foot of the ancient mountain. Fireflies emerged among the trees and underbrush. A circle of stones rested in the middle of the clearing, weathered and cracked. A few were missing, but wildflowers and toadstools had filled in the gaps.

Mathias placed his pipe to his lips and blew a solemn tune as he entered the circle. The mountain before him vanished, and in its place stood a great stone hall, grown over with clinging vines. Mathias lowered his pipe.

Auberon stood between the stone columns, glistening hair flowing back over his shoulders. "You have arrived," the Great Sylph said.

"Empty-handed, I'm afraid," Mathias replied.

"You bring no payment?" Cold light burned behind Auberon's eyes.

"The Governor refused. He seemed not to believe the magics had worked."

"The rodents fled the town, taking their pestilence with them, and drowned themselves in the sea. He can see that for himself.

35

"Unfortunately, sight does not always produce belief among mankind."

"And it is equally unfortunate for mankind that a lack of belief does not satisfy a contract. A boon was granted. Payment must be made. It is the law you agreed to when you accepted our instrument."

"I know, Your Grace. I respect the laws."

The hall filled with whispers carried from the unseen realm beyond. Auberon looked away from Mathias, listening. Then the light in his eyes softened. "Yes, Piper," he said, turning back, "you have always respected the magics. Our grievance is not with you but with the people of Hamlin. Ease your mind. We shall settle the debt ourselves."

Mathias shifted where he stood.

"You have more to say?" Auberon asked, raising a silver eyebrow.

"Begging your pardon, Your Grace, but there are many people in Hamlin. I don't think they should all be punished for the actions of the Governor and his council."

"The Governor is empowered by the people. Regardless, we do not deal in punishments, only payments. When the sun is high tomorrow, we will exact payment from Hamlin."

"There are children in the town. They have suffered much already."

"We have heard your petition, Piper. The laws must be answered." Auberon faded, and the mountain appeared before Mathias again.

He left the stone ring and wandered back down the foothills. Raising his pipe once more, he played a pensive tune as he looked for a tree under which to spend the night.

***

Sleep eluded Mathias. As the sun came up, he wandered the deer trails outside Hamlin. He clutched his pipe. He lifted it once—lungs filled with waiting notes—then silently lowered it again.

Cresting a low hill, he found a dark-haired girl sitting among the tall grass, a bouquet clutched in her small hands. She hummed softly to herself. "Good morning, little one," Matthias said, strolling to her side. "You are young to be out on your own."

"I always gather the morning blossoms," the girl said. "Mother says they help with the smells."

"Your mother will be pleased," Mathias said. "But she'll worry if you're gone long."

"I know. I just needed a rest." The girl pulled a short crutch from among the grasses and pushed herself up from the side of the hill. Tucking the crutch under her arm, she shambled toward the town, one leg hanging limply beneath her.

"You have a kind heart," Mathias said, though she had moved too far to hear him.

The girl's humming resumed, keeping time with her wobbling gait. Mathias raised his pipe again and mimicked the girl's tune. She turned back and listened for a few measures. Then she smiled at him and continued toward the town. Mathias blew a long, low note, then the tune shifted.

He thought of the other children in Hamlin who were probably waking now. He thought of those who had shivered in their beds while the rats plagued the streets. He thought of those who had watched their mothers and fathers cough out their last breaths. He thought of those who still cowered in the shadows, hungry eyes pleading with all who passed them. His pipe sang somber and dark, then paused as the girl reached the edge of the town.

"It would be better if you were not in Hamlin today."

Mathias blew through the pipe once more, and a new tune rolled and bounced along the breeze. The girl stopped to listen again. This time, her smile began slowly and spread until her whole face shone. A minute later, a boy wandered from the town and stopped next to her. As her smile spread to his face, another boy joined them.

The flowers dropped from the girl's hand as she turned her crutch and ambled back toward Mathias. The boys followed and quickly overtook her. More children emerged from the town, and the crowd pressed toward him.

Mathias turned and walked back into the hills as he played his tune, filling each note with laughter his heart didn't feel. He let his feet wander, heading nowhere in particular, just away. The children thronged around him, their laughter fluttering through the trees.

***

The tree line broke, and the mountain rose before them. Mathias paused, staring briefly at the stone circle, then turned back.

"Mathias." The tune caught in Mathias' pipe. Auberon stood in the circle. "We heard you playing," the Sylph said.

The children hung back at the edge of the clearing as Mathias lowered his pipe. "I used the magics, I know. I will make their payment."

"Yes," Auberon said. "This will suffice."

Mathias furrowed his brow. "What will suffice?"

"There are many ways these children can serve us, and we will watch over them. Hamlin's debt is paid."

"That's not—" Mathias began, but Auberon looked past him to the edge of the clearing.

"Come, children," Auberon said, raising his arms and taking a step backward. The tune Mathias had played surged from the mountain and beyond, carried by hundreds of unseen voices. Smiles returned to the children's faces, and they ran forward. One by one, they vanished into the stone circle at Auberon's feet.

When they were gone, Auberon lowered his arms and looked back at Mathias. The song still rang through the air. Mathias stared back, his pipe hanging limply in his hands.

"Fine," Mathias said, "you have your payment. Leave Hamlin in peace."

"There are more," Auberon said.

"What?"

Auberon nodded toward the trees. Mathias turned. The dark-haired girl still struggled toward them, her crutch sliding and snagging along the path. Behind her, two boys crouched and clung to each other. One of them stared at Auberon with wide eyes. The other angled his ear toward the mountain, his eyes looking at nothing.

"Their infirmities slowed their pace," Auberon said, "but we will tend to them."

"Leave them," Matthias said, turning back to Auberon.

"We will mend their ailments," Auberon said. "In our country, they will see and hear and walk."

"And there will be three more broken hearts in Hamlin. Your payment is satisfied. Leave these."

Auberon's head tilted as he listened to the voices carried from beyond the mountain, then his deep eyes stared into Mathias' heart. "The payment is accepted." And stepping forward into the ring of stones, Auberon was gone. The song died on the winds.

Mathias turned back toward the trees and

found the dark-haired girl just entering the clearing. A few wavering steps brought her to his side.

"Please," she said, "I want to go too."

"And what of your mother?"

"Please, I want to go."

Mathias looked into her eyes. "I don't know if I have saved you or condemned you, little one," he said. His hands tightened around the pipe. "Take the others. Return home."

***

It was three days before hunger drove Mathias back to civilization. He had wandered as far as he could from Hamlin, but he could not outrun the winds or the memories they carried. He didn't know the name of the town he had stumbled across, but he found his way to an inn boasting a sign of a black kettle over its door. He sat at a table in a dark corner, painfully aware that his purse was as empty as his stomach. The last coin he had seen had been left on the floor of the council chambers of Hamlin.

One hand rested on the pipe strapped to his belt. He had thrown it away once, but it found its way back to him. Magics weren't that easy to be rid of; he was as much their instrument as the pipe now. He should have known better anyway. One couldn't fool the magics. He had learned that long before he accepted the blessing of the Great Sylph. He leaned back against the wall, his hood pulled low over his closed eyes, and listened to the crowd.

Most of the talk was trivial—young men boasting of various exploits, older men complaining about their wives, and elderly men complaining about everything else. A lad whose voice had barely broken mooned over an unrequited love. Dull and hardly likely to pay well. And too young to understand that with which he bargained. A group of bearded men grumbled over corrupt officials. Tempting, but likely to attract more attention than he needed, at least until he had better motivation than an empty stomach. A merchant ranted to his underlings about highwaymen who had raided his caravans and made off with … his daughter. Mathias eyed the merchant. He was obviously well fed, and his cronies didn't appear to be starving either. Perhaps he could stand to see what magics would bring him if he had the disposition for it. And Matthias would need a hearty meal to face the will of the magics again himself.

Mathias approached the table. "You have a problem," he said.

"Who are you?" the merchant demanded, glaring at him. "Militia? Mercenary?"

"Just a man with a knack for solving problems."

"And you think you can solve mine?"

Mathias' finger traced one of the pipe's tone holes. "I can," he said, "for a price."

J. Anthony Gohier

J. Anthony Gohier has been a storyteller all his life. He received a degree in Film and Media Arts and has since returned to his first love, the written word. His writing has won awards in categories of short story, novel chapter, children's book, and poetry, as well as being published in several anthologies.

Which Shoes
by C.L. Steele

Surrounded by red brick stores and copious flowerbeds, Glinda sat on a black iron bench at an upscale outdoor mall. Her ginger hair blew in the wind of the upcoming storm. She laid her ruby red umbrella across her lap and adjusted her outfit so she would look the perfection of normal. Settling in, she lost herself in thought.

Perhaps I'm wrong to help her remember who she really is. But I miss her. Locasta was bossy, but she was down deep a good soul, a caring person who stood up and helped. Perhaps she just made a mistake. Well, there really is no choice. We sisters need her—I need her. But should I—can I—make her remember? It must be done gently after such a long time. I don't want to shock her.

A woman swooped around the corner; her head down and feet flying, she slowed as she looked up and noticed Glinda.

"Hello," Glinda said.

"Oh—uh, hi," sputtered the woman, catching her breath. "I practically ran from the parking lot. I'm late meeting my sister here. We're dress-shopping for a wedding," she said with open-eyed excitement. "Guess she's running late too. Thank goodness." She winked. "I'm Locasta," she said placing her hand on her chest, "but I go by Cassie."

"I'm Glinda. Please, catch your breath—take a seat."

"Thanks," Locasta said, falling into the comfort of the bench. Before she could even take a deep breath to release her anxiety, her phone chimed. "Oh, that's me. Sorry, this'll only be a second."

Glinda noted Locasta's black frizzy hair, which contrasted her pale face—the dark circles under her no-makeup blue eyes were disconcerting. The black sweats that almost hid the extra twenty pounds were topped with a ragged green sweater. Locasta looked disappointed as she finished her conversation and slid her phone into her triangular purse.

"Trouble?"

"My sister can't make it. Seems she has a flat tire. Odd for her brand-new car," Locasta said, her expression full of doubt. "I don't want to shop alone. Guess I'll just head back home."

"Why do that?" Glinda asked, pushing herself up from the bench using her long red umbrella with a curved hickory handle. "I have a great sense of fashion and will be happy to help. Besides, I'm going to a wedding soon and hate to shop alone too. I know just the place to start. It's near the old clock. A great store for shoes called Out of the Box. C'mon, let's get you dressed for the time of your life, starting from the bottom up. Whadya say?" Glinda could see Locasta thinking about it. She subtly turned her umbrella toward Locasta then back and smiled at the woman.

"Well, you certainly look nice. I love your blue shoes. Sure, why not. I'm here, right? Which way?"

Glinda pointed east with her umbrella toward a tall ornate 1900s clock, and they walked as the clouds darkened and the wind picked up. As they neared, the clock chimed, marking the noon hour.

"Oh no, look." Glinda pointed. A child's balloon, just purchased at a kiosk a few steps behind them, floated away. The mother yelled and the child burst into tears.

"That's not okay," Locasta said, removing her wallet from the triangular purse and going to soothe the situation with the purchase of a new yellow balloon.

In her absence, Glinda located the four bricks—marked with the four ordinances to the right of the timepiece and across from the space between Out of the Box Shoes and A Sprinkle or Two Ice Cream Shoppe.

Using the silver point of her red umbrella, she tapped the north brick twice and whispered, "One to the North, none to the South, one in the West, and the East is dead." She raised the umbrella point above the east and, tucking the umbrella under her arm with the point facing ahead, the bricks parted, and a wing of shops was revealed. A few figures dressed in black wandered among the shops and city trees. "Locasta, let's go. The weather."

Locasta waved and winked to the now happy family, then scampered toward Glinda. As they entered, the brick walkway turned from red to a warm golden brown. The wall closed behind them, allowing only their entrance, but from inside looking back acted as a window into the world of humans. Glinda checked the new clock to her east and pointed west at a storefront marked with a large sign above the door, announcing the store's name—*Out of the Box*.

"Here we are. Shoes for you," Glinda said, holding the door for Locasta to enter.

"Welcome ta Out of the Box," called a woman from the counter. "Glinda, good ta see ya, girl. Ain't that—"

"A friend of mine. She goes by Cassie. I'll take full responsibility in helping her today." Glinda smiled, hurrying Locasta along to a far aisle.

"Your friend from Jamaica? I like her

bohemian style. She moves like she likes to dance," Locasta rambled.

"What size?" Glinda interrupted.

"Eight."

"That would be this row." Glinda tapped the row with her umbrella, and the boxes jumped in succession all down the row. Locasta was busy looking around but jumped as she heard the dull, thumping noise of the boxes. "Does this place remind you of something, Locasta?"

"Cassie, please. Yes, it seems familiar. The stairway—the wood shelves and floor—the lighting. Oh, I know. It looks like the old library downtown. The old nunnery. Look, even the shoeboxes look like books. How fun."

"Do you remember the old fountain in front of the library?"

Locasta looked thoughtfully, her forehead puckered, then shook her head. "No, no. I'm far too young to remember a fountain. Perhaps I've seen it in a picture."

"Perhaps," Glinda said. "Now, which box calls to you?"

"What?"

"Just pick the one that calls to your instincts. I promise it's a great method of shopping. It works."

Locasta ran her hand along the row of shoeboxes. Stopping and picking up one, she opened it to find a pair of leather boots with pointy toes and a triangle cuff. "Not exactly wedding wear," she said.

"Well, with a long dress, they might be practical. Try them on." Glinda sat next to her on the bench bisecting the row of shoes as Locasta pulled on the boots. "Oh dear. A smudge on your forehead. May I?" Glinda placed her thumb in the center of Locasta's forehead, then whispered, "Remember the feeling, forget the details, let the boots lead you to healing." She briefly peered into Locasta's mind, then took her thumb away.

"What were we saying?" Locasta asked.

"You were saying the boots felt good. Walk around in them."

Locasta took a few steps, then rose into the air. Stepping here and there, she danced a little. "Feels like I'm walking on sunbeams. So much energy."

"Remember feeling that way before?"

Slowly, Locasta sank to the floor and plodded back to Glinda. She sat and removed the boots. Glinda touched Locasta's hand. Locasta looked around as if remembering.

"Well, you seemed to like those boots. Let's take those for every day, since there's a buy-one-get-one-free sale. But I think a wedding is a great time to be impractical. I'll put those away for you. Go choose another box."

Locasta ran her hand across a few boxes and chose a dark red box with an artistic "A" on its lid. The "A" looked like a shoe. Glinda pushed and shoved the enchanted boots back into their box as they fought to remain out. She slammed on the lid and grabbed the new box from Locasta.

"Pretty pink stilettoes," Locasta gasped as Glinda revealed and handed her the shoes. "I've never worn that high a heel." She rushed her feet into them.

Glinda watched the shoes take over. Everything about Locasta changed. Her lanky legs and branch-like arms moved as if they knew just how to sway and strut. There was a rhythm to her hips that danced with her shoulders. A commanding chin up with a slight tilt of the head was almost majestic in its appeal. As she turned, the power of her eyes—of her being—grew almost palpable.

"Man, you can smell the power," the bohemian counter clerk said. She lifted her brown prairie skirt, revealing her feetless legs, as she bounced just above the ground, trying to mimic the runway moves Locasta made and clearly enjoyed. "She's tranced, right?"

"Yes, Helga. She won't remember this—just the feeling of it."

Helga floated toward Glinda and took a seat. "I sure miss the power. Being human, ya know?"

"Yes, I remember it too well," Glinda said, admiring Locasta's pink-heel strut and lure. "Perhaps I'm wrong to help her remember who she really is."

"Oh, babble. She must remember the covenant, the sisterhood, the coven. Don't cha know. The people of the South need her. They's suffering without her justice. We be lucky to have you in the

North, now and then, to protect us. The poor West has gone wicked, and the East? Well, it be a battleground. We need her, and she be in there—in that brain of hers—waitin' to help. Ya know she'd give it all up— all of that feminine power—in order to wield her power for us downtrodden. Let those Warlocks know their injustice ain't gonna stand."

"It wasn't all of them. Just a few Warlocks caught in power's grasp," Glinda said, looking at Helga. "Now go. I have a wedding to prepare her for and memories to implant." Helga swirled off, and Glinda turned the handle of her umbrella.

Locasta inhaled a deep breath and let out a sensual sigh. She leaned against the shelving and removed the pink stilettos. "Wow, those can make a girl feel pretty…"

"Sexy and powerful?" Glinda suggested.

"Absolutely."

"Let me move that curl of yours. It keeps falling in your face," Glinda said as she guided the curl and Locasta to the bench, using her thumb on Locasta's forehead to peer into her mind again. "Neuron glowing in her brain, remember her power but hold its rein. Let it grow and slowly wake until the synapse of my wand it takes."

"I don't know where my mind is today. What were we saying?"

"We were just gathering our shoes and going to Hair Today next door."

"Hair Today?"

"Yes. Change into your shoes, and I'll take your choices to the counter. Quite the sale."

While Locasta put her shoes back on, Glinda paid for the boots and heels and removed the magic from them. "Let's go. I'm going to be late."

"But I haven't paid."

"Oh, they have a different way here. All the sales get scanned, then you pay and pick up at the exit. Free hands are free to shop more."

"Wow, cool."

They trotted to the storefront with the sign *Hair Today... Gone Tomorrow*. Glinda held the door, and Locasta entered the bright, ultra-modern store.

"Hello Glinda," the stick-thin woman in all black said, giving Glinda a hug. "Helga contacted me and said you were bringing a friend with you. So glad to see you. I'm Newena, but everyone calls me Newy. Locasta, right?"

"Cassie, please. Locasta makes me feel uncomfortable, like the quill of a feather sticking out of a down pillow. It's comfortably me but often makes me prickle when I hear it."

"Well, Cassie, you have some witchy hair going on there," Newy said, examining Locasta's hair. Then, realizing what she'd said, she mouthed, 'Sorry,' to Glinda.

"Did you call my hair witchy?"

Newy hustled everyone toward the back of the store. "*No*, no, no. I said bitchin' hair, but completely out of style. Here, sit. My store is called Hair

Today… Gone Tomorrow, because we used to get our hair done then go fly—I mean, go out in the wind and rain, and the nice hair today was gone, right? So, one day, I threw a few chemicals in the cauldr—I mean, black pot, and Voilà. Invented this."

Locasta took the white bottle handed to her and read: *'Witchypoo—straightener to make the witch in you unrecognizable.'* "Cute marketing."

"Yes, and the great thing is all you have to do is wash your hair, and it comes out your natural color and straight as a broomstick. I use it," Newy said.

"So do I," Glinda added.

"But you're a blond and Glinda is a redhead."

"Yes, that's the great thing. One product fits all. Your hair will be soft and shiny and raven-black," Newy assured.

"What's the price?"

"Well, free today, since I have a coupon. Buy one get one free," said Glinda.

"And since you're a new customer, I'll give you a complimentary mani-pedi."

"Can't say no to that," Locasta said.

"Very well, then. Let's get you washed, cut, and under the dryer."

As Locasta sat under the dryer, freshly washed and cut, Newy rushed to Glinda, asking, "Does she remember who she is yet?"

"Can't hurry magic or you'll chase it away. I used shoes to remind her about flying and how power feels. She remembers those things. The rest will come in time. What do you remember about that last day?"

"I remember them riding up on horseback, the red linings of their cloaks flapping as we stood outside the nunnery with its large fountain and oaks. The excitement of seeing him—I mean them—tingled through me, and a desire to look perfect for him—them. They gave us all bouquets of flowers that smelled of peace and serenity, like a fresh field after a rain or the wind at twilight, like pine, both sweet and clean. It made us lose ourselves. Most of us fainted and were dragged away. Thrown in a fire pit. Helga was pushed into the fire, ran out into the woods, her hem aflame. They caught her, then chopped off her burnt feet and hung her with me when she didn't die fast enough. After we died, our spirits rose and watched them lay you in that long, narrow cage, repeatedly dunking you in the fountain. The water would spark like lightning, and Locasta begged them to stop. They finally dragged her inside."

"They held me under for eleven hours," Glinda said. "Eleven. The final time, they left me in the water. Just before I drowned, she came to see me, calling my name and screaming, 'Sister, sister.' Her eyes seemed different through the silvery water. As she hauled me out of the fountain, the water splashed on her. Something odd happened. She suddenly couldn't remember anything. She also couldn't die. They abandoned her almost immediately, but over the centuries, I've made sure she had a place and a family. Sometimes, I've had to use the fountain water to make her forget the pain of being the last one of us alive. She has been an orphan, a slave, a bag lady, a lady of the night, a nun. This last time, I had to use my magic to convince a family to take her in as a foster kid. But at least she's alive. She eats and loves and sleeps—unlike us." She looking away, squeezing her hands together.

"We love."

"Yes, just not like she can. She is still human and filled with powers I would trade my magic for. Wouldn't you?"

"Oh, my dryer bell. She's done. Relax, Glinda."

Glinda caught her breath as Locasta entered the room. Newy, proficient as an artist, styled Locasta's hair into a beautiful up-do braid.

"You are stunning, my dear."

"I must have this shampoo."

"On the house if you allow me to do a before-and-after picture."

"Deal."

"Remember, never let them see you witchy, okay?"

"Send our bills to the front kiosk." Glinda winked. "We're off to Enchanting Attire."

Locasta looked in the mirror and tilted her head. "Do I even know who you are?" she said to herself. Glinda, standing behind her, met her gaze in their reflection.

"Perhaps it's working this time," Newy whispered. "Perhaps she will remember and help us." She hugged Glinda, who nodded with a small amount of hope.

Glinda and Locasta walked together in silence. Wide-eyed, Locasta rubbed her neck, stealing glances at the blank stare Glinda tried to maintain. Locasta blinked and rubbed her hands together in repeated anxiety, and Glinda tried to stop her own from doing the same. There was a strange sense of remorse building between them.

Both stopped in front of the store window of Enchanted Attire. A mesmerizing, bodiless red dress and tux danced and twirled beneath a crystal chandelier on a cloud of mystic fog.

"Magical—and a little spooky. How do they do that?" Locasta asked.

"Science. Tiny units inside the clothing blow air, making them look full, then small balls in the shoulders and waist and hiplines are programed to move in unison to the music. All Wi-Fi, and if you look at the floor, you'll see the air pump hidden near the fog machine. But yes, it all looks like magic, to those who believe. Witchcraft to the dubious."

"Or the malcontent."

"Do you remember?" Glinda asked.

Locasta swallowed hard and forced a poker face. A glaze passed over her eyes.

Why? Why doesn't she want to remember?

Glinda thought.

"I remember that I came here for a great dress. Something sexy and elegant," Locasta said, opening the door and allowing Glinda into the shop.

If the window was magical, the interior of the shop was bewitching. A grand spiral staircase flowed thought the middle of the shop. Glass catwalks stretched from either side of the second-story landing and emanated to various areas of the building. The second story had no floor other than these glass catwalks, allowing customers to see up to the dresses above while standing on the first floor. Occasionally, blue slivers of sky could be glimpsed between the attire from the above glass roof. The tuxes seemed to know to hide within the walls, while the dresses danced around, greeting the women with a curtsey. One sparkly-sexy number simply shimmied a welcome. Locasta startled as the disc she was standing on raised out of the floor. Grabbing the rising railing, she was swooshed out and into the dresses.

Behind her, Glinda called out, "On the panel, fill in the information. Select black for color and enter your size."

Locasta did so. Dresses flew up glass cylinder tubes while black dresses in a size six rushed into place from other cylinders, twirling and dancing. Each greeted her, then pirouetted from view. Locasta laughed in delight. "This is wonderful," she announced with youthful glee.

"If you find one you like, push the green button."

A beautiful dress with an empire waist and off-the-shoulder style required a green button push. Both the dress and Locasta were whisked to a dressing area. Moments later, Glinda joined them, holding a midnight blue dress of her own.

Myrna, the store owner, helped Locasta step up on a tufted stool. Quietly, she worked at measuring and pinning. Locasta turned to the mirror and caught a glance at Glinda in her blue dress with long Victorian sleeves and corseted waist.

"You look so beautiful, Glinda."

"You too, my dear."

"Beautiful, beautiful," Myrna sang like a Whippoorwill.

Locasta looked in the silver-framed mirror and a recognition of déjà vu seemed to flash over her face. "The black dress... the boots... Glinda's blue dress... red hair swimming in the fountain..." Locasta clutched her stomach and put a hand to her mouth as she gasped with remembrance.

Glinda had to hold back her own thoughts—her own anger. She had remembered the details years ago. She realized Locasta had never been held back by any of the attackers. She was only carried away to get her out of the way. Glinda's sister had come unattended to witness her dying in the fountain. Only after death did Locasta pull her from the water. Only then did Locasta lose her memory.

Why? Glinda raged, and although she knew she shouldn't—that this might cause Locasta to go back into hiding as Cassie—she cried out, "Why? Why, sister? Why did you betray us?"

"Why? Why?" chimed Myrna, watching this from her knees on the floor.

"It was him," Locasta said. "It was Ozcar. He convinced me to tell him about our magic."

Distraught, she fidgeted with a plain silver band on her left hand. "I loved him and thought telling him would help, not hurt. About our science and nature studies from the nuns and how we worked them into magic to excite and please ourselves. I thought if he understood... I had no idea he was planning on hurting us... you... our sisterhood. I only wanted to earn his respect. He said he just wanted to shoo witches away, not kill my friends. I didn't know. 'Shoo, witch, shoo,' they called as I ran from them." Locasta blinked, her face slackened into sadness and her neck blotchy and red.

Glinda's eyes darted from Locasta to the floor between them. She felt her forehead pucker and a small muscle in her jaw pulse.

"Eyes, eyes," Myrna mocked.

There was a long pause between them.

"I forgive you," Glinda said. "Centuries ago, I forgave you. Your explanation answered so many questions that have plagued me over the years. Seeing your eyes filled with tears that day through the silvery water, and seeing them today in the mirror, I knew. It wasn't your heart, but the betrayal pierces my own heart, sister." She rubbed her forehead as if trying to straighten the thoughts just behind the bone. "I realize I hadn't brought you to remember before now because I was afraid. That was my sin. I didn't believe in you enough to know for sure that you would not betray. That it was indeed him. I was afraid of what I'd learn. Bringing you back would mean facing that fear. It was easier to fight off the wicked witch of the west and cover all the North for you and the South and try to heal what the East has done. We need your help and good heart. Can I rely on you?"

"You kept me isolated from my powers for centuries? Centuries! You shut me out."

Glinda looked down. "I couldn't be sure. All of us are dead, just ghosts. You're our only living witch. You had to be protected, even from yourself. Now I see that was wrong. Our world needed you, and I needed you, and I should not have doubted you." Glinda caught herself pacing and rubbing her hands. She turned and faced Locasta, putting her hands behind her. "Forgive me, as I forgave those eyes that watched me die." Her hands ached from the tension, growing sweaty. "Can we forgive to unite against him? Will you fight against Ozcar?" she asked, looking boldly at her sister.

"Forgive, forgive," Myrna cried out, transforming to her black raven form and flying toward the door.

"Yes, sister. We will unite against him,"

Locasta promised, blinking and smiling sweetly. "In time, we will all heal." She stepped down from the stool and opened her arms to her sister. They embraced.

They would meet at Sprinkle or Two Ice Cream Shop tomorrow. All would be well, they decided.

As they gathered their things and left, Myrna called out, "Beautiful, why I forgive." Realizing Myrna had repeated their own words, they tittered and agreed that beauty was in forgiveness. They walked arm-in-arm as they meandered the golden-brown path to the windowed entrance. There was still a love between them. Glinda gave her sister a protective kiss on the forehead and handed her the red umbrella.

"All the instructions can be found inside. Think of it as a broom upgrade."

"How do I find this magical place again?"

"Magic can be found to the right of time, to the left of out of the box, and where a sprinkle or two can make you smile. It's all in the protection of the umbrella, Locasta. See you tomorrow."

Locasta opened the umbrella, pulling it overhead. Tied to the stretchers and ribs were red ribbons with plastic hearts attached. She reached up and touched one, and words appeared on the umbrella cloth before her.

To exit the window, walk straight through

with the umbrella's metal tip forward.

From the other side, Locasta laughed, and twirling the umbrella overhead, sent the hearts swirling. She smiled and waved to her sister, then turned to go.

Glinda wondered which shoes her sister would walk in now—the witch's boots or the pink power heel. *Give a girl the right shoes, and she can conquer the world,* she remembered Marilyn Monroe saying long ago. Glinda turned the ring on her right hand—a simple silver band that matched her sister's. After thinking a moment, she looked into her palm. A vision appeared. Glinda watched Locasta fiddle with the ring on her hand as silver tears fell and the rain patted the beautiful red umbrella protecting her.

CL Steele

CL Steele's epiphany to write came just two years ago. "Which Shoes" is CL Steele's second short story published this year. The world building was exciting writing. She would like to thank the editors of Chasing Magic for selecting "Which Shoes" from among the many submissions. You can also read her literary narrative, "Our Place In Time", in Once Upon A Wednesday, published by An Author's Tale. Her first novel, Paradigm Shift, is also scheduled for release this year. While writing daily, CL studies the

craft and participates in several writing communities. Discover more about CL Steele. Follow her at:
www.facebook.com/author.CLSteele

The End of Magic
by Jason Pere

"Our time is coming to an end. We cannot continue to exist in this realm," said Magic, a bottomless measure of sorrow in her voice. She looked over the faces of each and every one of her children gathered before her and shared in their grief. After soaking in the united lamentation of her offspring, Magic cast her gaze to the stone archway and the ghostly trails of silver mist emanating from its entrance.

"But why? What is the cause of all of this?" shouted Magic's eldest child, Time.

"The world shall pass to the humans. This in inevitable. They grow in numbers too fast and too great to overcome. We cannot remain here on earth with them," said Magic, crystalline tears forming in her eyes.

"If the humans are to fight us, I will stand against them. Nothing can defeat me!" roared Magic's largest child, who towered above the rest of his family, brandishing his sword and shield.

"Titian, my son, none of us will question your strength. You can vanquish armies with one sweep of your hand, but this struggle is not a contest of might. The humans mean no harm, and they harbor no ill will for our kind. They are forgetting us. That is why we can no longer share the earth with them," Magic replied. Her peaceful, soothing voice carried a subtle cadence of regret.

"How can they forget us?" came the melodic protest of one of Magic's favored daughters. "We have lived among them for so long. I sing to them every day and have guided many of the humans' tall ships safely to shore. If we go, who will watch over those who brave the waters?"

"You have been ever vigilant and protected many sailors from a treacherous fate on the waves. Siren, my child, it breaks my heart to say it, but there are few among the humans who can still hear your songs," Magic said gloomily. "Now, those who set across the oceans call on charts and the stars in the sky. Soon they will use machines to navigate the from port to port."

"Enough of the humans. What of my kith and kin?" roared Totem. "What is to become of the animals in my kingdom?" His long golden mane billowed and floated on the breeze, and his majestic antlers cast long and ominous shadows. Totem's feathered wings folded behind his back, and he fixed his keen eyes on his mother.

"Oh, my dear child, the animal kingdom you have guarded for ages is in peril indeed. Even with all your wisdom and cunning, there is little you can do for the beasts of the plains and the creatures in the sky above and water below. The humans have lost their reverence for animal kind. They no longer live in harmony with them. They hunt your progeny for sport and make trophies of their bodies. They poison the rivers and lakes where your offspring dwell. The humans now burn the forests that have sheltered your children. I grieve to say it shall only worsen," Magic lamented.

Each of her other children then launched their own protests, voicing their fears in turn, and Magic spoke with every one of them. It was the most sorrowful endeavor she had ever experienced, as she was unable to offer any comfort. After the last of Magic's children had spoken, several long moments of discord passed among Magic's decedents. Siren and her twin, Banshee, gave out a forlorn yet harmonious wail, which echoed up into the heavens. Fay, who was normally so joyous and spritely, only had tears to shed. Titian pounded his mighty fists into the earth with enough force to leave two craters. All these fantastical entities united in a singular display of hopelessness.

"Enough!" commanded Magic. In an instant, all was silent, and she had regained the undivided attention of those before her. "All is not lost," she added softly, offering a renewed sense of hope. "We can no longer share this world with the humans, but we shall not fade away into nothing. The humans may not hear our voices like they used to, but we shall not be fully forgotten."

"Mother, of what do you speak?" queried Sphinx.

Magic looked once more at the stone archway and the trails of otherworldly vapors emanating from its mouth. "Through this passage lies a realm where you all shall find refuge. In this place, you shall be safe from the forgetting of mankind. You may still communicate with the humans from this land, though not as before. Your words will be scarcely more than a whisper in a dream, but some—just some—of those left in this world shall still hear you." Magic's voice broke only a little, her eyes welling with tears once more.

"Will there ever be a return from this other realm?" asked Dragon as she raised her great, scaled head high, and smoke plumed from her nostrils.

Magic took her time in composing her response. "Yes. There will be a return... of sorts. The children of men will come to know of us in stories and tales told before sleep. I must warn you, once passage is made to the other side, those who travel there shall never again see the human world."

After a brief moment of tension, Kami broke the silence. "What is the name of this place to which we are banished?" it asked of its mother. Kami's skin changed rapidly from crackling flame to mountain stone, transforming in a splendid dance of elements.

"It is a place called Myth. In this realm, you shall all be safe and not forgotten by the humans," Magic said and wiped her eyes.

"I hear the choice of your words," said Magic's youngest, Reaper, as he lowered the hood of his shadowy black cloak and exposed his skeletal face. "You are not to come with us, Mother."

Magic wanted to break down sobbing in that moment, but she composed herself for just a while longer. "One has to stay behind and close the passage into Myth. I shall not join you on the other side." She closed her eyes. It was the only way she could say the words. If she had seen her children's faces when she told them this was a farewell, she would not have managed to go through with it.

A chorus of protest erupted from Magic's family. Hundreds of her children offered to be the one to stay behind and seal the gate bridging the human world and Myth. Magic put up a hand and signaled for all to be silent. She was quickly obeyed. "I am so proud of you all who would sacrifice yourselves for my sake. Sadly, I could not have any of you stay behind even if I wanted to. Only I have the strength to close the portal. I must be the one who stays. There is no more time for debate. You must go now." Magic glanced at the trails of mist receding into the archway.

One by one, each of her children bid their mother goodbye and started on the trail into Myth. Many tears and embraces were shared as a family was irrevocably torn asunder. When the last of Magic's children had disappeared out of sight, she used the last of her power to close the path between the two worlds. Before it was all over, she caressed her belly with a maternal hand.

"I am so sorry for both of you," Magic said to the unborn twins in her womb. "It is so cruel that you shall forever be separated from your brothers and sisters. Even crueler that I must abandon you as you are brought forth into this world. I wish I could be here with you, but it will take everything I have left to ensure the existence of your siblings on the other side. It will fall to you both to guide and watch over the humans in this world." The stone archway to Myth vanished after a wave of Magic's arms. Once the passage had been erased, she began to fade into the vapor. "The last thing I can do for you, my children, is give you your names," Magic said as she birthed her last two children into the world. "All will know you as Good and Evil."

All was gone from the hilltop where Magic and her progeny had just gathered. Only the whisper of wind blowing across the vast crests and valleys of tall grass remained. After moments of nothing, a small girl walked to the summit of the largest hill where the archway to Myth had been. She was bright and wonderful. Her eyes flickered with limitless joy and compassion. Despite the appearance of youth and her face set in the broadest of smiles, she carried an element of ancient empathy and understanding with her. The wind gently played with her long flowing mane of vibrant blond hair. The child's fair skin was flawless and smooth, but despite her pale complexion, an untold measure of warmth emanated from her being.

As the girl moved, each blade of grass on the hilltop bent against the wind and reached towards her inviting presence. Flights of birds soon gathered in the clear blue sky overhead. As the girl stood on the hilltop, she seemed to draw all things with living essence to her side. She laughed with the rich sound of a full orchestra string section as she saw the birds in the air and heard their songs. As her laughter rose into the heavens, it caused the sun to shine even brighter and cast its pleasant golden rays longer and farther across the world below.

The girl looked down into the deepest valley below the hilltop. She saw the villages of humans cradled within the protective, rolling hills of the countryside. For hours she watched them, entranced by the humans bustling about with the simple tasks of their day. The girl found herself consumed by the driving desire to be among them. It was only when the sun stopped casting its abundant light onto the world below and the birds above flew off for the horizon that the girl became aware of anything past her desire to walk with the humans.

The wind blowing the child's long golden hair now harbored a chill and hint of frost. The cold on the breeze foretold the coming of her brother. The girl looked back and saw her sibling coming up to join her on the hilltop. Her laugher stopped once she noticed the morose expression etched on her brother's face, but she kept smiling. The boy reached the crest of the hill and stood beside his sister. They shared a silent moment, both looking down on the humans below, her with love and adoration and he with malice and spite.

"Do you see? Do you see all the humans down there? They are wonderful, are they not? Evil, do you see?" asked the girl with excitement and joy.

"I see them, Good. I see them, and I hate them." The boy sneered as he spoke. His words came out with such brooding angst that heavy flecks of spittle flew from his mouth.

Good was taken aback by her brother's words. She nearly cried from his hurtful sentiment. "How can you say such a thing? Why do you hate them? You do not even know the humans," she said to her brother. Her eyes watered and lips quivered with sorrow.

"It is easy. I hate them because they are weak. The humans are so easy to destroy. They are worthless," said the petulant boy as he crossed his arms and pouted.

The brightness in Good's eyes rekindled as she replied. "Oh, I see, brother. You are right. The humans are weak. They need us to help them. It is just like Mother bid us. We must help the humans." She tried to take Evil's hand.

Evil recoiled from his sister and glared at her. "Help the humans, ha. They are beyond help and doomed to destroy themselves."

"We can help them. We can tell them stories. We can tell the humans about our brothers and sisters. We can tell them of Titian's strength, Fay's playfulness, Sphinx's mysteries... You and I, brother. We can tell the humans all the stories of our family. We'll help inspire men and women to shape their world into something great," Good said with unbridled desperation.

Evil let Good's words hang in the air until he finally spoke with a twisted and grotesque smile. "We will help inspire the humans. Oh, the stories I shall tell them. The world I see them craft will be a sight to behold. Truly a great sight to behold."

<u>Jason Pere</u>

Jason Pere currently resides in his home state of Connecticut with his darling wife, sweet hound dog, and duo of maniacal felines. He is a renaissance man, having dabbled in Acting for Film and Theater, Fencing and Mixed Martial Arts, Professional

Dorkary, and a bevy of other passions before coming to land on writing.

At first, Jason took a casual interest in writing, starting with poetry and journaling. Over time, he honed his direction and finally began writing larger works. In November of 2012, Jason self-published his first book, Modern Knighthood: Diary of a Warrior Poet. Since then, he has rapidly amassed many author credits.

https://www.amazon.com/Jason-Pere/e/B00JH63V0O

Emeline's Tree
by Liz Butcher

Emeline opened her eyes. Instead of her bedroom, there was nothing but darkness. She squeezed her eyes shut, then opened them again. This time, a haze moved across the blackness. Emeline stepped forward and was overcome with dizziness; enveloped by the dark, she had no sense of direction. Struggling to stay upright, she squinted as the mist parted before her, revealing a pinpoint of light.

The light slowly radiated outwards until it encompassed the space before her. Emeline held her hand up to her face, shielding herself from the glare. As her eyes adjusted to the light, she lowered her hand with a soft gasp.

A magnificent tree stood before her, majestic in its height, with a powerful trunk and hundreds of branches stretching out all around. Gnarled roots spread across the surface before plummeting farther into the transparent ground, until Emeline could no longer see their ends.

The hypnotic way the branches moved beckoned her to come closer; Emeline strained to listen, certain she heard a faint voice calling her name. As she neared the tree, she realized it was itself the source of the light surrounding it.

Drawn to it like a moth to a flame, she reached out to touch the trunk.

***

Emeline awoke with a start. When she sat up, light spots danced in her eyes, as though she'd stared at something bright for too long. She scanned the room as she ran her hands up her arms, trying to shake off the dream.

Her gaze fell upon the necklace sitting on her bedside table. She'd found it while sorting through the box of her parents' belongings. She'd wanted something small to take with her—a good luck charm to take to a new town, a new job. Though she'd gone through the box hundreds of times since her parents' deaths, she didn't recall ever seeing it before. Yet something within her recognized it.

Emeline stared at the large, oval-shaped ruby set in a filigree setting that reminded her of an old-fashioned mirror. It glinted in the early morning sun, and she blinked when she saw something reflected in it. Picking it up, turning it over in her hands, she decided her eyes had only played tricks on her.

Putting on the necklace, she allowed it to rest over her solar plexus. She smiled as a calmness washed away her anxieties for the day ahead.

***

After the ten-hour drive to Arbore Falls, Emeline felt as though she'd driven into an entirely different world. Main Street, the town center, was lined with family-owned businesses, their facades dating back over a hundred years. Beyond Main Street, the streets were heavily lined with trees all but hiding the houses behind them from view.

It took Emeline fifteen minutes to find her new place, despite it only being walking distance from Main Street. All the trees were a refreshing change, especially with the beautiful autumn colours of amber and gold.

Not having a lot of belongings, she was unpacked and settled in by dinner time. With her hands on her hips, she surveyed her new home. Happy with the work she'd done, she decided to treat herself to dinner at the diner. When she opened the front door, she cried out, her hand flying to her chest.

"Hello! You must be Emeline Coben. I'm so sorry I startled you!" exclaimed a rather short and stout woman of about forty; she had curly red hair and a warm smile.

"Um, yes. Hello."

"I'm Hannah Bishop. I'm the local historian and one-woman welcome party! I'm also a teacher up at Arbore Falls Primary, so we'll be working together."

"Oh! Well, it's lovely to meet a friendly face before I start."

Hannah held out a large, brown paper bag. "This is for you. I figured since it's your first night here, you're not likely to have stocked your kitchen yet."

As Emeline reached forward to accept the food, the necklace slipped out from underneath her cardigan.

Hannah lowered the bag, her expression darkening. "You're... that necklace... it's quite... interesting."

Emeline picked up the pendant, absently running her thumb over the gem. "Thank you. It was my mother's." With a sad smile, she looked up to find Hannah's eyes wide in alarm. The look was quickly gone, replaced by a smile, though Emeline couldn't help but feel it wasn't as warm as before.

"Well, that's nice. I'd best be going. Enjoy your food, and I'll see you up at the school Monday morning." Hannah handed her the bag and quickly backed away.

"Thanks again!" Emeline called out, staring after the woman who hurried down the street.

***

Surrounded again by darkness, Emeline was pleased she wasn't dizzy like before. She watched the familiar light grow in the distance before it faded away to reveal the luminescent tree. It was more magnificent than she remembered; its strong branches reached out on either side beyond her line of sight.

She seemed farther away from it this time around; she couldn't see the roots tunneling downwards. Taking a step forward, Emeline paused when she heard a rumbling in the distance. While she was unable to make anything out, she could feel the vibration carry through her feet before dispersing across her body.

The sensation sent a shiver of fear along her spine, and she wanted to run but had no idea where she'd go. She instinctively grasped her pendant, and calmness swept over her, clearing her mind.

Squinting into the darkness, she saw the debris flying up from the ground, like something was speeding along just under the surface. She stood her ground, more curious than afraid. The gleaming white tree roots broke the surface and reached towards her. They hovered at first, sensing her without seeing her.

Keeping perfectly still, she watched, intrigued as they neared her and wrapped around her body. The roots moved slowly, reverently, enveloping her in a gentle embrace. A great warmth spread through her, and Emeline felt sacred—like a great honour had been bestowed upon her. With the pendant held firmly in her hands, she clasped them against her chest and closed her eyes while the roots engulfed her.

***

Despite the dark clouds covering the sky, Emeline decided to walk to work for her first day. With a large coffee in hand, she headed for the school and tried to shake off the remnants of her dreams. She was unsure if the nerves fluttering around in her stomach were a result of a new job in a new town or from the intensity of what she'd experienced in her sleep.

***

Although Hannah introduced her to the other teachers and showed her around, her thin smile didn't reach her eyes. Emeline could swear the other teachers spoke in hushed whispers the minute they thought her out of earshot. She told herself she was imagining it, that it was nothing more than first-day nerves.

Once she entered her classroom, her trepidation vanished. Her first students. It made her smile to see their little upturned faces staring at her expectantly.

The morning passed without a hitch, and Emeline knew she was in her element. Yet after lunch, her mood dampened. A headache took over, spreading from the base of her neck and around to her temples. The sound of her own voice sounded like nails down a chalkboard, causing her to flinch as she talked to the children.

"Are you okay, Miss Coben?" a child asked. Emeline gave a small nod and what she hoped was a reassuring smile. Looking up at the clock, she was relieved to see there was only an hour and a half left before the children went home for the day.

Rubbing her temples, she tried stretching out her neck to relieve the headache. It was then that Emeline saw her. Standing outside, at the far edge of the playground, was a young woman. She stood perfectly still. A light wind blew at her long dark hair and her white tattered dress with its high neck and full skirts.

The woman stared straight at Emeline. Despite the distance between them, Emeline could saw the wounded expression on the woman's face; she felt the pain resonating from her. It reached outwards, cinching her heart like a vice.

Emeline stepped around the children sitting on the carpet. Their questions of concern fell on deaf ears, and she made her way to the window for a better look. With languid movements, the girl raised her arms out, her palms facing up, and Emeline found herself placing her hands against the window in response.

She braced herself against the glass as a wave of dizziness engulfed her. A buzzing sounded in her ears, and pressure built in her head, causing her temples to throb. She stared at the woman with the distinct feeling the stranger was trying to show her something.

Closing her eyes against the building pressure, Emeline found herself still looking at the woman. Only now, the sun was shining and she stood in a field of long grass and wildflowers. A young man was with the woman, and as Emeline watched, they danced and weaved around each other before he succeeded in grabbing her around the waist and pulling her close. As their laughter fell away, their gazes intensified, and the man leaned in for a kiss that was eagerly reciprocated.

"Emeline!"

She spun around, disoriented, as the vision disappeared. In its place stood the headmaster.

"I'm sorry, sir. I didn't see you there."

"Exactly what the hell is the matter with you?"

"I'm sorry?" Taking a quick glance at the clock on the wall, she balked. "Is that time correct?"

she asked in a whisper, realizing her classroom was empty.

"Yes. It is. Which means, if I've been informed correctly, you've been standing there for an hour."

"That can't be…"

"Two of your students went to Hannah next door, frightened because their new teacher was staring out the window, non-responsive. Hannah came to see for herself, and when she was unable to rouse you, she sent the children outside to play and came to me. I only succeeded in getting your attention after considerable effort."

"I… I saw a woman. Young. Over there…" She pointed at the window, lowering her arm when she saw the headmaster had no interest in looking. Emeline cleared her throat, steadying herself. "There was a young woman. I came to the window for a closer look. She seemed distressed."

"So where is she now?" he asked in a voice both stern and patronising.

Emeline glanced out the window once more, certain the girl must have run off once their bond was broken. Struggling to come up with an answer, she could think of nothing but the hour of time she'd lost.

"Go home, Miss Coben. I will dismiss your class. I don't think I need to explain the repercussions of a repeat performance tomorrow."

Emeline could only manage a small nod as she watched the principal stride out of the room.

Hurriedly, she grabbed her bag, not wanting to see the confusion or fear on her students' faces when they returned to collect their bags. Tomorrow would be soon enough.

***

Sitting on her small back veranda, staring out at the forest of trees surrounding her house, Emeline ran through the afternoon's events.

"What's happening to me?" she whispered to the trees.

With a sigh, she picked up the phone and called in a takeaway order from the diner. Knowing that in a small town her behaviour was likely common knowledge by now, she didn't want to draw further attention to herself by eating in.

It took no time at all to reach the diner, and she yanked open the door, dismayed to find herself face to face with Hannah Bishop. Forcing a quick smile and hello, Emeline went to the counter to collect her order.

As she handed over her money, the doorbell jangled. She instinctively looked up to see Hannah hurriedly exiting. Emeline clutched her bag of food and dashed out after her.

"Wait!" she called out. Hannah stopped, and Emeline walked briskly towards her.

"Emeline. Hello. Nice to see you, but I'm in a hurry."

"I want to know what I did to offend you. You made all that effort coming to introduce yourself, but then you've acted strangely around me ever since."

"It's your necklace that I find offensive. You have some nerve wearing it around here."

Emeline's mouth fell open in surprise. She wrapped her fingers around the pendant. A soothing warmth engulfed her hand, giving her strength to press forward. "I don't understand. My necklace offends you? I'm sorry, but that's ridiculous! It's just—"

"How much do you know about that necklace?" Hannah interrupted.

"I can't see how it's any of your business, but it belonged to my mother. No, I don't know a thing about it, since my parents died a long time ago. All I need to know is that it was hers."

Hannah's eyes widened in unmistakable disbelief. Her skin paled as she gave a shake of her head. "You don't know..." she whispered, barely audible.

"Know what?" Emeline asked, confusion overriding her frustration.

"You're..." Hannah turned on her heel and hurried down the street, leaving Emeline staring after her.

***

Emeline sat on the veranda in the darkness, admiring a spectacular view of the moonless, star-filled sky. Yet she was unable to completely enjoy it. Absently toying with the pendant, she told herself Hannah was mistaken. There was no way Hannah knew of her mother—she'd grown up on the other side of the country. At least, that was what she'd been told.

Opening the browser on her phone, she searched for her mother's maiden name—Abagail Thomson. She scrolled through the hits, her frustration increasing as not one was related to her mother. With a huff, she tried changing the search to Corban. Emeline sank back into her chair. Her brow furrowed in confusion as she stared at the only related hit—a wedding announcement.

Emeline sighed. She'd never known much about her mother, but she'd counted on the little she did know. What if none of it was true?

A rustle in the tree line at the edge of the yard distracted her; she squinted in the darkness, half expecting to see an animal. A strange movement between the tree trunks caught her eyes: a flash of something pale. Emeline leaned forward, her breath caught in her chest. A cool shiver ran down her spine as a pale hand crept around the side of a trunk. The hand was followed by an arm.

She found herself torn between wanting to move closer, and wanting to run inside and lock the doors. Instead, she remained frozen in fear; the only sound was her heart pounding in her chest. As she watched, transfixed, the young woman appeared. Despite the darkness, Emeline could see her as clearly as if it were daylight. A light shone from within her, radiating outwards like a beacon in the night, drawing Emeline in.

Before she knew what she was doing, Emeline walked briskly across the yard. The woman retreated into the trees. "Wait!" she cried out, stumbling over the sudden rough ground, the close proximity of the trees intensifying the darkness. She was reduced to a snail's pace as she tried to navigate with her hands outstretched in front of her. The occasional flash of light ahead was the only indication she was going the right way.

Finally, the trees thinned, and Emeline gasped, almost losing her balance and falling back into them. In front of her was a large clearing, hidden all the way around by a perimeter of trees. But what stopped her in her tracks was the enormous tree in the center.

It was the tree from her dreams.

Its pull strengthened the closer she got. So enamoured by it, she didn't notice that she'd lost sight of the woman. Reaching out her hand, Emeline leaned in to touch the trunk.

A piercing beeping sounded, breaking the spell. It took her a few moments to realise it was her phone, and she reached into her pocket to find her morning alarm sounding.

5 a.m.

Startled, Emeline looked up from her phone to find herself standing in the middle of the backyard. She frantically looked around for any sign of the woman. She was alone. From the pallid skin tone of her hands, she knew she'd stood outside all night. Shivering at the realization, she hurried inside to get warm.

She struggled to make sense of what happened while she allowed the hot shower to soothe her. As she felt herself warming up, she decided she couldn't go to work—she had to figure out who the woman was and what she wanted.

Emeline decided to sit outside in the hope that the woman would appear again.

With a strong, hot cup of coffee beside her and the laptop in her lap, she wracked her brain for the right keywords to type. Finally, she searched for any reported sightings of a mysterious woman in the area. Surprised the search came back with nothing, she found herself questioning her own sanity. Trying 'ruby', 'heirloom', and the like provided no help either. Looking down, she saw the pendant resting on the laptop, and it dawned on her to search for 'ruby' and 'Arbore Falls'.

Her mouth fell open when a picture of her necklace was displayed on the screen. She scrolled down and clicked on the article, "The Putnam Ruby", and skimmed it.

'Brought over from England by the Putnam family in 1629...'

'Passed down to the eldest daughter of each generation...'

'Family suspected of witchcraft...'

'Prominent family feared...'

'Mystery surrounds deaths of Putnam family rivals...'

'Fruitless investigations...'

Emeline slowed her reading. *'After the death of the only son of the prominent Bishop family, an angry mob abducted Temperance Putnam, who was believed to be in a secret relationship with the young man.*

With her parents away, Temperance had no one to defend her. The death of John Bishop was the final straw in decades of discontent and suspicion towards the family. Temperance was accused of witchcraft and went without a trial; the mob in their anger lynched her from a tree before burning her body where it hung.

It was presumed Temperance wore the ruby at the time of her death, for there is no record of its whereabouts since.

After her death, the Putnam family left Arbore Falls after 285 years.'

The article finished with a Putnam family photo. Emeline immediately recognized the young woman as her mysterious visitor.

It was Temperance Putnam.

Emeline sat back in her chair, letting the information sink in. She felt agitated and on edge, unable to sit still. Putting her laptop aside, she paced along the veranda, her hand pressed against her forehead as her mind raised one question after the next.

It makes no sense. Why do I have the necklace? My mother wasn't a Putnam. I don't understand...

Without realizing it, Emeline had crossed the yard and navigated her way through the trees. It was easier to move with the little daylight piercing the canopy of leaves. After a few minutes, Emeline stepped into the clearing. For a moment, she was frozen, awed by the magnificent tree. Tears pricked her eyes; she was relieved to know it was real.

She admired the beauty of the elegant branches while she walked towards it. A faint hum floated towards her. Emeline paused and strained to listen. Picking up the pendant, she realized the noise came from the ruby, and as she watched, the stone swirled beneath the surface. Emeline let it fall from her hand as the ground trembled.

She forced herself forward; the tremors strengthened the closer she approached. She paused, bracing herself when a large crack raced upwards from the base of the tree. Barely staying on her feet, Emeline watched two hands emerge from the crack, placing themselves firmly on either side of the trunk.

The pendant rose from where it lay against her chest, reaching out for the tree as much as it could without breaking the clasp. Raising her hand to grab it, Emeline thought twice and let it be, enthralled by what was happening.

The hands braced against the tree before a head slowly followed, the unmistakeable long, dark hair spilling forwards. Next came one blackened leg, then the other, before the body of Temperance Putnam, clad in her torn dress. She stood there for a moment, and Emeline felt the flutter of fear and nerves in the pit of her stomach. Temperance walked towards her, and Emeline's heart pounded against her chest.

But she held her ground, and as Temperance stopped before her, Emeline reached up and unclasped the necklace from around her neck. The pendant still hovered in place, its chain dangling behind it. Temperance held her hand out beneath it, and the stone gave a flash of light before falling into her hand. Temperance smiled at Emeline, but it was a smile full of sadness.

Emeline flinched as Temperance reached out and placed a palm on her forehead, eyes bulging with the sudden flood of imagery swamping her mind.

She saw Temperance standing in the same field as before with the young man she now knew was John Bishop. Temperance beamed with happiness, wide-eyed and smiling. John reached up and tucked a piece of hair behind her ear before stroking her cheek with his thumb. She grabbed his hand and placed it on her stomach. While it was easily hidden by her layers of skirts, there was no denying Temperance was pregnant.

John leaned in and kissed her, his hand still on her stomach. When he pulled back, his eyes brimmed with tears, and his face contorted with grief. The smile fell from Temperance's face; the light in her own eyes dimmed. He gave a quick shake of his head, glancing over his shoulder towards the town. Bringing her hands to his lips, he kissed them, no longer able to meet her gaze as the tears spilled.

He turned his back and strode away, the heartbreak evident in Temperance's eyes. They were like shattered mirrors, never to be intact again. She wrapped her arms around her stomach as her chest heaved and tears streamed down her face. Tugging at her neck, she pulled the pendant from where it hid under her dress. Holding it tightly, she pressed her head against it in prayer, then she fell to her knees and wailed. In the distance, John hesitated, just for a moment, before continuing on his way.

The ruby flashed, and a calmness swept over her. She lifted her head. The tears were still wet upon her cheeks, but her eyes now held a defiant, angry glint. She raised her hands up, directing them towards her love, and spat out a quick succession of words.

John's body seized where he stood, his eyes wide with surprise. He clutched at his heart and collapsed to the ground as the life vanished from his eyes.

Temperance stared after him, her arms still outreached. Her bottom lip quivered, and her eyes welled as the magnitude of what she'd done set in.

With a brilliant flash of light, Emeline found herself watching a noose being placed around Temperance's neck. The woman's eyes were wide with fear, but it was not fear for her own life. She clasped her hands against her chest, feeling for the pendant hidden under her dress. As the mob pitied what they perceived to be a last-minute prayer for her damned soul, Temperance closed her eyes and cursed her revenge upon them all.

Another flash, and Emeline witnessed the heartbreak of Temperance's parents retrieving her blackened body. Holding her grief at bay, Temperance's mother released the ruby from her daughter's neck. Gripping it tightly, she lay both hands upon her daughter's stomach. When she closed her eyes, she chanted her incantations, and her husband kept an eye out. Though it was too late to save their daughter, the glow from the ruby assured them they could save their grandchild.

Emeline watched them leave their family home for good—the only way to protect Temperance's daughter. She then watched the girl grow into a young woman, passing the ruby onto her own daughter, who also grew older and passed it on to hers. So it went, one generation after the other as the years spanned onwards, each owner keeping the ruby and their powerful magic a secret.

Before she knew it, Emeline saw her own mother proudly receive her birthright, and a longing sadness tugged at her heart. She felt cheated out of the family tradition—out of the defining moment between mother and daughter. Anger filled her as she thought of all the times she didn't belong, the uncertainty about who she was, of feeling her life had no purpose.

"We can take it all back. We can make them pay," Temperance whispered, removing her hand from Emeline and looking straight at her.

Emeline gave a nod. With a smile, Temperance clasped the necklace around her own neck. They embraced, and a brilliant flash of light engulfed them.

Temperance blinked to clear her vision. A new power surged through her, and she said a prayer of gratitude to Emeline. With the two women now one, the Putnam magical line was stronger than ever. As a ruby glint flashed across her eyes, Temperance smirked. She set off back through the trees and towards the town.

<u>Liz Butcher</u>

Liz Butcher resides in Brisbane, Australia, with her

husband, daughter, and two cats, Pandora and Zeus. While writing is her passion, her numerous interests include psychology, history, astronomy, the paranormal, mythology, reading, art and music—all of which help fuel her imagination. She also loves being out in nature, especially amongst the trees or near the water. Liz has published a number of short stories in anthologies and currently has a multitude of projects in the works, including her upcoming novel, Fates Revenge. Website:

http://lizbutcherauthor.wix.com/lizbutcher

The Talking Cedar
by Britt Haraway

I was surprised when my mother's three-hundred-year-old Cedar tree began yelling at me, although quite pleased to be in the middle of a real enchantment. I had thought a tree would be like the ones in the kids' movies, wisdom sprouting from its mossy ears, this deep-rooted patience we humans should learn from. This tree, a Lebanese Cedar my mother had bragged about since my youth, had been planted to commemorate Louis the XIV's birth, and it now towered over our yard, outliving all French kings. Its voice startled me, coming down invisible as if from the sky. My brie and wine tipped over into the shallow grass as I backed away, and I dropped the

Rumi I'd been reading out loud. The tree was angry. His curses grew convoluted and extreme. By the end of this confusing and frightening speech, his mouth was so raw that sap bled on the grass and flew out, spraying my white t-shirt, the sight of which calmed him and drove him to an equally confusing shame.

I'd been so good, he said. The relapse of rage caught me off guard. He apologized repeatedly, the first of his sentences that I truly understood, and I assured him I hadn't taken his insults personally. "But now that you mention it," I said, "you don't sound like a very happy tree." He said he wasn't always like this. Once, he'd been quiet like other trees and in love.

He invited me to sit back down and enjoy my cheese, only facing him this time instead of the world. He told me about his love for a Sequoia tree my mother used to have in our yard, one he'd first met when he was only twenty-five, not yet secure in his own branches. He marveled at the speed at which the Sequoia grew beside him. He described the redness of the bark, how it looked so warm in the morning light. He told me of its scent, but here he had to stop himself, moved as he was at the memory. I waited and could hear the wind coming through his limbs, and it amazed me how that happens. When the earth will accompany your feelings, the rain leaking down your collar as you watch an old lover from the bushes.

Her scent, he finally managed, was like travel.

He said her mind grew, even outpaced the rapidity of her outward development. She learned the habits of the squirrels more quickly than he had, and he only had to tell her the name of a bird's song once, and she knew it forever—really knew it—and would call it out first. "Oh," he said, "and such a wit, and meshed so well with my own silliness. When a woodpecker flew by with its looping flight, she called it Woody, managing to evoke the easy innuendo and also to associate it with the obstinacy of the trees in our region. The Grackles she called Gra-kel—Welch, get it?—and remarked on the shapeliness of their bosom. Sweet jokes too. When the Whip-poor-will started to call at night, she would remind me it was my birthday, to make a wish, anything I wanted, she'd do what she could, as long as it didn't require public singing or feet." He paused again in memory, and then with tender simplicity said, "It was nice to have someone remember my birthday."

I was a little impatient at this point, so I asked what happened to the lovely Sequoia. "Your mother chose me," he said. "I was a historic tree, a fine example, rare and fully mature. That was what the tree doctor said—that's what his truck called him. It was me or her, is what he said, just room for one in the garden."

I apologized for my mother's choice, guessing rightly, I think, that he'd rather have shortened his own life to spend time with the lovely Sequoia. "I try not to blame her," he said, "but like you saw, I'm not always on top of my anger. You see, this isn't the first time. Sequoias don't ever really die. Their roots are stubborn. They keep growing back and up, like weeds, and there is no space for grief. I've had to re-meet her three times. She goes away for a while and then she's back again, and I fall right back in love with her, the anger vanishing with each of her new discoveries, with each of her new and fascinating personalities. She is never the same. How I love that about her, how she makes my world mysterious again, then dooms me without knowing it. Without the memory of any of the crimes.

"Sometimes," he said, "I wish your mother had made the more expensive decision to rip up her roots, every fucking one of them. Go ahead, get your mother. You tell her. Turn the goddamn bulldozers back on. Fucking bitch. Get your own fucking yard." His mouth was getting pale again, his eyes not locked on mine but searching the yard, looking up at the sky. I was not sure if he was looking to curse my mother or the yard or the old Sequoia tree.

I knew it was time for me to leave. He was waiting for her to grow up again, keeping his veins pumping until he could see her in the familiar light, impatient for that last adulthood. And maybe her voice, which must sometimes be small and curious, would sound out loud this time and remind him of something he'd forgotten, like an old joke which was not a joke to anyone but them, the one about the squirrel that fell inside the swimming pool. About what a beautiful thing it was when someone came along in time to push the water out of its lungs.

Britt Harraway

Britt Haraway's book of short stories *Early Men* was published September 2016 by Lamar University Literary Press. His stories have appeared in *Moon City Review*, *Great Weather for Media*, *New Madrid*, *BorderSenses* and elsewhere. His work was selected for The Best of Small Fictions 2016, guest-edited by Stuart Dybek. He holds a PhD from the University of Southern Mississippi's Center for Writers. Currently, he is an assistant professor in the creative writing program at the University of Texas Rio Grande Valley, where he is the fiction editor of *riverSedge* literary magazine.

Orion and the Dream-Eater
by Heather M. Holmes

"For Dustin, who believed in my dreams even when I did not."

The newborn was naked and alone, squalling in the mud. Rigel did not see him. The rain beat down from a cloudless violet sky, nearly drowning the infant and his cries. Maretta shouted at her husband from inside the wagon, but her voice was lost in the din of the storm. Pulling back the heavy curtain of blue dragonhide, Maretta cupped her hands to her lips and tried again.

"Stop the wagon!"

"What?" he shouted back, glancing over his shoulder.

Maretta screamed with all the force she could muster. "Stop!"

Rigel pulled on the reins, and the nite mares halted to graze in the sparse teal grass. Maretta sprang from the wagon, rushing past them. Rigel could see the child now, flailing on the cold ground. He shook his head and smirked, watching his predictable wife run towards the babe. He almost laughed at her desperation, but instead, he called her name sternly. "Maretta. It's just a dream. It ain't real."

"Oh, yes, he is. Just as real as you and me."

"He don't have to be!"

"He don't have to be left out for that Dream-Eater, neither!" Maretta knelt beside the infant, gathering him into her arms. As she cradled him to her chest, she felt her bosoms swell with milk, and suddenly the world was still. The child stopped crying, staring up at her with stormy blue eyes. The rain stopped falling, and Orion shone overhead like a guardian among the stars.

"Orion." Maretta smiled down at her son, sealing the magic. Rigel beckoned her back into the wagon with a tilt of his head. Maretta climbed aboard, clutching her new treasure. Rigel dipped his head to hide his grin. When his wife had disappeared behind the dragonhide, he shook his head again and chuckled to himself.

"Yah," Rigel called to the nite mares, flicking the reins. The wet smacks of their hooves in the mud echoed all around as the Dreamscape unfolded before them.

Maretta took to motherhood like a swan to water. Rigel would have preferred to wait a few years before tackling fatherhood, but life happens as it will. He had to admit it was rather nice having the lad around—not the smells so much, but the sounds. The babe had an easy laugh and rarely fussed. Maretta spent hours singing to the boy and telling him stories as the wagon bumped along.

"Stop!" she shouted. "Come back, Orion!"

Rigel dropped the firewood and darted after the toddler, who had wandered too close to the nite mares' powerful legs. He caught him under the armpits, swooping Orion up and passing him into Maretta's outstretched arms. He tossed the logs into the flames, then sat beside his wife, who struggled to keep the determined child in her lap.

"Sit still, Orion! How about a story, love? Yes?"

"Yuss!" called the boy, popping a finger into his mouth and grinning around it.

"Once upon a world, there was a star—and not just any star, a *shooting* star, who chose our planet for her home. For centuries, she granted wishes to all who saw her and had the heart for wishing. She lived a life of gaiety, flitting Above and Below, in and out between the Dreamscape, reality, and the other layers of the world. Her joy was complete when she birthed her first starling.

"But the world is an onion, and you never know when it will peel back a new layer for you. It was time for the star to know grief, for it is pain that makes joy so precious. The starling did not live. It crashed to Earth, landing in reality, where it was a mere rock.

"The star was devastated. She sacrificed her life force to grant herself a wish—her child's life for her own. Engulfing the planet in magic, she cast her spell on us all. When a grieving mother dreamt of her lost babe, the infant would appear in Nite, and when he had found a mother here, his old mother in the real world would have peace for her suffering.

"The starling was raised by a pack of nite howls, and that was the beginning of the Dream Children. We are like humans, but we aren't, just as Nite is like night, but it isn't. And that, my darling, is how you were born."

Orion had curled up beside Maretta, his head in her lap, and fallen asleep long before the story was told. She still stroked his golden curls. Rigel had puffed his pipe and stared at the stars, lost in Maretta's voice. He passed the pipe to her and leaned back on his palms in the grass. "That boy's grown restless."

"'Course he is. He's got all that energy, and he's cooped up all day!"

"I suppose we'll need a house," Rigel said after a moment.

"You suppose right." A cloud of purple smoke escaped Maretta's mouth.

"Life changes suddenly, like the Dreamscape."

"And to think we almost didn't hear him underneath that murderous rain."

"That was some fierce sorrow. I'm glad she has peace now. You were right to take the child."

"I know."

"Perhaps, after we've settled, we could have another by means of a more… *traditional* kind of magic." Rigel glanced at Maretta out of the corner of his eye, his lips curled in a half-smile.

Maretta blushed. Rigel leaned in to place a kiss on his wife's scarlet cheek, and she turned to meet his lips with hers. He gently hoisted Orion over his shoulder to carry him to the wagon. Maretta puffed on the pipe, blowing purple smoke rings at the moons as they circled each other in the purple sky. Then she doused the fire and joined her family on the feather down mattress inside the wagon.

Six years passed in the blink of an eye. Orion had crossed his arms on the kitchen table of their little cottage. Maretta held up each letter, identifying and pronouncing it. She was nearing the end of the alphabet. His foot tapped on its own, but when his mother cleared her throat, it stopped. At long last, she reached the final, wonderful letter Z—and then she held up "a". Orion made a small sound of disgust.

"And b is for—"

"Boring!"

"Orion!"

"But why are there two sets of letters? You only need one."

"Because uppercase and lowercase letters mean different things. Capital letters show you when a new sentence begins or when a word is more important than others, like a name. You need to know both to read or write."

"I just want to scavenge with Paw. I don't want to do words."

"Suppose you get lost. How you gonna know where you are?"

"I'll ask someone."

"What if no one is around? What if a sign says 'Keep Out,' but you can't read it? Now you're trespassing. Besides, there is knowledge in books—anything you could ever want to know."

"Like what?"

"What makes suns and stars burn. How to tame and slay beasts. All that has been. All that could have been but wasn't. Why the twin moons are locked in their embrace. How to bottle wishes and visit the Palace of the Stars—"

"Okay, I get it. Can I go now, please?"

"After your letters. Paw won't wanna hear you were being disagreeable when he gets home."

"Yes, mother."

Though his glum tone suggested he was only

humoring her, Orion secretly finished his lesson in better spirits. He did want to know how to slay beasts and bottle wishes. Someday, perhaps, he would read in books how to do both, then find the Dream-Eater. The people were already cheering Orion's name in the back of his mind when Maretta dismissed him.

On his eleventh birthday, Maretta gifted Orion with a Grounding Stone, which would repel the Dreamscape during travel and allow him to fade out of dreams if he was in danger. The translucent white crystal was wrapped in copper wire and dangled from a thin leather cord. Orion grinned as he held it up to admire it, but then his face fell. He turned to Maretta. "But Mother, this is *your* Grounding Stone."

"I don't need it. I can borrow your father's if need be, but I won't be wanting to leave the house much for a while." Maretta glanced at Rigel, a half-smile on her lips, then back to Orion. She put her hands over her belly, cradling it with her palms. A slow smile spread across Orion's face as his father spoke.

"You see, Orion, your mother is going to have a baby."

"And since the baby will keep me very busy, you will join your father on his outings."

"Awesome!"

"You will still have lessons at night," Rigel added.

"Aw." Though Orion sighed, his grin was

stubborn, and soon the whole family was hugging and smiling together.

Rigel and Orion loaded the wagon early the next morning. The Dreamscape stretched out before them, random, infinite. There were layers within layers of dreams, all converging together, each one a different world. Orion watched the scenes change as the wagon rumbled along. A railroad in the distance, spanning a golden desert, became an ocean horizon beyond a beach of sparkling sand. Skyscrapers loomed on either side while a sea turtle swam overhead.

"When can we stop and explore?"

"This excursion is going to be hands-off, a bit look but don't touch, I'm afraid."

"But I've ridden through the Dreamscape before! I'm ready to dream walk."

"Tomorrow, perhaps. Today we're going to the city."

"The city?" Orion gasped. "The Spinning City?"

"That's right. We're off to buy a wish."

"Aren't they expensive?"

"A safe delivery for your mother and the baby is well worth the cost. Whoa!" Rigel pulled on the reins, bringing the nite mares to a halt.

On either side of the wagon, rows of halls stretched into the Dreamscape. Rigel touched his Grounding Stone, and it went dark. He nodded to Orion, who did the same. The Dreamscape swallowed them, and Orion found himself in the main aisle of a massive underground library.

"What luck! Your mother's been asking for new books, and here's some for free. Let's have a look around."

The great wooden shelves loomed over them. The floor and ceiling were both a phosphorescent tan rock, whose golden glow lit the room. Orion headed down the aisle with a bronze placard that read "Non-Fiction: B." He ran his fingers over the spines of a dozen baby books, as well as more interesting titles like *Bastard Stole My Candy* and *Booger Recipes for Every Occasion*.

His fingers slowed as he found the books about beasts—*Beasts of the Arctic, Beasts of the Deep, Beasts of Narnia*. Orion pulled *Beasts of Nite* from the shelf and flipped through the Ds. There was a detailed explanation of how to capture a Dream Sprite, but there was no entry for Dream-Eater. Hearing his father call, Orion snapped the book shut and hurried back to the wagon.

They did not stop again until they reached the city. It appeared out of nowhere, the Dreamscape parting to reveal its glowing crystal towers. They were the biggest Grounding Stones Orion had ever seen. Above them, the Dreamscape twisted and changed, touching only the city's spinning spires. Patchwork metal walls surrounded the city, though the great steel doors stood wide open to travelers.

The buildings were assembled haphazardly

from every kind of material—wood, crystal, gold, even seashells. The crowd was just as eclectic, a melting pot of the many races of Nite. Rigel steered the wagon with purpose into the heart of the city, a square with a broken marble fountain. The silver water lay stagnant, reflecting the spires and towers above.

"Good dreams to you," said a quiet, deep voice from beneath the brim of a bowler hat. A tall, slender man in a purple suit stood in front of them. He had dark eyes, wild hair, and a youthful face with a sharp nose.

"And to you. It's been a while. How are you?"

"Same old tricks, same old hat." The man in the hat grinned wide. "How's the old bat?"

"She sends her love. Says she can still clobber you at chess."

"You see? Delusional."

"This is our son, Orion." Rigel laid a hand on Orion's shoulder. "He's just had his eleventh. This is my friend, Saiph."

"Good dreams, sir."

"And to you. Eleven is a big year for a lad. What brings you to the Dizzy City?"

"My mother, sir. She—she's going to have a baby." Orion's eyes gleamed with pride.

"Another batling? Marvelous! You'll be needing this, I presume?" A clear vial appeared between Saiph's thumb and index finger. Orion could see the magic swirling inside. Saiph tossed it to him.

"Only the best for my Maretta."

"Indeed. You know, for a small added fee, I can use the Sight to see the child's gender."

"Maretta would scold me for wasting money on foolishness. How much for the wish?"

Pocketing the vial, Orion wandered to the fountain as the adults completed their transaction. He peered over the rim, expecting to see colorful fish or scattered coins. The pool was a perfect mirror. Then the reflection changed. Instead of the Dreamscape, the twin moons of the Nite sky hung overhead, and the overlapping rooftops of the Spinning City became treetops.

"I see you've discovered the Reflecting Pool. Always a favorite. It shows you a glimpse of your future, but only a random moment. What do you see?" asked Saiph.

"I'm standing in the woods, holding some kind of plant."

"How mysterious!" Saiph smiled broadly.

"What do you see, Paw?" asked Orion, and Rigel joined him by the water.

"Nothing." Rigel shook his head after a moment, looking to Saiph. "Damn thing must be broken."

"Nonsense. You're as batty as your wife!" Saiph closed the gap between them with a single step, flashing towards them in a blur. Looming over Rigel and Orion, he peered into the pool at their reflections. Orion could only see his own. He looked up at Saiph, whose face had fallen as his eyes darted back and forth over the water.

"It's just a parlor trick." Rigel faced Saiph, meeting his eyes. "I'm sure you can fix it."

"It isn't broken." Saiph's gaze went distant, as if he were looking through Rigel. Rigel broke the trance with a blink, and Saiph stumbled back a few steps. "My friend," he gasped, ashen. Saiph put a hand on Rigel's shoulder. "There's *nothing there*."

"I must be in your blind spot." Rigel cracked a smile.

"Nonsense. My only blind spot is—"

The Oracle was interrupted by a metallic moan, followed shortly by a deafening crash and a roar of screams. In the distance, one of the spinning spires fell in a cacophony of breaking glass and crumbling rock. Behind it, there was a hole in the city wall where the gate had been. The ground shook beneath the destruction.

Rigel hurried everyone into the wagon and veered right at a canter. The street was empty, shutters closed. Ahead of them stood another city gate. They raced towards it as a panicked mob rounded the corner behind them. A savage shriek pierced the din of the crowd, echoing off the city walls. Orion's heart pounded in his chest and yet felt frozen, cold.

He shot a glance at the crowd running behind them. Orion watched in horror as a giant set of jagged jaws opened, swallowing an entire group of people.

He screamed as he saw the beast, a giant, inky black orb, swirling and gyrating like a storm—a great black hole with great white teeth. The mouth snapped shut again, devouring the last of the survivors.

They lurched to the left as the wagon hit a bump. Saiph was thrown out to the side. Rigel thrust the reins at Orion and leapt out after Saiph. Orion looked over his shoulder to see Rigel hit the ground in a roll. The beast hurtled towards them, its maw agape. Saiph was dusting himself off, oddly oblivious. Rigel lunged at the Oracle, knocking him out of its path. Orion screamed as the jaws closed and his father disappeared.

With tears streaming down his face, Orion spurred the nite mares onward. They took a sharp right, steering the wagon off the main road into an alley. He pulled hard on the reins and jumped out of the wagon, running towards the road. The Dream-Eater roared by, leaving a trail of debris in its wake. Orion shouted and cursed at it until he was sobbing on his knees in the dirt.

They did not speak during the journey home. Maretta was waiting on the front porch. Saiph took off his hat as he climbed down from the wagon and faced her. Her hand went to her heart. Saiph flashed to her side and embraced Maretta as she wept.

Orion watched his mother and the Oracle go into the house. It was near dark when they emerged. He was still sitting in the wagon, staring into the Dreamscape. Saiph appeared beside him, his hat in his hands. Orion did not look up.

"I don't understand. Why didn't you just flash out of the Dream-Eater's way?"

"I did not see it."

"But you have the Sight!"

"There are blind spots. It is a child of Chaos. I cannot perceive it, only its effects on Nite."

"What is it?"

"It is a creature called a Despair, a manifestation of human suffering. The world is an onion. If one layer goes bad, the others soon rot. Most Despairs die before growing big enough to eat whole dreams. This particular Despair was spawned by a long and bloody war that has devoured dreams across reality. When the war ends, it will weaken and die... along with everything it has eaten."

"I'm gonna find a way to get Paw back, and then I'm gonna kill that horrid thing."

"Are you, now?" Saiph asked softly, his expression impassive as he looked into Orion's eyes—through them, as he had done with Rigel.

Orion searched Saiph's eyes for some small glimpse, like in the Reflecting Pool, but found only his dark pupils, like two black holes.

"Eleven really is a big year. A big year deserves a big gift." Saiph snapped his fingers. A furry, golden-eyed creature appeared between them. It was navy blue with tufts of white fur sticking from its pointy ears. The animal was the size of an adult wolf, but Orion could tell from its clumsy movements it was still just a pup. It licked his hand as he ran his fingers through its thick fur.

"Oh, good. She likes you."

"A nite howl? Do you have any idea how much those things eat?" asked Maretta, coming to stand at Orion's side. Her eyes were still wet.

"That's what makes it such a great deal for me." Saiph winked at Orion, then vanished into the Dreamscape in a blur.

Maretta embraced Orion, and the two held each other for a long time. Her eyes brimmed with tears again when he pulled the bottled wish from his pocket. They unloaded the wagon together. Maretta smiled weakly as she touched the books Rigel had taken from the archive for her.

Orion took *Beasts of Nite* to bed with him that night. He found only a few brief paragraphs about Despairs. There was nothing about how to destroy them. The book offered little hope. *'Everything they eat is suspended in an infinite world of limbo until the Despair dies, destroying everything still inside it.'*

"If only I could just make it throw up," Orion sighed, scratching the nite howl pup behind the ears.

The pup grew as tall as Orion, her form less lanky, her gait steadier. He named her Artemis. Maretta grew, too, her energy waning as she neared her due date. It fell to Orion to tend the garden and animals. The wish ensured a safe, painless birth, and Maretta delivered a baby girl. She named the child

Hope, because the family needed more of it.

Orion was woken often by his new sister. Groggy, he would wander onto the porch to watch the Dreamscape from the swing. On one such night, just days before his twelfth birthday, Orion waited for Artemis to fetch a ball he had thrown into a dream. He called, but she did not come. Orion threw an uncertain glance over his shoulder, then stepped into the Dreamscape.

The dream closed around him. He found himself standing in a courtroom before a judge wearing only a white wig. Everyone was naked—the jury, the spectators, even the lawyers. Orion touched his Grounding Stone, and the teal grass of Nite reappeared at his feet, the naked court curving around him. He called for the nite howl as he walked between dreams, searching the changing landscape.

Ungrounding again, Orion found himself surrounded by staircases going in all manner of directions, even the nonsensical, like upside down. A portly man in a black suit, his thin white hair combed over his balding head, sat in a gilded armchair on a platform across from Orion. The bottle in his hand swirled with magic. He offered it to Orion, but when he reached out, it disappeared.

The man laughed. "You thought I was gonna just give it to you? The world is an onion. You can't get your slice without a few tears."

"What do I have to do?"

"Just meet me over here."

"That's all? It's not even that far of a jump."

"No, no, no." The man laughed again. "No shortcuts. You have to solve the maze, boy!"

Orion looked around the labyrinth. The staircase to the second platform went up, which meant he needed to get down. The stairs behind him led upstairs, then branched to the left and right, sideways along the walls. He tried to map a path with his eyes but couldn't keep track of the angles. The man in the suit looked smug.

"Have you ever done it?"

"Me? Of course!"

"How long does it take?"

"My best time is fifty-seven minutes!" The man grinned as he boasted.

"It's rigged."

"What?"

"Dreams only last half an hour, at most. Even if a dreamer knew the path, they would wake up halfway," explained Orion.

"*You're* not a dreamer."

"When the dream ends, this world disappears, leaving me on Nite. I still only have thirty minutes."

"Well, I've done it!"

"No one can do it but you. You're always here, no matter where the dream moves."

"This is preposterous!" the man in the suit sputtered, his forehead creased with frustration.

"Give me the wish."

"I am bound by this dream's magic to give

this wish to the one who solves the maze!"

"You're a cheat if you don't! I *have* solved it."

The stone walls shook, rumbling all around. A staircase fell away from the wall behind him, crashing into the stairs to Orion's platform. The man in the suit shouted as a crack split the floor between his feet. Above Orion, another staircase crumbled, breaking into falling chunks. He ran at the ledge, leapt across, and held out his hand, shouting at the man. "Your world is breaking because you are breaking its rules. You have to give me the wish to satisfy the dream magic!"

"Here! Take it!"

Orion snatched the vial from the man's hand and touched his Grounding Stone as the platform fell away. Nite bubbled around him again. He slipped the little bottle into his pocket, smiling. Calling for Artemis, Orion wandered further into the Dreamscape, his imagination already toying with the wish's potential.

Hearing a bark, Orion let the Dreamscape enfold him. He stood in a forest, dark and thick. Crooked, skeletal trees stretched gnarled branches towards a black sky with a crimson moon. They shook in the wind as thunder rolled in the distance, then the dream fell eerily silent. A growl split the air, and Orion hurried towards it.

He found Artemis crouched low, her teeth bared. The nite mare before her was the largest Orion had ever seen. Its crystalline, sapphire scales glinted in the wan light as it grazed. A little girl in a shimmering white dress cowered behind Artemis, her back against a hollow, wilted tree. The nite mare raised its head, fixing its violet, fly-like eyes on her, and the girl screamed.

Orion pulled a pouch of sugar cubes from his pocket. He approached slowly, his hand outstretched with the offering. The nite mare rolled its many eyes, taking a step back. Orion paused to pet Artemis' head, calming her. When the nite mare took the sweets, the dream changed, all the hallmarks of horror melting away to reveal a colorful, thriving wood bathed in golden sunlight.

"Um, little girl?" Orion knelt beside the silver-haired maiden.

"I'm not a girl. I'm a star! What is that horrible beast?"

"It's just a nite mare. They use fear as a defense mechanism, like a shield. They're harmless, just shy. Are you okay?"

"No, I'm not! I've fallen."

"Can't you fly?"

"Not here. I'm stuck in your stupid gravity."

"Wish yourself back into the sky."

"I can't use my magic for myself, or I'll *die*."

Orion's face fell as the girl started to weep again. Artemis whined at him. Orion slipped a hand into his pocket, curling his fingers around the vial. He pictured himself standing before the Dream-Eater, armed with the weapon of its destruction. But that was two wishes. His heart sank as he handed the bottle to the fallen star.

"You've got a wish! This is wonderful. Thank you!" The star pressed a quick kiss to his cheek.

"I reckon the world needs a shooting star more than a hero."

"But you are a hero, *my* hero! I'm Glimmer."

"Orion." He dipped his head to hide his flushed cheeks. "And this is Artemis. She's a nite howl. They're like wolves, but they're not, just as Nite is like night, but it's not."

"She's lovely."

"As are you." Orion pulled the blushing star to her feet.

"I can never tell day from night here. The moons are always in the sky. How do you tell with no sun?"

"The Dreamscape is most active during the day. It all but disappears at night, because the humans are all awake during their day."

"Interesting. The world *is* an onion." The young star let out a whimsical laugh. "Well, a wish for a wish is only fair, I think. What is yours?"

"A poison, toxic enough to make any creature of Chaos vomit," Orion decided after a moment. A noxious green flower with a spined stem appeared in his hand.

"You have my favor. Call on me anytime I streak across your sky, and I will shine on you." The star uncorked the bottle.

"*Any*time?"

"On your mark, Orion." With a mischievous grin, she closed her eyes to make her wish.

The star shot into the air in a flash of light, leaving a trail of flickering stardust. Orion closed his fingers around the blossom's fuzzy petals, watching her disappear into the purple sky. He held his breath, searching the heavens. When the star blazed across the sky, he squeezed his eyes shut and made a second wish. He opened them to face the Dream-Eater.

Its primal shriek sent chills through him, but Orion stood his ground. The Dream-Eater barreled towards him, gnashing its teeth. Its cavernous mouth opened, and Orion saw oblivion—the infinite, black nothingness of its maw. He threw the poisonous plant, and the Despair's jaws closed around it. Artemis barked as it neared, and Orion leapt out of the way.

The Dream-Eater twisted and shook, then exhaled a breath like a hurricane wind. A torrent of dreams spilled from its mouth in every direction. The Despair shrank as it spewed its innards. The dreams floated upward, separating into imperfect bubbles of every size and drifting away into the Dreamscape. As the dreams rose, Orion noticed dark, moving shapes on the ground—people, struggling to stand.

The Dream-Eater hiccupped, releasing another dream. It had lost half its size, and as it vomited again, it deflated like an old party balloon. The Despair shuddered and writhed, grinding its teeth, then belched a giant bubble of dreams clustered together. All that remained of it was a bouncing black spot, no bigger than a lump of coal. Orion stamped it out of existence.

"Orion!" a familiar voice called, and Orion turned to see his father staggering towards him.

"Paw!" He ran to Rigel, throwing his arms around him.

"My boy!" Rigel pressed Orion to his chest. "I never thought I'd see you again. I missed you so much."

"I missed you! I killed it, Paw. I killed the Dream-Eater. Poison!"

"You clever boy!"

"It's too bad no one will know but us."

"I wouldn't say that." Rigel gestured to the crowd that had gathered around them. Cheers rang out as Orion faced them. Someone called out his name, and it echoed through the crowd in a slow ripple. The people chanted his name until they were shouting. Orion stared at the crowd, speechless. A slow grin spread across his face, and he turned to his father. Their eyes met, and they embraced again.

Artemis howled, and her brethren joined their voices to her song all over Nite. Above them, the constellation Orion stared down, a watchful guardian flickering in the violet sky. A sparkling star flew past the twin moons, disappearing in a wink. In reality, a woman sat down to write a forgotten story she had dreamed as a child but lost to despair after the war. On the other side of the globe, tanks opened fire.

Heather Holmes

Heather Holmes is both an atheist and a devout believer in magic, whose stories blend fantasy with reality to make observations about the world and the human condition. Despite being the height of a fifth grader, she's actually pushing thirty and is prone to understatement. She is a mom and college student by day and a madwoman at night, plotting evil schemes and killing darlings. She likes to touch her readers in weird ways. Heather lives near Charleston, SC with two cats, a beagle, and a bunch of nerds.

Born of the Elements
by Laura Callender

Soren looked up at his mother with the wide eyes of innocence, refusing to go to sleep until he had a story. His tummy let out a rumble, but his smile masked the hunger they both felt.

"Tell me about the Elements," he said, almost pleading.

His mother looked at him, sighing; she wasn't going to get an early night. She knew that if she had no food to offer, at least she would feed his dreams. "All right," she said. "A great while ago, the world was full of wonder. The ocean and the land stood divided under the breath of the harsh winds and fires raging above." She paused, wondering if her son was too young for the old tales.

Soren soaked in every word, pushing his mother to tell him more.

"The Elements divided, starting a war that ravaged the earth until the birth of Irvina, the child of the four. She was an Incidental, born despite all four Elements trying to claim her. Fire licked her skin as Wind blew back the severity of its touch. Irvina was dragged away from her birth mother, across the crippled land towards the sea. Baby Irvina plopped into the water, her life only moments from being consumed. It has been said that salty liquid traveled over her tongue, threatening to squeeze out every last drop of air within. Water was winning. She would claim Irvina—or so it was thought."

Soren lay back, stretching his feet under the blanket. He carved out a comfortable position as he listened with interest. "Go on, Mother. More, more."

"The punishing death baby Irvina endured before her final fall left scars from all four Elements. It is said that when baby Irvina's spirit, which was left to roam the sea, finally matures, she will rise like a God to bring peace to our land."

"Will she come, Mother?"

The very question saddened Gaity as she tucked the blanket around her boy's shoulders. No child should have to witness the brutal conditions they endured daily. "No one knows for sure, but we hope these old tales hold some truth. If Irvina ever comes to shore, she will always be welcome here."

Soren smiled, somewhat satisfied by her answer. "Goodnight, son."

"Goodnight, Mother."

***

She walked with no particular aim or direction, elated to feel every new sensation each step brought. She stole glances at her puddled limbs in wonder. She saw the reflection of the clearing sky in her liquid outline yet still felt connected to the ocean—the only home she had ever known.

As she manifested into human form, she found she could command the air and quell the burning forests. Her spirit had come of age, manifesting great power that could bring peace to the land she was so ready to explore.

The jutting remains of charred forests alongside wind-battered buildings mesmerized the girl. The dark, dull colors should have signified something sad to her but didn't. She lacked any understanding of what she saw. Her eyes took in only beauty in the devastation humans had endured for so long.

She was unable to quantify how far she had wandered but saw the sky change in intensity many times. Both were equally as beautiful but one discernibly quieter than the other. It appeared that land creatures thrived in the brightness of the fire in the sky. When the bright ball dipped low towards the horizon, she saw anxiety in the eyes of every living thing she encountered. She could sense their hesitation as they stalked her curiously. She kept walking until the scent of the ocean had faded to reveal the musk of the earth beneath her feet.

She felt a pinch on the outer layer of her being. Raising her hand to her eyes, she twisted her limb in wonder. Skin formed over solidifying water, giving her the first glimpse of what her human form would look like. The swift changes confused her. She felt a rush of joy as she examined the smooth flesh, hardly noticing the person walking towards her. She took in his tiny frame, bouncing along with a degree of caution. His floppy hair mimicked the color of the decaying trees. It rested on his ears, which barely met the height of her chest. He scanned her with intent, like he was looking for a lost toy, before locking eyes with her. He gaped at her in astonishment.

"You were glowing, Miss."

Words fell from the boys mouth faster than a passing school of anchovies. She couldn't make sense of the noise. She twisted her head in an attempt to catch something understandable.

The boy reached out his tiny hand and stroked her arm. Her indifferent reaction allowed him to behave more daringly. He turned and prodded the limb, almost shaking it uncomfortably. His touch sent a burst of energy through the girl's entire body. She let out a loud gasp as air filled her lungs and awakened her mind. When the boy spoke once again to ask if she was all right, she knew exactly what he was saying.

"I'm fine" she said, laughing wildly. "I feel wonderful." She tugged her hand away from the boy, who seemed reluctant to let go. She thrust her arms up to the sky, feeling a connection with the Element as she felt Air caress her bare skin. Contemplating life outside the ocean had always sent a pulse of panic through her. Now, standing on the land, the girl knew she had nothing to fear. She was one with her creators, making her feel safe and strong.

Kneeling, she registered the boy's anguish and delight. "You are correct. What you saw was the inner me. I come from a place far from here. Have you ever seen the ocean?" she asked.

"I know how the sea can destroy the land. I've tasted the salt after it left. But I've never seen the ocean in its home."

She sensed the boy's sadness. He had experienced pain while she had roamed unbidden in the ocean depths—unaware of the war raging above. "I am here now." She spoke with conviction. "I promise to one day show you the ocean in all its wonder. You will like it, I'm sure."

The boy didn't seem excited or dismissive of her suggestion. He still looked at her with awe. "Will you come and meet my family? I know you will be welcome, Irvina."

Responding with a wide smile, she took the boy's hand and allowed him to lead her to his home.

"Irvina, you say. I like that name and will keep it."

***

The man stepped towards her. Irvina's skin tingled before gradually darkening in tone to match that of the visitor. He stood still, appearing somewhat offended by the woman's chameleon abilities. Irvina let out a small gasp, twisting her arms before her. Despite knowing he thought she had mocked him, she could only smile. "Beautiful," she added, speaking with such innocence and sincerity.

"What are you?" The man's voice trembled with uncertainty easy to miss. He held himself tall, giving no sign to anyone else of the fear he carried so close to his heart.

"I am you. I am them. I am everyone. I have come to calm the Elements that have been waging war on earth for far too long. I was born a human, like you. The Elements claimed me, resulting in what I am today. Please have no fear."

Gasps followed in response to her precise telling of the old tales everyone had hoped to be true. It was a quick burst of information but answered every possible question they had. She was no longer a strange woman, from a strange place; she was their God, their leader, their savior.

Irvina looked around, taking in the shelter they called home. They had opened their broken, panelled door and ushered her to a bench. The mud walls were neat, and Irvina enjoyed how earthy their home felt.

"We would offer you food, but we had a scorching and didn't reach the crop in time. It could be a few days before we get something from our neighbouring village."

"You must eat to survive?" Irvina asked, devoid of any expression.

"Yes. We have watchers who observe the Elements. We track patterns and changes and have somehow managed to navigate the brutal onslaught. We trade skills, and we do all right."

Irvina noted how good the surrounding energy felt. The people here chose to be happy through their difficulties. She warmed to them with ease, feeling like she could stay here and get to know each of them.

"I find you quite remarkable. Thank you for your generosity."

The room quieted, then one by one, the patrons dropped to their knees, signifying their respect for Irvina. She understood the meaning. The hope they carried traveled deep into her soul, showing her how much they needed her help.

Soren meandered between his family and guests, jumped into Irvina's lap, and rested his head on her chest. She held him there and closed her eyes as she set to work on fixing the damage the war had wrought.

Her lap felt suddenly lighter. She looked down to see the boy fading before a burst of energy took him from the room. "Soren," cried Irvina, reaching out to the empty space and looking for something to hold on to.

Screams echoed around the room. Gaity stood before her, seething anger rippling across her lips. "What have you done to my boy?"

Irvina couldn't think straight; she drew in too many emotions she wasn't used to. She focused hard on the howling wind before allowing her shoulders to slump with understanding.

"He is gone." Irvina didn't cry. She sat, saddened and contemplative. "My help comes with a price, it seems. To end this war is more complicated and painful than even I realized. But now I understand. I have to deliver willing sacrifices to bring about change. Soren is gone and cannot return. He placed his heart and trust in my hands, and…"

The crying intensified. Gaity lunged forward and slapped Irvina with such force that her baby-fine skin tore under the pressure.

Two men jerked Gaity back while she kicked and screamed, "You killed Soren! You murderer! He was my baby! He was all I had left—and you took him!"

Irvina stared at her empty lap with a sense of loss she did not comprehend. She felt no urge to fight, only that she—like Soren—deserved to be gone from this world, too.

"You are not my God. You are not welcome here. You are the devil. Leave."

Irvina stood and left pain in her wake. She now accepted she should not have taken for granted her first days on land. The excitement she'd felt clouded her purpose. To fulfil the prophecies whispered in the wind, she would need to manipulate all creatures on land. Her journey would be riddled with pain and loneliness of which she didn't feel capable.

Dropping to her knees, she scraped her hands over the earth. Salty tears dripped amongst the debris. Her one hope of a happy future was now gone, and her anger fermented deep inside. The rumbling terror translated into an earthquake that trembled across the terrain. Her anxiety crumbled towns and flattened villages. She sought out every inch of her power and sent it upwards before pulling it towards her with incredible force.

A burst of water came hurtling from the ocean, engulfing Irvina. The wind kicked up and thrust the wave high, spitting Irvina out onto a nearby mountaintop. Flames engulfed the Redwood Pines, and the ground fell away, sending Irvina tumbling down a rocky ravine.

Her crumpled body lay motionless. The Elements were in angst, but Irvina's soul had already left. Their efforts to stop what was coming were all in vein.

As the last of her combined power came to fruition, Irvina obliterated her human form. Along with Earth. Her decision to take everything and free everyone of any further pain had been her chosen path.

Irvina felt her spirt disconnect from a heavy burden. She accepted she would be lost to the universe, forever alone in the darkness.

Laura Callender

Laura spends much of her day chasing two young toddlers around, stealing the odd moment to write, publish, or create cover designs. She is the proud founder of CWC, a collaborative writing organization that is now in the planning stages for Project Eight. Born and raised in the UK, Laura finds herself back 'up north', having traveled extensively for many years. After working in various professions, Laura has found a renewed passion in life, having immersed herself in the writing community. She is home.

Email: bitbybitbook@yahoo.com

Damsel in Distress
by M.W. King

Oryon stood at attention outside the ornate wooden door leading to the throne room, wondering what to expect. He'd never been in the presence of royalty before. He looked down at his clothing—his best but still tattered.

His eyes widened as two soldiers of the royal guard walked past him, side by side, one of them carrying a charred helmet. The other guard lifted the golden knocker on the door and let it fall; it clanged loudly against the base. The noise echoed for a few seconds before the door opened with a groan, scraping against the stone floor. The guards marched through the threshold without acknowledging the king's usher. After they had passed him, the usher stepped out and motioned for Oryon to follow.

He wiped his sweaty hands on his trousers. *Well, that probably just made them even dirtier,* he thought, staring at his palms. *It's too late to do anything about it now.* He smoothed his hair back and entered the throne room.

He tried to focus on the tapping of the usher's shoes on the floor in front of him to distract him from his racing heartbeat. At the base of the throne stairs, the usher dropped to a knee and briefly touched his forehead to the floor. "Your Majesty," he said before standing. "Oryon of the village Brassles."

Oryon bowed with his hands clasped at his waist as King Nicholas looked him over. The king let out a sigh and rubbed his temple. His queen stood beside him, staring forward with a blank expression. With such statuesque beauty, red-rimmed eyes were the only indication of emotion on her face.

"What brings you to my court on this day," the king began, staring at Oryon with narrowed eyes and continuing in a mocking tone, "Oryon of Brassles?"

"My King," he said, bowing. "I come in regard to the royal decree."

"So you wish to defeat the dragon, save the princess, and collect the reward?" The accompanying sigh made it sound more like a statement of disappointment than a question. "Tell me, what is your trade?"

"A shepherd, Your Highness."

"A shepherd," King Nicholas scoffed. "Do you need bravery to be a shepherd?"

Oryon hesitated, not wanting to admit the answer. "I suppose not as much as a knight, Your Highness."

"How about strength?"

"I must be strong enough to lift the sheep—"

King Nicholas cut him off, seemingly oblivious Oryon had even spoken. "Or agility?"

Oryon shook his head and tried to steady his breathing.

"Sword handling? Speed? Determination? Anything?" The king raised his voice. "Please tell me how a *shepherd* will defeat a dragon. What could you possibly know that they did not?" He pointed to the wall where dozens of various pieces of armor hung from spikes, all charred or crushed and one helmet still smoking.

Oryon's breath caught in his throat. He was unable to take his eyes off the tribute to fallen soldiers. His confidence faltered; how could he prevail when no one else had so far? He thought of the reward. Three chests full of gold coins could last him for the rest of his life, maybe even liberate him from the slums.

"My cleverness, Your Highness," he said, finally prying his eyes away.

"Cleverness?"

"Yes." Oryon squared his shoulders and stuck

out his chin. "It takes much cleverness to be a successful shepherd. I must tend to my flock and anticipate the care they require. I must be clever enough to keep up with their foolishness and be sure they do not die from their own stupidity. Not only that, but I must be clever enough to stay ahead of the animals that prey on them." He paused, looking back at the helmets for only an instant. "I'd be willing to wager that all of these men were chosen for their brute strength or sword skills, but none for their ability to outsmart beasts. As far as I can tell, I am the best man for the job."

"Perhaps there is some truth to your words," the king said, folding his hands in his lap.

"And furthermore, Your Highness," Oryon's façade of confidence got the better of him as he blurted out, "I believe a reward of only a few gold-filled chests are a bit underwhelming, considering the stakes involved."

"And what would you propose to be a satisfactory reward?"

"The princess' hand in marriage." The last bit of confidence drained away, along with the color in his face.

King Nicholas shifted on his throne and scratched his beard. Although he still stared at Oryon, a different emotion shone behind his eyes. He glanced at his queen, whose expression remained unchanged. He turned back to Oryon. "I will approve this… if you fulfill these promises you've made. *If* you return.

And as there's a great possibility it's too late for the princess, try to bring the dragon back alive, but alive is not a necessity. The mages tell me there are as many uses for dead dragons as there are for living ones."

The queen's eyebrows raised as she leaned over and whispered into the king's ear. King Nicholas looked up at her with his mouth agape. "What does it matter? First off, he probably won't return at all."

At this, the queen's eyes shot to Oryon. He sensed a pitying agreement in her gaze.

"And second, you seem to forget you have two other daughters to take care of. Perhaps you need to learn to accept the fact that Princess Leyla is gone. Either way, this beast will pay for what it's done to our daughter." The king motioned for his ushers without waiting for a response and looked back to Oryon. "I will provide you with a horse, armor, and weaponry of your choice. My royal guard will escort you through the forest to the castle in the kingdom of Dunstable, where the dragon has taken up residence. You will be on your own from there."

The king stood and stormed out of the room through the door behind the throne. The queen seemed frozen, looking at him. Her eyes were glazed and her chin quivered, as if she were using all her effort to keep the tears from spilling over. Finally, she blinked, returning her face to its stone elegance, and turned to follow her husband.

The ushers stood near the door Oryon had

entered through, holding it open and waiting for him. Just as he was about to exit the room, the queen's voice caught his attention. She rushed across the throne room, and when she got close enough, she spoke frantically in a hushed voice. "Oryon of Brassles, I need you to understand how imperative this quest is. The king may have given up, but I have not. It can't be too late." She wrung her hands, and her eyes shifted downward. "There's something the king didn't tell you. She's not well. There may not be much time left for her before she succumbs to her illness and we lose her forever." She took Oryon's hand in hers. "I'm begging you. Please find a way to bring her back."

"My Queen." Oryon squeezed her hand and looked straight into her eyes as he bowed his head forward. "I'll do everything I can. I pledge it on my life."

"I don't want your life. I want my daughter," she said, wiping a tear from her cheek.

***

As the sun began to set on the second day of their trek, Oryon and the soldiers escorting him set up camp to rest for the night in the forest. The most difficult part of the journey so far had been carrying the sword in the scabbard on his waist and wearing the chainmail and metal vest. He'd chosen the lightest breastplate available instead of the full suit of armor, but even that was hard to get used to. The silence was the second most difficult part; of the six men escorting him, only Reginald, the First Guard, would speak to him. The others either grunted one-word responses or completely ignored him.

He sat down on a large stump and pulled out his water canteen. As Reginald sat nearby, Oryon was captivated by the scars on his face. A strip of gnarled, melted skin stretched from just below the outside corner of his right eye to his jaw line, cutting a vertical stripe through his red beard. The awkward silence was exacerbated when Reginald caught Oryon staring at his face.

"This is nothing like how I imagined it would be," Oryon finally said to break the silence.

"What did you expect?" Reginald asked. He lifted his wineskin to his lips and took a long swig, holding a loaf of bread out for Oryon to rip off a piece.

"Well, fending off wild animals, for one thing. Or enemy soldiers. Why haven't we crossed paths with any soldiers from Dunstable? We're within a quarter day's march, are we not?"

Reginald let out a long breath. "The first handful of times I led my men through this forest, we fought off many animals. The place was teeming with beasts of all sorts, all determined to have one of us for a meal. Such as the three-headed wolf. That's a beast made of nightmares. Or the double-fanged serpent—a seven-foot-long snake with a head on each end of its body, complete with fangs as long as my finger." He held up his finger and stared at it with a half-grin, as if he actually enjoyed facing the dangers he described. "Most of the animals that attacked were brought back to King Nicholas to feast on or display. Attacks became less frequent with each trip until they stopped altogether." He paused to take another sip and wipe the bread crumbs from his beard. "And as for the soldiers..." A small chuckle escaped his lips. "The dragon took care of most of them when it razed the castle and took it up for a nest. Any who remained were either eaten or unlucky enough to cross paths with us."

Oryon took a small bite from his hunk of bread. As much as he tried to distract himself, his mind kept wandering back to what he was about to do. When the royal stewards had stopped in his village, it had seemed surreal. None of the villagers had ever seen a dragon, never mind fought one. But it had attacked the castle, and the king was desperate to get his daughter back—desperate enough to make her savior the richest man in the kingdom.

The steward had said, "It may not have been your village yet, but who's to say it won't be in a fortnight—" he paused, presumably for dramatic effect "—or tonight?"

Admittedly, Oryon wasn't much interested in saving his village, but the prospect of a better life was something he couldn't pass up, even if it meant risking his life.

"I see you chose the sword and shield," Reginald said, looking at the items sitting on the ground beside Oryon. "The popular choice."

Oryon nodded, swallowing a lump in his throat. There was something about the way Reginald had said it that made him second-guess his choice. "Why don't they send the royal guard in with the hopeful champion?" he finally asked, picking at his bread and avoiding eye contact.

"Do you see this group of men?" Reginald pointed at the handful of men huddled together a few feet away, each eating and drinking silently. "There were a few covert missions trying to rescue the princess. None of the knights ever returned. That's when the king began sending men from all over the kingdom. Just about anyone who was willing. When we escorted the first quest seeker, we fought with him, and our group was four times as many. These are the men who managed to escape. From there on, King Nicholas refused to send his guard in with a *hopeful* savior. Especially when it takes half a year to train a common knight well enough to be worthy of his guard."

"But how do we even know the princess is still alive? Why hasn't it eaten her?"

"I don't know," Reginald said, standing abruptly. "Maybe it only likes the taste of men or it's keeping her as a trinket. You ask too many questions. Focus your remaining energy on figuring out how to outsmart the beast. That's what you're good at, isn't it?" He wiped off the front of his tunic, took another gulp from his wineskin, and walked over to sit with the other men.

＊＊

News of the dragon's attack on Dunstable had spread fast, but none of the stories could prepare him for what lay ahead as he stood on the hilltop at the tree line of the forest. Less than a mile of charred grass stood between him and the stones that used to be the front gate of Dunstable's citadel. The castle, renowned for its elaborate masonry and massive size, had been reduced to only one full tower, a handful of half-toppled structures, and piles of blood-splattered rubble as far as the eye could see. Scorch marks riddled each structure, and small, scattered fires seemed to ignite from thin air. His heartbeat echoed in his ears as the royal guard reached the hilltop to stand next to him.

Oryon surveyed the area, hoping to figure out where the dragon might be hiding. Looking to the solitary tower, he saw Princess Leyla standing just inside the highest window, staring back at him. Her long dark hair cascaded over her shoulders and danced with the wind. She pushed a strand of it from her face and turned away from the window, disappearing from sight.

Don't worry, Princess. You'll be leaving this wretched place today.

"Well, this is it," one of the men said, patting him on the back. "You're on your own from here."

It was the first time any of the men aside from Reginald had spoken to him. He swallowed the lump in his throat. "Any words of advice?"

"Yeah, stay away from the fire." The guard turned and walked back the way they had come.

Reginald lingered as the other men walked away. "Do you have a plan, Champion?"

Oryon shook his head, eyes still trained on the ruins. "I've never needed a plan before with any beast. I just had to be clever enough to spot advantages in my surroundings."

"Well, the only guidance I can give you is to aim for the eyes. Seems to be the only vulnerable part of the whole beast. I hope you have at least enough brute strength to do that," Reginald said over his shoulder as he walked away.

Oryon's feet felt like lead as he took his first step alone. It only took him about fifteen minutes to reach the stone walls surrounding the castle—or at least what remained of them. A layer of gray ash covered the ground. The wind picked up small whirlwinds of it, forming them into drifts. With his next step, a thin branch cracked beneath his foot. As he looked closer, he realized it was a blackened bone. Holding back a shudder, he pressed on.

He walked with light footsteps, not wanting to announce his presence. The element of surprise was imperative, especially with larger beasts. His eyes darted back and forth, taking inventory of any vantage points or hiding spots. A former tower structure swayed in the wind; more than half of the foundation bricks were missing. He looked toward the tower where the princess had been, examining the path he would have to take to get to it.

I wonder if I can make it up to where the princess is without being seen by the dragon.

He froze as a brick crumbled on a nearby pile of rubble, the pieces rolling down the sides and knocking along the ground. Once the noise stopped and all Oryon could hear was the whistling of the wind through the open space, he took another tentative step. He glanced back and forth, trying to keep his eyes on everything in his line of sight. The more his gaze passed over the landscape, the more he noticed scattered remains—the last resting place for men much braver than he.

He jerked his head to the left when something passed just out of his line of sight. As he inched his way closer to the tower, he stopped to study a print in the ash—a dragon's footprint. Stepping into it, he pushed his heel to the back and positioned his other foot heel-to-toe. He took one more step inside it, plus another foot length and a half for the longest toe of the beast. Stepping away, he noticed several more leading him in the direction of the princess' tower prison.

This must lead to the dragon.

He sidestepped past a flaming pile of rubble

and saw what he had been looking for. A tail covered in iridescent blue and green scales and purple spikes dragged along the ground, disappearing behind the tower. Wrapping his hand around the sword at his waist, he tiptoed along the wall in the same direction. If he could sneak up behind the beast, maybe he could get in the first attack.

With the next step, the dragon came into view, standing only a few yards away. Its head swiveled back and forth, searching for something. As Oryon reached to grab the shield from his back, his foot kicked a piece of rubble, sending it skipping along the stone ground. The dragon's head snapped to look in his direction, instantly catching him in his tracks. The mighty beast roared. Oryon stumbled, trying to run the other way as a blast of fiery breath spewed from the dragon's mouth. He ran back along the wall of the tower, hiding himself from view.

Oryon estimated the dragon's height to be about three times his own, its neck being a third of it. It was small compared to what he had imagined, though. The dragon's galloping footsteps grew closer. He pulled the sword from its sheath and planted his feet into the ground, holding the sword above his head with two hands. When the dragon's head came into view, he swung the sword down with all his might onto its neck. The blade shattered, but the dragon recoiled, letting out another roar.

Oryon grabbed what remained of the sword— the hilt and about half of the blade—and jumped away from the safety of the wall. Feeling he had a clean shot, he threw the broken sword as hard as he could. It whistled as it cut through the air and sailed straight past the dragon's head.

The dragon's eyes narrowed, focusing on Oryon. Was the creature grinning? He grabbed his shield from his back.

Just as the dragon took a step forward and opened its large jaws, Oryon's sword hit its intended mark—a vulnerable spot in the half-ruined tower just behind the beast. The ruin rocked back and forth as the inside of the dragon's mouth illuminated. Oryon held the shield like a discus. He took half a second to aim it at the tower before releasing it. Grazing the side of the tower, the blow gave just enough leverage that the stones toppled onto the dragon.

Before the dust had settled, Oryon ran around the other tower that held the princess, searching for the door. Once he found it, he tried to turn the door handle, but it was locked.

He stepped back and kicked it. The frame shook, but the door didn't budge. He picked up a brick and bashed it against the door handle until it broke off. The door swung open, and he sprinted up the spiral stairs.

He ripped open the door at the top of the tower, letting out a plume of dust. Rushing into the room, he could barely make out the silhouette of the princess. He scooped her up into his arms and, without saying a word, carried her down the stairs.

She coughed as the dust cleared and put her arms around his neck. "No one has ever outsmarted the dragon and gotten to me before."

Oryon found himself speechless in her presence with her bright violet eyes trained on him. He exited the tower cautiously, looking around for the dragon. It looked as if it had not escaped from the mountain of rubble yet.

"Let's get you home, Princess Leyla." He set her down and led her by the hand.

"I can't go home," she said, pulling her hand away.

Oryon turned and took both her hands in his. "Why? Your mother is desperate to see you again. Do not lose hope because of your condition."

Her face softened. "You know?"

"We will find you a cure."

"There is no cure." There was a hardened finality in her voice.

"Then why not live out the rest of your days with those who love you?"

A half smile appeared on her face as she took a step toward him. "And what do you get from this? What is your reward, my savior?"

"The bounty was for three gold-filled chests, and…" His face turned scarlet, and his eyes wandered down to her hand, still holding his.

"My hand in marriage?" she asked. "You would marry me, even with my condition?"

"Of course." He closed the gap between them

with one stride and tucked a strand of hair behind her ear. "Now, hurry, before the dragon wakes. The royal guard waits just beyond that hilltop and they can help chain it to bring it back."

"The dragon?" the princess asked, pulling away from him again and stopping in her tracks.

"Yes, your father believes it might prove useful." Oryon stepped toward her, but she matched him with a backward step. "What is it, Princess? Have you grown fond of the beast?" he scoffed.

Her eyes watered as she took another step back. She pursed her lips, her violet eyes now boring into him with an intense stare. She let out a hearty laugh. "There is one thing they must have forgotten to mention to you, my dear, naïve savior." Her laughter grew louder into a cackle, and her eyes shone like daggers. She seemed taller, suddenly. Her lips spread into a grin, revealing razor-sharp teeth that had not been there a moment ago. The skin on her arms rippled with goosebumps, then shimmered, giving off blue and green hues. "I am the dragon."

M.W. King

M.W. King is a writer who dabbles in many genres, her favorite being fantasy. After six years in the Navy, she decided one tour on a ship was enough and now squeezes her writing between work, school, and other hobbies, which include daydreaming, crafting, and napping. She currently resides in New Hampshire with her husband and three little monsters. She's been published in two CWC anthologies and one anthology put together by the Authors' Tale writing group.

Briar Rose
by Amanda Linsmeier

I was the huntress. I ate thorns to break my fast, sometimes ground to powder but often whole. I bound my breasts with strips of cloth and refused to back down from anything. My people respected me. Some feared me. I was what the weak aspired to be.

Behind my back, they called me Briar Rose, but I considered it a compliment. The former part of the name fit me better than the latter. There was nothing about me resembling the soft, beautiful bud. Nothing.

***

It was the blood I smelled first. The metallic sweetness of it filled my nostrils until they flared with warning. My skin prickled as I notched my arrow. When I stepped silently around the tree, his body came into view.

Lowering my weapon in disappointment, I sighed. I had hoped for a stag; I'd thought I *smelled* a stag. My people would've been glad for the meat—I hadn't caught more than a couple hares in days. If it had been a stag, I would have killed it quickly, thanked the animal for its sacrifice, and taken a bite of the heart. It was the way of the hunter, though I always had to work myself up a little to do it. I didn't like to admit that weakness even to myself.

I could have shot this man, just on principle. He was trespassing on our land. But he was too easy a target. I knelt, soaking my knees with his blood, and felt for a pulse in his neck. It was strong, surprisingly.

Nudging him none too gently, I frowned. "Wake up. You're alive."

He grimaced but didn't open his eyes until I slapped him. He jerked his head with a growl. "Stop."

"Are you stupid?" I said, staring into his dark eyes. "Why are you just lying here, waiting to be eaten?"

"I'm injured."

"You'll be more injured if you don't get your arse off the ground and find shelter."

"Who are you? Why do you care?"

"I'm Rose. And I don't." I got up and began

to walk away.

"Wait!"

I looked back and sighed in disgust. "Why should I?"

"Because," he said, "I need you."

***

I hated being needed. I was happier to be feared, to be revered, to be respected.

Yet, something inside me gave in. It could have been the healing blood from my mother. She had healed those who were hurt—physically or otherwise. My father had been a warrior. But they couldn't save themselves against the wrath of King Rufian. He'd cut their lives short without so much as a cursory glance backwards. I had been only twelve, and I watched both their bodies fall to the ground before it even sank into my brain.

They were dead by the time I got to their sides, and it took three grown men to pull me away screaming. Two years later, I took up my bow the way my father had taught me and began to hunt. I didn't admit this to anyone, but in the darkest recess of my mind, every kill had the king's face on it. Every beast I felled was practice for when I would someday, somehow, come across my chance for revenge.

***

I fed him bone broth and warm milk from my goat until he was so drowsy, his eyes would not stay open. I had had no man, and never would I marry. Yet I was drawn to him. Touching the side of his face, running my fingertips along the brown of his beard, I lost myself for a moment. He moaned in his sleep, and I jerked my hand away as if caught. I assessed the long, jagged tear to his side. It had missed his organs by a scant inch. I cleaned it, bandaged him, and waited for him to wake.

I told myself I would feed him again, then send him on his way.

***

Two days later, he was still there. His wound was healing nicely, and his eyes were bright. We talked, though something put me off. I told myself I was uneasy only because I was attracted to him. When he jested, I laughed. When he told me Rose suited me, my long, red hair, I blushed. I would have normally punched a man in the jaw for that, but I resisted my instincts. Somewhere between finding him in the woods and sitting with him on the edge of my bed, where he rested, I had let down my guard. What's more, I had softened for him.

When, on the third night, he pulled my hair into his fist and tugged my head back to expose my neck, I let him kiss me there. I pulled his own hair into my hands and found it hard to let go. When he tasted my lips, I did not resist. And when he peeled off my clothing and parted my thighs with his rough hands, I let him. Smelling his somehow familiar scent, I shut my eyes and moaned.

***

In the morning, I was awoken by a shout outside.

"Aye, Rose!"

Flynn. Of all the people I would *not* want to find me naked, tangled up with a man, it would be Flynn. He would see me as vulnerable. I had trained him, and he looked up to me.

I threw on my clothing and closed the door to the cottage quickly as I walked out, in case he happened to crane his head and notice the lump in my bed.

"What is it?" I said. "We're not hunting so early." The sun had barely begun to pink the sky around the edges. I preferred to hunt after I had my morning meal of porridge, goat milk, and thorns, which Flynn refused to add to his regimen, even though I insisted they would strengthen his aim.

"Nah," he said. "I only came to tell you what I heard." He ran his fingers through his light hair and tried to look more solemn—which was pretty useless; Flynn looked perpetually jovial. "They say there's a man-beast running 'round these parts."

I frowned. "Who says? What kind?" I hadn't heard of man-beasts in years, not since the tales my mother used to tell me at nightfall.

"A stag," Flynn said. "Bruke caught him a couple days ago. The stag changed... before his eyes, right after he'd stabbed him. Bruke was so shocked, he dropped his knife. He was afraid. Thought the lot of us would think he'd lost his mind."

I gritted my teeth. "If he would have said something, it would've saved me some trouble, the stupid arse!" I went into my cottage, slamming the door behind me.

***

He didn't deny it. He almost seemed surprised, like I should have guessed it. I was furious with myself. How had I *not* known? I'd smelled a stag. I'd known there was something not right about him. And still, I had cared for him. I had let him into my bed, my arms. I had fooled even myself.

"Get out," I hissed. "Forget last night ever happened."

"Ah, Rose," he said, pulling me in again by my long hair. "Don't be cross. I didn't think you'd mind so much."

"Oh? You thought I'd be fine rutting with a wild animal?"

"Did I not feel like a man last night? Both times?"

I flushed with anger. "Shut up. Get out."

"All right. Thank you for your hospitality. I'll have my father's men bring your village some food as a thank you. It's the least I can do."

"Your father's men?"

"His soldiers."

"Your father's... soldiers?"

He stared at me like I was daft. "I'll have them bring food from the castle. As a thank you."

"Your father is King Rufian?" I said the last word like it was poison in my mouth, but he didn't seem to notice.

"Of course," he said. "Didn't you know I'm Oren?"

"I didn't realize it was common knowledge that the prince was a man-beast." My throat tightened.

"It's not. I only assumed you'd recognized me. Thought that's why you'd saved me."

"I don't know why I saved you," I said dully. I stared at him until he blinked.

"Well... I thank you." He bowed his head, and then he was gone.

***

I gave him a head start.

His trail was sloppy, and though it seemed like forever, it must have been only minutes until I caught up with him. He didn't hear me, though his head perked up, antlers majestically curved. He had chosen to travel as a stag. It made no difference to me whether he was human or animal. I had two arrows notched. One for my mother. One for my father. When I let them fly, he didn't know they were coming. Before the light left his eyes, I drove the dagger through him.

***

I was methodical, neat, as I carved the stag's heart from his body.

"Thank you for your gift," I said automatically.

I leaned in and took a bite until the red ran down my chin like a river. My parents were avenged. The king had paid for his deed. I took another bite— didn't even shudder.

After all, this was no big deal.

I ate thorns for breakfast.

Amanda Linsmeier

Amanda Linsmeier is the author of *Ditch Flowers* and many short stories. Her writing has been featured in *Portage Magazine*, *Literary Mama*, and *Brain Child Magazine*. Besides writing Women's Fiction, she loves reading and writing fables, fairytales, and fantasy, and sometimes she pretends her Hogwarts letter is still coming. She can be found blogging about writing and books at amandalinsmeier.com. When she's not writing, she works part-time at her local library and brings home more books than she has time to read. Amanda lives in the countryside, surrounded by trees, with her family, two dogs, and two half-wild cats.

Wayward's Beacon
by E.R. Smo

Jaune leaned against the headboard of his bed, his notebook computer seated on his lap. Tear-soaked tissues lay next to him while he watched a video of her, just another in a long list he'd watched that day. He'd often recorded her—or them together—on his phone, then uploaded the videos to watch later.

"Come on, tell me something funny! You always have some weird story to tell," Jade said in the video.

He sniffled and smiled, looking at her pretty face and long, wavy black hair. She had always been playful and loved hearing him tell her stories of all sorts, whether they be from his life or not.

"All right, all right. Let's see… Oh, I don't think I've told you this one yet. For good reason, so you don't go telling other people, got it?" He watched his hand poke her nose after asking, which she swatted away.

"All right, fine. Sounds like this'll be good."

"Okay, so, I went golfing with my dad and brother once. We were at the driving range, and there was a wooden roof above us held up by support beams. Long story short, I smacked a ball, it ricocheted off one of the beams, came right back and hit me square in the nuts!"

He chuckled along with her on the video as she erupted into giggles.

"Oh, my God! Oh, I have to tell everybody!"

"Don't you dare! You promised you wouldn't!"

"I didn't promise anything."

The phone had fallen, but he could hear the wrestling and laughing, remembering how he tried to get her phone away from her so she couldn't send any texts to anybody. They were so happy to have found one another, and to each of them, the other's happiness had become priority. He gripped his blonde hair tightly, trying to keep his breathing under control. Nothing could be done for the tears streaming down his face. He had to close the laptop and take deep breaths to maintain what little composure he had left.

Nobody attempted to visit him anymore, and

he preferred it that way. Nearly every day since his wife's death, family and friends had come to try to console him. Their attempts only aggravated him, just making him want to be alone, even if all he could do was cry, question life, and sleep. Out of the corner of his eye, he saw a pill bottle on the table next to his bed, the contents of which he had yet to have the courage to consume. His religious late wife would have thrown a fit if she knew his thoughts. He did not share in her beliefs.

His eyes fell upon a small box on the dresser. Neatly wrapped in purple wrapping paper and a yellow ribbon, it had been left for him before her passing, a gift from her to be opened on their anniversary—two days after the accident. She always did like to tease him. As of yet, he had been unable to bring himself to open it.

He stood from the bed and approached the dresser, reaching for the box, but retracted. There sat the last thing he'd ever be given by his beloved. Once opened, never again would he receive any gift from her. Therein lay part of the reason he had yet to open it. The other—he did not believe he could emotionally handle it. But he also saw it as an insult to her not to have opened it. Minutes passed as he contemplated what to do with the box. His eyes never left the lightly dust-coated gift.

He snatched the box from the dresser. His breathing came slowly while he tugged at the delicate ribbon, untying it and gently setting it upon the dresser. Every motion made his heart pound in his chest, and he took care not to rip the paper at all. He wanted to keep every bit of this present forever, including the wrapping.

Inside of a plain white box lay a book, though not a real one. It seemed a small decoration for a desk that fit in the palm of his hand. He flipped the box over, the toy-like gift landing in his hand, sending an unusual shiver through his spine and forcing a short gasp. The sensation quickly passed. To most, it wouldn't seem like much, but he immediately knew what it represented. Jaune clutched it tight.

Their first meeting flashed in his mind. Out with friends, he had been telling them a funny story from a previous day, and a giggle came from not far away. She had overheard, and his eyes fell upon her for the first time. It was not a spark but a roaring flame between them as their relationship—and love— quickly blossomed. Through the years they'd been together, she'd sit with a smile and listen to any story he had to tell, oftentimes forcing him to come up with one on the spot.

Eyes on the ground, mind distracted, he shuffled to the bedroom door always kept closed for the past month—a habit he'd developed due to wanting solitude, even though there was no one to intrude in the first place. He opened the door and took several steps before the realization of something amiss tore him from his thoughts.

He gazed up not at the upstairs hallway of his

home but at a field of lush, green grass and vibrant flowers of every color he could imagine. The sky above held only as many small clouds as he could count on one hand. He turned his head to find the door he'd walked through had vanished. In every direction lay more flora as far as his wide eyes could see.

His heart raced with a flurry of emotions. It was strange, frightening even, and yet something so beautiful couldn't possibly be terrible. "What's going on?" he whispered.

He dared to take a single step forward, then bent to caress a flower with his fingertips. It felt real. The sweet aroma of the pollen filled his nostrils, his skin soaking in the warmth of the sun. It felt too real to be a dream, yet it could only be that.

"This makes no sense." He once more turned to look behind him, hoping to see his bedroom door, yet there lay only the endless field. "What do I do now?" he muttered, so caught up in the confusing but fantastic situation, he hardly noticed his eyes were dry for the first time in a month.

He glanced to his hand, which clutched the gift and shook, but not of his own doing. It trembled harder, forcing him to open his hand and nearly drop the palm-sized book. Slowly, Jaune opened it, nearly falling back in surprise when a ball of light burst forth. It hovered for a moment, then zipped from side to side and quickly around him as if examining him. He turned his head and body, trying to keep it in his sights. The light stopped in front of him, leaving him starring in awe.

"What… are you?" He reached for it, but it darted away before contact could be made. "W-wait!" Jaune tried again to catch the tiny ball of light, but it proved too quick, always remaining just out of reach. It had come from the book, the gift his wife had given him. The idea there could be a connection drove his pursuit. He chased for as long as his body would allow, until his chest felt as heavy as his breathing. "Hey, slow down."

The orb weaved in front of him, as if taunting his failed attempts. Slowly, it backed away, descending to the ground. Then, before his eyes, it exploded. The result was not force, nor fire, but an image. Those dry eyes moistened again as he stared at a ghostly image of himself and his wife, seated amongst the grass. They were smiling, laughing.

He smiled—the first genuine smile since before his wife's passing. No sound came from the moving image, or perhaps memory, but that mattered little. Jaune fell to his knees, so close he could touch her. And he tried, though his fingers passed through her image. Disappointing, but not enough to force away the smile upon his lips. There she sat, his beloved, happy and with him.

Hard to tell if what played before him was a specific memory or a jumble of multiple. Picnics in a field not far from their home were had more than once, and he couldn't place which of those times this moving image displayed. He remembered a time it began to rain, forcing them to take refuge under a large tree. The memory widened his smile and forced a chuckle.

"I love you," he said to the image of his wife. Of course, she gave neither response nor acknowledgement, but he knew she wouldn't.

Jaune sat and watched, for how long he could not say. Hunger never pained him, the sky never darkened, yet hours passed without him noticing. His focus remained only on his wife and how happy she seemed with him. He refused to leave. This was as close to his wife as he could ever get again. Tears welled over the hours—days—he'd spent watching her. At no point were his eyes dry, but he felt such a sense of happiness.

The more time passed, however, the more that happiness died down, the smile fading. His hand more frequently tried to touch his wife with no success. The desire to hold her in his arms, for her to hear him, interact with him and not his ghostly self, desperately grew.

"Please! Look at me! Say something to me!" His tears were once more tears of grief. "Please. I can't stay this way." No sooner had he spoken those words than the image faded, the orb of light returning to its original form.

"Wait! Bring her back!" His pursuit of the orb began again, never quite closing the gap as he ran. Flowers were trampled in his mad attempt to catch the orb, though he knew not what he would do with it if he caught it. What he *could* do with it.

The shift happened so quickly, he didn't recognize it until it had already happened. No longer was he in the gorgeous field of vibrant colors and sweet aromas. He ran upon a beach, the sky choked with dark clouds. The waves crashed upon the sand, more so as his frustrations grew. "Let me see her again!"

To his surprise, the orb stopped and once more exploded into a new image. An image he did not wish to see. He could hardly contain the tears, the trembling of his body, as he gazed upon his wife lying in a hospital bed, he at her side holding her hand. Again, he couldn't hear anything said by the apparitions. This time, he focused not upon his wife but himself.

"You idiot. Why didn't you do more?" he yelled. His fist thrust through the image harmlessly, only strengthening his rage. He punched and kicked his own image, threw handfuls of sand at it, and yelled in his own face. The waves roared, and thunder followed his every bellow.

"You could have saved her, right? You should have done more research, looked at more options, more hospitals!" His knuckles turned white, teeth bared at his own image. "To hell with money. Maybe if you tried harder, she'd still be alive! She'd still be here!" His vision blurred with hot tears.

He'd done those things he yelled about, lost

countless hours of sleep searching for the smallest bit of hope to save his wife. After the fact, it never seemed like enough. His misguided rage manifested around him. Lightning cracked across the sky, thunder roared, a torrential downpour soaked him in seconds. The harsh storm grew more violent the more his anger increased and the louder he yelled. Raw emotion held in for a month let loose all at once. With nothing else around, he continuously punched the sand, needing a way to expel the excess energy born of his rage.

Jaune hated himself, and at the same time, he hated himself for hating himself. Somewhere deep in his mind, he knew he'd done all he could, yet there always remained doubt, and it consumed him. "Why did she have to go? Why her? Why not anybody else? Why not me?" He yelled as loud as he could, eyes clenched shut, body tensing and trembling, crying harder than he ever had before. "Why not that drunken idiot who crashed into her? He deserved to die. He should have died horribly in her place!"

The minutes passed, his energy exhausted, and with it the storm around him. He knelt upon the sand, motionless save the rise and fall of his chest. When he lifted his head and opened his eyes, the image vanished, the orb of light once more in its place. It remained close, hovering.

"Can't you do something?" he asked in a meek, desperate voice. "Look at what you're doing. It's unreal. Can't you bring her back? Give her one more day? Something?" Jaune shifted to a kneeling position, reaching and successfully cupping the orb in his hands, holding it close to him. It had come from the book, the gift, so he surmised it must somehow be a part of his beloved, connected in some way.

He paid no attention to the shifting scenery around him, the chaotic, dark beach giving way to a house of worship. The orb lay cradled gently against his chest like a child. "I'll do anything. Please. You can take half my life. You can end it after I've had time with her. I don't care what you do, just give her back to me."

Breathing slow and deep, he managed to control his emotions, to calm himself to the point he could stop the tears. He adjusted so his back sat against a pew, quickly gazing around him. He'd never been religious, so unlike most, he didn't have the comfort of believing in Heaven. The truth of the afterlife, if one even existed, could be something humankind had not thought of yet. Whatever it was, he hoped it gave him a way to see her once more.

"If it means I'll see her again, then it's all right. You can kill me right now, and it'll be fine." Still, he attempted to convince this magic orb to let him see her, the real her, no matter what the cost. Any idea he could conceive was offered up to the orb, yet instead of responding, it shot from his hand and exploded into yet another scene of his past.

His eyes widened seeing her in her wedding gown, standing with him at the altar. They looked so happy, their faces smiling so wide there could be no mistaking their joy. This scene he had seen numerous times over the past month, watching their wedding video repeatedly.

"See? That's how we're supposed to be. Even if it's in the next life, please make it happen. You must be capable, right?"

When it became obvious the orb wouldn't grant any of his requests, he sighed, leaning his head back against the pew. "I feel so bad that I'm still here and she's not. We were supposed to grow old together, have kids, enjoy a happy life. She wanted two kids, one boy, one girl. A dog too. The cliché happy family. It would have been so nice." No more tears were shed. It didn't seem as though he could produce any more, though his eyes felt puffy and heavy.

"You know, I tried killing myself a couple times, hoping I could be with her if I did. But I just couldn't do it. I'm such a coward." His arms fell to his sides, the orb halting mid-fall. Looking down, he watched the wooden floors give way to dry, desolate earth, the desert now surrounding him.

"I don't know what to do with my life anymore." Jaune brought his knees up, resting his arms across them and his forehead on his arms. Without her, he found no more reason to live. The point of his life was to be with her, and he doubted he could find another purpose.

"If you're not going to help, just leave. Don't

even bother sending me back home, if you were going to at all." He fell to his side, curled up on the hard ground, staring at nothing.

Illusion or not, the arid wasteland on which he lay brought intense heat. It mattered not. If he were to die here, it would be a welcome escape from the harsh reality to which he'd otherwise return. Sweat dripped down his face, though he hardly seemed to notice. Nor did he notice the orb of light zipping this way and that in front of him.

"Don't worry so much. We'll see each other again. I promise."

The voice—his wife's voice—roused him from his mental shutdown. He glanced up to see another image of the past, slowly sitting up to get a better look. His wife sat up in the hospital bed, with his help, and held his hand. For the first time since arriving, he could hear her voice. This time, he wanted to look away, to not see her final seconds of life yet again. Already, the tears swelled in his eyes.

"How do you know that? Why do you believe that so much?" his image asked with a shaky voice.

"You need more faith, Jaune. There is so much more to this world than you know. You'll see, one day." Her eyes closed as she took several slow, heavy breaths—the last breaths she'd ever take. "I'll be waiting for you, love."

Watching the most tragic scene of his life play before his eyes for the second time, he was grateful he didn't have to hear the heart monitor flatline. And yet, for some reason, he didn't lose it, didn't bawl like a child as he often had in the past month. He sat and stared as the image faded away, her final words echoing in his mind.

The orb returned to him, gently hovering before his eyes and not making any attempt to move when he reached for it. "What are you?" The orb responded by floating around his right hand—the hand that had once not let go of the small book. He opened his hand, then carefully opened the book. A message appeared inside, in her handwriting, but glowing a brilliant gold. "I'll be waiting for you, love. You'd better have a lot of stories to tell me."

Before this day, he would have dismissed her words as misguided religious belief, faith in something of which she had no proof, just because it made her feel better. That was how he always regarded it, though he never said so to her face. Still, perhaps it wasn't merely blind belief.

He cupped the orb in both hands, the book lying open in one. His barren surroundings shifted back to the place of worship. Jaune still had no idea what had just happened, or how—an experience he could not explain through means other than those he knew were not real. No dream could be so vivid, where he could smell the flowers or feel the rain hit his face.

"How are you doing this?" he asked the orb as his environment once more shifted back to the stormy beach, though it did not remain there for long. The dark clouds above him lightened, the rain ceased, and the waves calmed. "How was she able to do this?"

The clouds gave way to a bright blue sky, the sand parting for the colorful flowers and rich grass of the field. The sweet aroma filled his nostrils again, bringing new energy to his body weakened by depression. "She gave me that book. The book you came from. That all of this came from. How did she do this?" For the first time, he could truly think through this otherworldly experience, undistracted by the images that caused him so much anguish.

"There is so much more to this world than you know," he whispered, quoting his wife and giving those words serious thought. Those words, this experience—there was an obvious connection. He realized she hadn't spoken on blind faith. Whether it was religion, or something more magical, his wife must have been the cause of this. A loud shiver in the air behind him caught his attention. He turned to stare at his bedroom door standing among the flowers.

Jaune hesitated, knowing what he would return to if he stepped through the door. For a long while, he just stared at it. He couldn't stay here forever. Or perhaps he could. He'd felt no hunger or thirst since arriving; perhaps he wouldn't age. He could stay here and watch images of their past forever, in a way no camera could have ever captured. The thought seemed appealing, until he remembered the first image, how frustrated and angry he became that he couldn't touch her or speak to her.

The things she'd always believed that he hadn't were being reconsidered. Perhaps he would see her again, but this place could prevent that. Jaune stood, debating his options, weighing the pros and cons. With a deep breath, he walked the short distance to the door and grasped the doorknob, turning to gaze upon the stunning field one last time. In his mind, he also stared at the other places he'd visited. He turned and opened the door to return home.

***

Jaune tied the laces of his boots, mentally reminding himself where he had to go. He'd never been hiking before, but it could be fun on such a nice day. He had a small bag set to the side, holding water and food, his phone ready to serve as his GPS so long as he maintained signal. Though he wasn't worried, getting lost while hiking would be just one more interesting story.

He decided to go hiking alone, not ready to interact with others for long periods of time just yet. He still needed time to think, to sort through his emotions, and time alone in case he broke down again. The tears hadn't stopped, though they'd slowed. He doubted such emotional tremors would ever completely go away and knew he would never stop missing her terribly. But the time had come to get back into the world and live his life. Jaune intended to live his life as fully as he could, even if by himself. After all, he insisted on creating enough stories to last an eternity.

E.R. Smo

E.R. Smo is an author who likes to dabble in various genres, though he primarily writes fantasy. Much of his inspiration comes from other forms of media, such as television shows and videogames. He is currently working on his first novel, a fantasy adventure heavily inspired by the old JRPG style of videogames. His desire to write began when a greatly admired animator passed away and fans were asked to do something creative in his memory in lieu of traditional flowers or cards. You can follow E.R. Smo at https://www.facebook.com/ersmoauthor

Grenadine's Charm
by W.S. Moye

Grenadine frowned as she grabbed Moonbeam's loose lead and guided her back to the small paddock on the downriver side of the farm.

You're an old fool, girl. That's the third time you've taken her cowbell for the clanging of pots on Ebbo's walking tub.

She rounded the front of the house, shooed the chickens, and collected a few yard eggs. She took another long look at the forest path. It was still empty.

She'd been at this house for three years now and had made it into a proper witch's home. She ducked her head inside and went over to the hearth, inspecting the eggs by holding them up to the lamplight and looking for a dark silhouette. The third egg manifested a partially formed chick inside, so she put it in a clearly labeled jar on the materials shelf and placed the other eggs into the wire basket over the sink basin. Grenadine checked her reflection in the bit of water at the bottom of the basin. She wasn't old or ugly. Her skin was smooth, and her eyes were big and bright. They were her favorite feature. She wasn't too big or too little; though she had never felt sexy, she was healthy. She wore a nice underlayer of practical dress, with a bit of gypsy flair in the headband, the shoulder scarf, and the golden belt she wore over her clothes. When she dressed this way, she felt exotic. Smiling, she smoothed her tawny hair back again. She wanted to look nice if Ebbo ever came by.

***

Grenadine had met Ebbo ten months ago, when she'd signed up on the Registry. Being a witch was a time-consuming process, and sometimes, the rarer ingredients called for long searches to locate. Some of the components could be harvested from her farm or garden, sure, but others were impossible to find locally. The Registry allowed for her home to be a stop on Ebbo's standard route, so she could buy, trade, or sell goods directly with him. Ebbo only dealt with those who performed magick and so specialized in magical materials. She remembered the first time she'd seen him, his lithe form moving quickly up the forest path and keeping time with the pings and knocks coming from the walking tub that carried the supplies. Of course, he could have ridden a broom or a cauldron—or a carpet, if he'd wanted—but he seemed to enjoy walking. He had bowed deeply, introduced himself, and given her a once-over of his current inventory. That day, she bought three feathers from an eagle's tail and the worn-out spindle of a blind widow.

Since then, he'd been through a couple times. She had made it a point to see him, and it was the highlight of any moon when it happened. Last time, she ordered a tome and *Magicks and Relics of the Ancient World*, and now she looked forward to reading it during her nights by the lamplight.

The next time through, Ebbo came up the path, whistling like he always did, and he had her book in hand and ready for her to use. She'd first realized how she felt about Ebbo then. She was standing on the path, excited to see him until she realized she'd completely forgotten about the book she'd ordered. Blushing, she feigned excitement for the book. He worried his stovepipe hat with his hands and displayed a broad smile, like usual.

"Ah, that one wasn't an easy find, but I have an archivist friend who specializes in Ancient tomes," he said. "I had to trade out an aragonite fire crystal and a yew wand for it, but it was easy enough."

"Oh goodness!" She hugged the book across

her chest and looked him in the eye. "I didn't realize it would be so much! Please, let me give you some extra for your troubles… it's the least I could do." She reached into a satchel she wore at her hip and pulled out a handful of coins to count.

Ebbo put a hand up and simply smiled his usual dashing smile. "Oh, it wasn't any trouble at all for you—" he caught himself "—a customer like you. Please consider it a sign of our friendship."

Blathering old ninny… this man is a salesman. He isn't flirting with you, he's making money. He's making money right off your feelings!

"Anyway, do you have any imbued ink?" She focused on nothing in particular in the orchard. "And a new quill… turkey, preferably."

Ebbo paused, looking at her for a moment. He shuffled about and stared at his hat before answering. "Certainly."

He produced the items, and she quickly counted out the coins and pressed them into his open hand. Bowing deeply, he thanked her. She marched into the house and watched until he was completely out of sight. Grenadine sat down and tried to cry, but she was so stubborn that no tears would come.

For the next moon and a half, she tended to her farm and home and tried not to think. She was certain her foolishness had driven him off for good, and she'd barely known his name. She had no idea how to find him. She wasn't entirely sure how he'd ever found her. All her life, she'd thought she was a loner. Meant to be alone, and happy to be alone. But there was a quality about Ebbo that rocked something in her. He made her feel alive just with his presence. He gave her a hunger to know more of him. She wanted to know his thoughts, to hear his opinion. She'd give anything to see him again, but she had to be practical. He had been kind—she had not—and she hadn't had the good sense to at least order something else so he'd have a reason to come back through. He was gone.

She used her new quill to transpose her old Book of Shadows and keep her mind busy. She copied spell after spell, needlessly taking up more parchment to record the same things over again, but it kept her from thinking too much. Idle hands weren't the devil's workshop, but a mind with too much time to think certainly was.

Everything worked against her. Springtime was here, and the world was abloom with vibrant color. She could gather many spell components right here in her very own woods and have enough to dry or preserve for later in the year when the weather turned harsh. If only she could stand to be out. The animals were accustomed to her, and though she normally enjoyed seeing them, now it was painful. Every him had a her, and every she and he were so obnoxiously happy that Grenadine loathed going outside at all—this was not good for a witch.

After she'd spent entirely too much time inside and failed to keep the sadness at bay, she went out to sit on the porch and analyze her situation. She lit a pipe, which was uncommon for a woman—even a witch—and after a time, the smell of cherry cavendish tobacco and some easy rocking had soothed her nerves. She decided she had two options. She could continue the way she was and be of no good to anyone—she hadn't even been into town to smudge the new homes or tend to the sick in these last two moons—or she could hold on to the hope that she would one day find a way to see Ebbo again. Hope was always the better choice. Since then, she had been a woman on a mission, and if Ebbo ever came back, she'd order the world to keep him from going away again.

***

She had just come back from picking mushrooms outside one of the local fairy rings when she remembered she wanted to add soapstone to her list. By now, her shopping list for Ebbo had grown so long, she wasn't sure his tub would hold it all. But adding things to the list added to her hope. She stopped to pick a lilac for her hair and rub honeysuckle on her skin and lips. It had been a hot day, but she wanted to smell good if Ebbo was about.

She came in from the riverside, away from the path, and skirted the stone wall that dammed the river and forced water over the wheel. She heard a distant ting-tang and shook her head. Moonbeam must have gotten out again. Still, she smiled. She set her basket down by the door and wandered through the front garden, which was now blooming beautifully, to the path.

"Well, good afternoon, Madam Grenadine," Ebbo said, bowing deeply, hat in hand.

Grenadine was taken aback to see him and searched for words. "Ebbo! I mean, well, good afternoon to you, too, Mr. Ebbo." She curtsied as best she knew how. Witch social skills were only upheld for solidarity in the Covens, but she had been in town often enough to know what regular women did when greeting others. "I'm surprised to see you here!" She kept her eyes on the ground.

"Why, I wouldn't miss this stop for all the world," he said, fiddling with his hat again. He brushed some unruly brown hair from his eyes and adjusted his rounded spectacles so they were once again straight on his nose. "I mean, you still wish to be on the registry, do you not?" From somewhere in the back of his tub, a pair of mandrakes shrieked. Their cries did not cause madness—that was an old commoners' tale. Both Ebbo and Grenadine ignored them.

"Oh," she started. "Oh! Well, yes. Of course I would! I have a few things I'd like to order … just one moment while I fetch my list?"

He nodded, smiling.

Grenadine, nearly tripping over her basket, scrambled in the door and grabbed the list—

the very long list. She fretted; it was too long. After a quick dab of lavender oil beneath the nose and on the temples, she was able to regain her composure. She then quickly wrote a couple of the items down on a new piece of parchment, smoothed her dress and hair, and went back outside.

Ebbo took the scrap and used two long, thin fingers to adjust his glasses again. "Ah, well, the blood of a werewolf I have right here..." he said and brought out a tiny box shaped like a treasure chest. The fingerless gloves on his hands allowed his fingers to remain agile as he walked them expertly through a set of slides to produce the requested item. "But the astrolabe will take me until next time. No worries, though. Ebbo always delivers!" He smiled at her and bowed again. Then, he and his tub clamored down the path. Ebbo whistled a tune of moon-dancing as he went.

Grenadine watched him take every last step until he was out of sight, then ran into the house, bringing the materials basket in with her. She set it down and examined the slide.

The two thin glass pieces held a large, deep red drop between them and were labeled in what she could only assume was his immaculate handwriting.

Werewolf blood/ non-rabid 1/60 DRAM

She set it up on the mantle, where she could see it from her workbench, and just admired it. Hope lived here again. That little slide represented hope. That was when the makings of a plan appeared in her head.

***

It would doubtless be a few moons until Ebbo came back by again with her order, and by then, Summer would really be cranking down on them. He'd be thirsty, and she would too. She had time enough to gather materials and get her plan in order, so she set about busily preparing.

Most people think magick is an exact science, when in fact it's much more personal than that. Magick is about finding your niche in the universe and learning to jive with it. It's like learning to dance. Even similar dancers have slightly different movements and work in slightly different ways. It's about what feels good. It isn't about bending the world to your whim, or taking the easy way out, or a kind of domination. It's like the wind that pulls free a single seed and carries it along on barely a breath, until it is gently placed in a new home.

She intended to make a love spell. This wasn't the kind of thing you did to overpower a person. She would drink it too. All it really did was allow them to relax a bit, postpone worries, and grow any hope they had inside them. It was a love spell in the same way ale was a courage spell. Liquid hope.

She wanted good, fresh ingredients. The basil

and fennel would be easy; she grew them herself right in the kitchen window tray and kept them healthy. With Summer approaching, they would be fully grown when she was ready, with a day to dry out for the freshest herbs possible.

Verbena would be similarly easy to get. She used her front garden to grow a variety of flowers, for both appearance and spell components. Spring had brought about a healthy flower garden, and she could clip a small sprig of Verbena and have it drying from the rafter over the mantle. Drying was nature's magick—it had its own way of locking in everything good in a plant and separating out everything bad. A day's press under some heavy books would leach the impurities out into the paper, and the sprig would be ready to use in a spell or for preservation in dry bins.

She went to the root cellar on the downriver side of the house and found a bottle of very nice red wine she'd been saving. She dusted it off and placed it on the rack near the door for when the time came.

The nutmeg wasn't grown locally; it didn't like the temperate climates. Her own nutmeg would, of course, still be good, but it was old, and she was going to so much trouble to get the very freshest and best that this was no exception. After searching in the local towns, she found a shop in Butterfog with a fresh supply of nutmeg. They said Ebbo had just delivered it to them on his previous visit, and after some talk, she discovered that this was the stop he made right before heading to her house. She bought more than she needed, as a thank you, and took it back to her home.

One more ingredient would be all she needed. Fresh honey. She eventually intended to get her own apiary started, of course, but these things took time. The day started with her in her sun hat, sitting out on the porch, relaxing and rocking—and watching. She had already collected a half bucket of pine needles and some old citrus peels she'd strung up from last Spring's orchard haul. These materials didn't need to be fresh. It wouldn't affect anything. Through patience and diligence, she watched several bees come to visit her flowers then head off down the path. She quietly got up, grabbed her pail, and followed them.

Following a bee takes patience, also. They're much smarter than people give them credit for. They know where their hive is, but they may take scouting detours on the way back as they fly. Eventually, though, all bees lead to the hive. She was lucky. It was in an old tree stump and not too high off the ground. She dropped the netting down off the brim of her hat and tucked it into the top of her dress. Then she took out a match, lit it, and dropped it in the bucket. Before long, a sweet, thick white smoke rose up and through the hive. The bees seemed to settle down. They crawled all over her, but the trick was not to panic. That would get her stung. She slowly and carefully scraped a small corner of the hive, scooping out the rich golden honey into a small vial, which she slowly placed back in her pocket. She covered the hive back over, said a quick, silent thank you to Nature for her goodness, and took her pail in hand.

The trip back home was also slow—she didn't want to seem threatening to any bees that might have stayed with her—but by the time she got home, she was clear enough to hang up her sun hat and go inside without incident.

She'd already been downriver to see Marjoram McJade, a fellow witch who lived about a day's walk from her. She'd taken her broom, of course, and turned it into a two-hour flight. It took some courage and a lot of trust to work things out with Marjoram, but they had known each other since they'd apprenticed with the District Coven, and she knew Marjoram would not betray her wishes. Marjoram was more excited to help her than Grenadine had ever seen. Hope was winning.

Another two hours found her home again with nothing to do but wait, and that was probably the hardest part yet.

***

It was a warm Summer's day, and Grenadine was at the well, drawing some water to soak beans for that night's stew, when Ghost, Marjoram's snowy owl, came in for a silent landing on the well's edge. He swiveled his head around and shook his leg. Grenadine wiped her hands and carefully untied the tiny piece of parchment from his leg. It simply read:

He just left me! He's looking in good spirits. He'll be in Butterfog tonight and to you on the morrow.
Best wishes!
M. M.

She scribbled a quick thank you on the back of it, rolled it up, and tied it back to the owl's leg. Ghost let her. When she was done, he took off from his perch, circled the area, and flew off in the direction of Marjoram's house again.

The day was spent as usual, but with Grenadine smiling ear to ear. The next morning, she awoke, fixed and scented her hair and skin, put on her best dress, and wrapped her head in an exquisite scarf with gold accents. She went to the cellar and fetched the red wine, went upstairs to her worktable, and prepared the ingredients for the love spell.

That day, when Ebbo came clanging up the walk, she met him at the path with her tray and asked him to have a drink with her. He sat down and took a sip. He chuckled a bit, nodded, and finished the drink off, asking for more. They talked for hours until it was nearly dark, and Grenadine barely remembered to order another book from him before he slipped off into the twilight, walking backwards away from her, slowly, and smiling.

***

Ebbo was a natural salesman and had the easy charm that came with it. Talk was how he made his living. But ever since the day he'd met Grenadine, his words had failed him.

He knew what he wanted. He wanted to spend his evenings with a woman who understood him. Someone he understood and with whom he could relate. Someone with whom he could laugh. Yes, he knew what he wanted—but he couldn't figure out how to say what he wanted to say.

He'd ordered a basket filled with supplies from the shoppe in nearby Butterfog to be delivered to Grenadine. One day after this, they had shared a drink together.

***

Grenadine carefully unwrapped the basket that had just been delivered. Inside was some fresh fennel and basil, a bit of dried Verbena, some nutmeg, some red wine, a small jar of honey, and a parchment that just said:

–Ebbo.

She smiled.

W.S. Moye

W.S. Moye is a lover of stories and of worlds of wonder, of humor and glory, and of things that go hex in the night. He typically writes Fantasy, Sci-fi, and Humor—novels for fun, short stories to really challenge himself, and both for punishment. You can find more of his nonsense here:

https://www.facebook.com/WSMoye

The Sidewinder and the Buffalo Child:
A Prairie Tale
by Mary Lucille Hays

The Sidewinder came to the prairie from the western country of hot, dry winds and sparse, bitter herbs. She was a beautiful snake–sleek with pearly scales, a wide jaw, and an arresting pattern of topaz spots studding her back like precious stones. She was smaller than her cousin, the Timber Rattler, and her rattle was tender, little more than a button, for she was young.

The Sidewinder had not been long in the grassland when she gave birth to a Buffalo Child. She was much surprised, as she had expected to bear a dozen or so jeweled wrigglers—miniatures of herself, who would skim over the sand in a rapid, sideways motion. Except here, there was no sand, only grass. And nestled in the grass lay a quivering bag of bone and horn and bloody wool and foreign limbs.

The Sidewinder had heard of snakes whose habit it was to lay a clutch of eggs instead of bearing live young, but she had always imagined these clusters to be pale and luminous, with leathery shells as soft as the petal of a rose. The birth sack which enclosed her Child, the Buffalo, was large and pulsing and purple, veined like the leaf of an oak. The Child inside began to kick, and the Sidewinder slit the sack with her tooth, in one line, smooth and swift.

Upon release, the Buffalo Child rolled onto her back and shook her four legs skyward. She turned her face, moist nose and sweet brown eye, toward the snake, and with that look, as sometimes happens between a new mother and her babe, the Sidewinder fell into an irrevocable and terrifying love.

The Buffalo struggled to her side and lay panting and kicking for a moment. The Sidewinder swayed cautiously, flicking her tongue to catch the warm mammalian scent of her strange daughter, keeping carefully out of reach of the hooves like polished tortoiseshell. Next, the Child rolled onto her knees, and in three movements—clumsy but swift as the prairie wind—she was on her feet, legs splayed, knees quaking.

The Child's girth and stature were as frightening to the Sidewinder as her sharp scent and hooves had been. But when the Buffalo looked at her mother and offered a bleat, the Sidewinder knew that this one would not make a zig-zag path through the grasses to fend for herself, and she went to find food for her daughter.

As the days on the prairie lengthened and warmed, so did the Buffalo Child grow. Her mother fed her on mice and voles and moles and sometimes a sweet gopher, but her favorite foods were the very grasses and clovers and thistles of the prairie. She loved the scent of the sun on the grass and the lacy wild carrots growing everywhere in abundance, and when she found a patch of hyssop or pennyroyal, she would paw the ground, crushing the herbs with her hooves until they'd yield their sharp, minty odors. Then she would roll and wriggle on her back, snorting in an ecstasy the Sidewinder could watch only from a careful distance.

This ceremony puzzled and frightened the snake, and when her daughter began to pick mouthfuls of timothy and goatsbeard and leave the bundles in secret at the doorway of the Sidewinder's hole, she was bemused but graciously accepted the gifts and brought them indoors to cushion her den.

Sometimes in the spring, the two would set out together. The Sidewinder would say, "Let us go to the creek and see if I can catch some frogs for supper," and they would set off in the direction of the creek. But somehow the path would shift, and the Buffalo Child would see that they were heading for the old oak. If the Buffalo Child asked when they would arrive at the stream, the Sidewinder would say, "Nonsense, Child. I said we were going to the tree to catch mice."

The Buffalo Child found this very confusing, and she could never guess, when she set off with her mother, whether they would end up at the little wooded spinney of locusts on the hill or the big rock by the pond.

Whenever her mother went alone to hunt, the Buffalo Child amused herself by running on the prairie, chasing rabbits and bumblebees. Chasing butterflies, whose twisting flight reminded her of her mother's zigzag trail through the grass, made her head ache with dizziness. But she loved to run in a straight line, the thundering rhythm of her hoofbeats echoing in her powerful shoulders, making her heart pound and her woolly coat damp with sweat.

One day, of crystalline blue sky and light, puffy cloud, while she was rolling and nuzzling in a spray of bergamot quite near her mother's dooryard, the Buffalo Child heard the sound of thunder—a long, low rumble that seemed to come from the bowels of the earth itself and seemed to have no end. Startled, for she had not smelled the rain coming, the Buffalo Child lumbered to her feet and scanned the horizon for the approaching storm. But in all directions, the sky was a peaceful blue, and still the sound continued.

The earth beneath her feet gently shivered. Then, to the north, she saw the dust rising and the dark shape moving toward her like a rolling river. She felt her heart swell and thrill to the sound and musky smell that was strange and somehow familiar. The thundering grew louder, and a rabbit scattered past. Her legs quaked with excitement, or perhaps because the ground was now genuinely shaking, and she felt the urge to run as far and as long as the earth stood steady beneath her pounding feet. But then the Buffalo Child saw her mother winding faster than ever before toward her hole, her eyes wide and glazed.

"They are upon us," she cried. "Oh, we must get down. We will be trampled. Get below, Child! We will be crushed." And she dove into her hole and lay coiled and quaking among the aromatic herbs.

Of course, the Buffalo Child could not fit into her mother's tunnel, and she pawed the ground, snorting and turning this way and that, for the river of creatures was indeed almost upon her. She saw no place to hide, no hole in the earth that could swallow her as it did her mother. And so she ran.

The thundering engulfed her, and she became part of the thundering. Running like a crazed thing, with no hope of escape, she was frightened as never before. A massive brown shape passed her on her left. From some small corner of her awareness, on the edge of her fury and fear, she noted horns curving inward. Then, two more overtook her, and she veered to the right but felt something brush and bump lightly against her flank as it passed, steering her back straight ahead. On all sides, the world became dust and rumble and horn and pounding hoof, and the Buffalo Child was swept along with the current. She became part of the rushing river and lost all sense of her four legs and her separateness. Her terror gradually gave way to exhilaration, for though her speed could not match that of the passing creatures, and she knew instinctively that to stumble or hesitate would mean her doom, the current parted to allow her a running space, and she felt the pulsing, thunderous rhythm match the song of her own blood.

She did not know how long she ran, but as she finally became aware of her own labored breathing, she noticed a thinning of the herd around her. And just as she realized that she was indeed falling behind, she stumbled and fell heavily to the ground.

She pulled herself immediately to her feet, but the herd was already far to the south. She could see a few stragglers, and she watched until she could see only a cloud of dust on the horizon. Then she nuzzled the gopher hole that had tripped her and turned her nose homeward.

She was thoughtful on her journey. Her heart was still full of wonder and excitement, and though her legs took her back to her mother at a limp, some part of her still rolled over the prairie at a gallop.

It was twilight when she arrived back at her mother's door, and she could hear the Sidewinder wailing, "Oh, my Child. She is lost. She has been trampled. Oh, what shall I do?"

"Mother, no! I am here. I am all right," called the Buffalo Child. And the Sidewinder left her weeping and slipped out of her hole. When she saw that it was true, she wept anew, and twining herself around her Child's legs, she flicked her tongue in and out of her mouth to taste her daughter's scent lest her eyes fool her. When she was satisfied that it was her own daughter returned to her, unhurt save a small swelling above the hoof, she asked the Child to relate how she had escaped tragedy. But instead of answering, her daughter asked, "Mother, who were they? Those creatures?"

The Sidewinder looked at her daughter and shook her rattle ever so slightly. "They are the Buffalo."

"I think they are like me," said the Buffalo Child.

"Yes, Child. I fear they are like you."

The Sidewinder waited. The Buffalo looked up at the moon.

"Mother, I felt so odd, running with them. It was as if I were running home."

Still the Sidewinder waited.

"Mama? I think I would like to try to find these Buffalo."

The Sidewinder gave a long, low sigh, then stared hard at the shadow the moon made with the red clover.

"Daughter, I love you, and my only wish is for your happiness. Go, if it will make you happy, and find a home with the Buffalo."

The Buffalo knelt and gently nudged her mother's face. "Thank you, Mother," she said. "I will head South in the morning." And making a cushion of her weariness, she curled her legs under her and went to sleep.

The Sidewinder listened to her daughter's breathing for a moment, then turned to her hole and went down to nestle in the sweet grasses.

Had the Buffalo been awake, she would have heard her mother's keening wail lifting to the moon. "Surely my daughter hates me," she cried.
But the Buffalo was dreaming of running, and running, and running on the prairie.

Mary Lucille Hays

Mary Lucille Hays has lived most of her life in the Midwest. She was named for both of her grandmothers and teaches writing at the University of Illinois. In 2015, she was Murray State University's Jesse Stuart Fellow. Mary has published work in *Quiddity, ACM, Broad!, The Mid-America Poetry Review, Blue Violin, Coal City Review,* and other publications. In 2007, The Illinois Center for the Book presented her with the Gwendolyn Brooks Award for her poem, "Tippet Hill." A founding editor of *New Stone Circle*, she raises chickens on her grandmother's farm in Central Illinois.

Her work can be read at:
tamingjunkyarddog.blogspot.com

Daphne, the Girl in the Armor
by Amanda Luzzader

Alessandro rose before the sun, while the air was still invigorating. He loaded his donkey Mackamae and led him out of the village to the top of a hill. There he stopped and turned back to look over Tazah.

It was a village he loved, where he had many friends, and where he had been very happy.

"Why must you go, Alessandro?" his mama had protested.

"Because she is not here," he answered.

Even though there were more animals than people living in Tazah, there were still many lovely girls there.

"What about Edita?" his mama had asked.

"She is more beautiful than a flower, and I see her waiting for you at the well every day."

"Edita is very pretty," Alessandro admitted.

"Well, then?" His mama stood with her hands on her stout hips.

Alessandro shrugged. "She is not the one."

His mother pulled a dishrag from the waistband of her apron and hit him with it. "Do you want to break my heart? Is that it?"

For months, his mama and friends had coaxed Alessandro to reveal what exactly it was he was looking for, but he could not say.

"Do you like the fair-haired girls, Alessandro?"

"I don't know. Maybe."

"Are you looking for a girl who can cook? One to satisfy that insatiable appetite of yours?"

"Perhaps."

"A buxom girl. Surely, that's what you want."

Alessandro shrugged. "I'll know her when I find her," he always declared.

His friend Zack accused him of being too choosey. "You could have your pick of any girl, but you say none of them are good enough. You may be good-looking, but you're not one of the gods."

As it grew closer to the day he would leave, his mother experienced many crying episodes in which she wailed so loudly, it spooked the horses.

"Why? Why are you leaving me, Alessandro?" she muttered between sobs.

"For love," Alessandro answered. "For love."

And finally, there was nothing more his mama or friends could say. Alessandro was leaving to find love, and he vowed that he'd search the entire world if needed to find her.

The roosters were crowing when Alessandro finally turned his back on Tazah. He patted Mackamae on the back and said, "When we return, it will be with my one true love."

Mackamae shook his head and grumbled. He was less than interested in Alessandro's love life. He walked ahead of Alessandro, trying to pull him along. Mackamae was a donkey who wanted to see the world.

For many days, they walked. Sometimes in cold rain. Sometimes in blistering heat. They visited an island where there were many women who seductively shook their hips when they danced. Mackamae fell in love. With pineapple. He licked and smacked his lips and was thoroughly disappointed when Alessandro led him back onto a boat to leave the island.

Alessandro smiled as they sailed away. "We're one step closer to finding her," he said.

Mackamae hung his head. He was sure he'd never find something as delicious as pineapple ever again.

They crossed over valleys and climbed up mountains. They stopped in a snowy village where the pink-cheeked daughters of the plump villagers brought them hot cacoa. The girls wrapped Mackamae in warm blankets and braided his hair while they joked with Alessandro. Mackamae was delighted, and when he caught Alessandro's eyes, he perked up his ears, raised his eyebrows, and smiled. But Alessandro waved him off, and the next day, they left again.

The duo walked so much that Alessandro's olive skin browned to a mocha color, and Mackamae grew lean and strong.

They visited cities and towns, and everywhere they went, Mackamae fell in love with the food and the people and the music. He'd buck up onto his hind legs to dance to trumpets or drums or banjos. He would hee-haw and laugh, and sometimes Alessandro, with maybe just a little too much to drink, would hold his hooves, and the pair would dance together until they collapsed.

But always in the morning, Alessandro would say, "All right, my friend. It's time to go." And Mackamae would wave his tail goodbye to the friends they'd made as they journeyed on to the next town.

For five years, three months, and twenty-four days, they traveled the world—eating and drinking and laughing at the stories their newest friends would tell. But after all that time, Mackamae was ready to go home. He was a donkey who had seen the sun rise and set in all corners of the world. A field of wild flowers had taken his breath away. He'd thrilled when they stood atop a mountain and could see so far they actually saw the curve of the Earth. But he missed his friends in Tazah—duck and pig especially, and even the horses. Mackamae was tired of traveling day after day. So he walked a little slower and he bickered with Alessandro and his ears didn't perk up anymore at the scent of new food.

Alessandro didn't seem to notice though, because he walked a little slower himself. And sometimes, when they came across another town, he'd just sigh and keep on walking.

"Mackamae," he said, "what if there's no one out there for me? Or what if I've simply missed her? In all these places we've been… was she right there waiting for me, and I simply passed her by?"

Mackamae rolled his eyes and kept walking.

There was an ache in the pit of Alessandro's stomach. He thought about going home, too. He missed his mama. He missed his friends. He missed the way the sun filtered into his bedroom in the mornings to wake him and the smell of the wet alfalfa in the fields. But mostly, he was afraid that he was wasting his life chasing something that didn't exist.

That night it rained, and Alessandro was thankful because the raindrops on his face concealed his tears from Mackamae. The last thing he wanted was for that jackass to see him cry.

In the morning, Alessandro rose and stretched. He smiled and breathed deeply. He'd decided it was good that he hadn't found her. Because things easily obtained are taken for granted. The difficulty of finding his true love would only make him value her even more.

After all, Alessandro believed in love. From the tips of his toes and all through his body, he believed in love. It wouldn't matter to him if she was one hundred years old or if she was ugly or if she was lazy. The heart knew what it wanted, and his heart would tell him when he found her. And if he never found her? That was all right, too. Because it was a truly noble feat to spend one's life in pursuit of true love. And just because he hadn't found his love yet, he knew she was still out there, somewhere.

Mackamae and Alessandro traveled for another two years and forty-three more days, and by then, they had become the best of friends. They could finish each other's sentences. When Alessandro grew a long beard, Mackamae grew one, too. They'd fall asleep in hay lofts, passing gas and telling jokes. Mackamae would never admit it, but he wanted Alessandro to find his soul's mate, too, almost just as much as Alessandro. Not because he wanted to stop their travels, but because Alessandro was his closest friend.

That day, they had wandered off the road and were meandering through a shady grove of aspen trees, where the birds sang, purplish-pink flowers bloomed, and low ivy bushes spread over the ground. The trees opened into a meadow, and as Alessandro and Mackamae approached, they spied a soldier engaged in a great battle.

Alessandro stopped short.

"My God, what a woman!" he cried.

Mackamae brayed. It was unclear to the donkey how his friend knew it was a woman. The soldier was clad entirely in armor.

"Of course it's a woman," answered Alessandro. "See the grace of her movements. Hear the softness of her voice."

Mackamae brayed again. Hee-haw, hee-haw?

"I'm not sure, my friend. She fights magnificently, but I see no opponent."

The soldier thrust swiftly, and she swung smartly. She brought her great shield up to defend from attacking blows, but neither Alessandro nor Mackamae could see anyone else in the field.

"Her enemy must be invisible," Alessandro told Mackamae.

Mackamae didn't hear him, though. He could only stare at the lady warrior, his mouth open, buck teeth showing. In all their travels, they'd never seen such a person. She was astounding. Maybe a little crazy. But his heart was beating hard because he knew this girl wasn't like any of the others Alessandro had turned down. And when Mackamae finally composed himself, he looked up at Alessandro to see him staring at the girl, too, his eyes glowing. And Mackamae knew they'd finally found her.

"We'll wait," Alessandro said without looking away. "When she's finished, we'll introduce ourselves."

But the fight with the invisible foe continued all morning. She swung her sword valiantly, drew back, and parried an unseen blown. The sun moved across the horizon as she lunged and twisted and thrust, and still she fought.

She had fought for so long that Alessandro and Mackamae had grown tired and lay down in the cool grass while they kept watching her. They ate a small lunch of cheese and bread, and Alessandro wished to share it with the girl, if only she'd notice them. He was afraid to distract her from the battle because she fought with such ferocity, he knew it must be a difficult fight.

Finally, Alessandro stood. "We can't let her fight this alone," he said. He found a stick by a tree and rushed into the meadow to help the girl.

Just as he arrived, she had fallen backwards onto the ground and held her shield up to protect herself. Alessandro swung the stick wildly, hoping it would connect with whatever the girl was fighting.

It swished through the air, and at first, Alessandro thought he had missed. But then the girl sat up and lifted her visor. Sweat beaded her forehead, and her dark hair was matted against her skin. Her eyes were moist, and although Alessandro couldn't see what color they were, he was certain they were the most beautiful eyes he had ever seen.

"I'm Alessandro," he said.

"I'm Daphne," she replied, then she slapped the visor shut and resumed the fight.

All day long she fought. Sometimes she did well, making great strides across the meadow as her sword slashed through the air, and during these times, Alessandro and Mackamae would run behind her, cheering her on. Other times, the invisible foe forced her to the ground, and she'd struggle even to raise her shield. During these times, Alessandro would stand in front of her, hoping to protect her from whatever it was she feared. Mackamae would kick wildly, but the enemy they fought was apparently personal to Daphne, because she alone could fight it.

Daphne kept fighting. For days, then weeks, then months. She never stopped. Alessandro and Mackamae had to stop for rest, food, and sleep, but Daphne never stopped, and this made Alessandro love her.

One day, Alessandro drew close to Daphne as they fought. "You know, Daphne," he shouted, "I love you."

For just a moment, she paused. She lifted her visor and turned to Alessandro. "I love you, too," she said.

The words filled Alessandro with such joy and lightness that he floated off the ground for three days.

Daphne continued her battle, and Alessandro and Mackamae stayed with her, wanting nothing more than to help her succeed.

After an entire year, on a particularly rough day, when Daphne had fought nearly to her breaking point, she stopped abruptly.

Her sword dropped from her hand.

"I'm done," she said. She lifted her visor. "I don't want to fight anymore."

"Come home with me, Daphne," said Alessandro. "Let me take care of you." He felt as though there were pins in every part of his body. All his hopes and dreams for the future rested in her answer.

Daphne looked back at him. Her eyes were brown and her lashes long.

Alessandro was certain the silence would cause him to burst, and even Mackamae froze in anticipation.

"I think," she said, "that I would like that."

And so they began the long journey back to Tazah.

Daphne didn't remove her armor, but even still, she and Alessandro held hands most of the way. The trip back to Tazah would take them six months, and the pair talked the entire time. Alessandro told Daphne about how much of a jackass Mackamae was, and then Mackamae told Daphne how much of a jackass Alessandro could be. Mackamae warned Daphne of the horrible smell of Alessandro's feet when he removed his shoes. Alessandro said Mackamae passed gas in his sleep all night.

And Daphne told them many things—about her childhood and her home and her family, but she never spoke about her battle and she never said who or what it was she fought.

Every day, they grew more in love, until Alessandro was convinced he was the happiest man alive. Daphne would not remove her armor, but Alessandro didn't care. He liked her just the way she was.

When they finally made it to Tazah, Alessandro was so excited to introduce Daphne to everyone. It would be the beginning of their perfect life. They would marry and have babies and raise pigs, and Alessandro would have everything he ever wanted in life.

"We're here! We're here!" Alessandro shouted as they walked into the village.

There were a few more houses and a lot more animals, but it was the same home Alessandro remembered. Mackamae galloped off to find his friends.

In his excitement, Alessandro pulled Daphne along, but she could not move very fast in her armor.

Soon, the villagers stepped out of the houses, calling back to others inside, "It's Alessandro! He's come home." But as soon as they stepped out and saw him with Daphne still wearing the coat of armor, they scratched their heads.

"He turned down our daughters for this?" a mother whispered to her husband.

Instead of being greeted with exclamations of joy, as Alessandro had expected, the villagers seemed … perplexed.

"I found her," he called to them, as if they

simply didn't understand. But they only stared quietly back.

Daphne shrank inside her armor. She stood very close to Alessandro, as though she were afraid.

At last, they made it to Alessandro's hut, and there waiting for him was his mama, looking as portly as ever. Alessandro dropped Daphne's hand to sweep his mother into a big hug. "I found her," he declared. "And you're going to love her. You're all going to love her! She's perfect."

And everybody turned to look at the perfect girl, who stood alone now with her head bowed and her armor shaking.

"This is why you were gone all these years?" His mama scowled. "You can't even see her! Why is she hiding behind all that armor?"

It was only then that Alessandro sensed Daphne's discomfort, and so he gently grabbed her by the arm and quickly led her inside, where he shut the door and all the shutters to keep the neighbors from staring anymore.

Other than Mackamae, none of Alessandro's friends could understand why he was so interested in Daphne—the quiet girl who wouldn't take off her armor even after being there for weeks.

"What's with the armor?" they'd ask Alessandro. "Is she frightened of you or just scared you can't protect her?"

"She will take it off when she is ready," he answered. But even he began to wonder if she'd ever take it off. He longed to be close to her. To feel her in his arms. But the armor made that impossible. Still, he loved her more than life even with the armor, but he'd say to her, "Daphne, you don't need the armor anymore. You're safe here. I'll protect you. You don't need to fight anymore."

But Daphne would shake her head. "You don't understand. I can't take it off."

Alessandro's mama felt it was her duty to protect her son. She took him aside one day. "Don't you see?" she asked. "She's playing you for a fool. Sleeping in your house, eating your food, but never taking off the armor. That's not love. She's taking advantage of you. If she really loved you, she'd let you see the real Daphne."

"She just needs time, Mama," said Alessandro.

"Six weeks maybe. But this? She's been here six months, now!"

Alessandro grew angry. "This is between us," he shouted. Still, Alessandro went to the shop and bought the most beautiful and expensive dresses. He laid them out on the bed for Daphne to see.

"They're beautiful," she said.

"Put one on," he said.

"I can't," she said, shaking her head.

Alessandro knew what people were thinking. He heard the things they whispered. And he wondered himself. Why wouldn't Daphne take off the armor? Hadn't he fought beside her? Hadn't he proven his love and devotion to her? He'd given her everything, even his very heart. So why did she keep the armor? Did she not love him? Surely if she loved him the way he loved her, she would take the armor off so they could be in each other's arms.

The more Alessandro thought about it, the angrier he became. He sulked around the house. He pushed Daphne's hand off him when she touched his arm.

"What's wrong?" asked Daphne.

"Don't you get it?" he spat. "I don't want to be touched by your armor. I want you. The real you." He'd go off drinking with Mackamae and not come home until the next day.

Daphne would cry behind her faceplate, but still she would not take it off.

Finally, Alessandro had had enough. She didn't need the armor. He would protect her! If she would just take it off, he was sure he could get her to see that.

And so he issued an ultimatum. "Either you let me take off the armor, or you get out."

It wasn't that he didn't love her, because he did. With all his heart and soul he loved her. He just didn't understand why she was so guarded, why she didn't lose the armor. He didn't want her to leave, but he didn't want to go one more day without being able to hold her.

"I thought you loved me," said Daphne.

"I do," said Alessandro.

"Then don't do this," she pleaded. "I can't take it off. I just can't."

"If you love me," Alessandro said. "If you really love me, you'll do this for me."

"It will kill me," Daphne said.

"No it won't!" Alessandro said. "I'm going to protect you! Don't you see? You don't need the armor because I'm here! If you love me, if you truly love me, you will do this."

"Is this the only way?" Daphne asked, crying.

Alessandro paused for a moment, because he loved Daphne even with the armor. Even without being able to see anything but rusted and dented plates, he loved her for her. And he wondered if that wasn't enough.

"Yes," he finally said. "That's the only way." And he said it because he was so sure that things would be better without the armor.

"Then take it off me," she said.

She lay down on the bed, and Alessandro removed her helmet and visor, her breastplate and gauntlets and tausset. He removed it all, and for the first time ever, he saw her.

She was beautiful.

And she was broken.

White cracks crossed her skin. Everywhere. She looked like a porcelain doll that had been fractured and then glued back together.

Daphne sat up. Seeing Alessandro staring at her, she laughed nervously.

"What is this?" said Alessandro. "These marks. What are they?"

"Alessandro, I tried to tell you." She smiled and laughed her nervous laugh again.

And then a piece of her cheek fell off. Like a piece of eggshell. It came away from her cheek and fell to the floor, leaving a black space.

As though by instinct, she covered the void with her hand, but the sudden movement started a chain reaction. First, her fingers broke like icicles and fell to pieces with the tinkling of broken glass. Then her arm fell apart.

And before Alessandro's eyes, the love of his life crumbled. He reached for the pieces, trying to hold them together, but he could not, and they fell and splintered into dust.

It was only then that Alessandro realized Daphne's armor had held her together. He understood then that it was not his place to remove her armor before she had healed.

At last he understood her, because he felt a great crack form in his heart. He looked at Daphne's armor where it lay scattered. He felt the crack spread within him.

Once again, he packed up his donkey Mackamae for a long journey. He first visited the village blacksmith, who fitted him with his own suit of armor. And then he left, this time to fight a battle with a foe nobody else could see.

Amanda Luzzader

Amanda Luzzader is an award-winning writer and poet. She loves rain, a perfectly brewed cup of tea, and free two-day shipping. Amanda's fiction can be found in numerous collections, including Volatile When Mixed: An Anthology of Poetry and Prose (2016 LUW Press), Apocalypse: Utah (2016 Griffin Publishers), and The Helicon West Anthology (Helicon West Press 2016). She also writes creative nonfiction and poetry, and feels that high-quality writing is equal parts tension and passion. Amanda is a grant writer for a nonprofit organization and is the proud mom of two incredibly bright boys.

Find Amanda on Facebook at:

www.facebook.com/authoramandaluzzader/

The Night Shift
by AJ Millen

A fox barks, and a distant owl hoots somewhere across the playing fields. I peek out from my shelter among the roots and watch the darkness rapidly cover what's left of the damp day like a shroud spread over a dearly departed. The glare of a streetlight pokes jagged fingers through the branches above me as I wait for dusk to give way to night.

Out there, humans are returning to their homes. Closing heavy curtains against the unknown night. Enfolding them in the comfort of their own homes, where they'll grab a few hours with their loved ones—and maybe a take-away as they watch a TV movie—before seeking solace in the safety of their beds. At least, that's where they think they're safe.

There's no home our kind hasn't visited. No sleep we haven't shattered with a spasm of fear and panic. No locked doors or barred windows that can keep us away.

Ironic that they've started hanging up ineffective spiders' webs of wool and trinkets bearing our own name to keep us out.

But we're not the ones who conceive and give birth to the night terrors haunting them; they manage that just fine all on their own in the depths of their hate, their bitterness, their buried hopes and fears.

We just gather them, take sustenance from them, and use them to build our dark subterranean kingdoms.

We are the Dreamcatchers.

***

A shriek rang out from the upstairs bedroom, interrupting the sullen squabble being fought out below.

"Daddy! The monster! It here's again. Make it go…" The words faded away into muffled sobbing.

James got up abruptly, knocking his chair backwards as he did. The tear-streaked woman opposite him rolled her eyes.

"You spoil that child," she spat. "How is she ever going to learn to stop being afraid of the dark if you go running at every whimper?"

"Come on, Holly. She's just a little girl. Weren't you ever scared of something you thought was hiding in your bed? I'll just go show her there's nothing to worry about."

"It's about time she grew out of it," replied his wife of nine years. "It's not the imaginary monsters she needs to be afraid of."

"She's just six, for Christ's sake." James shook his head in disbelief. "When did you become such a cold bitch?"

"Round about the same time you lost everything we'd ever worked for and didn't have the balls to tell me about it." Holly took an angry drag on her cigarette, the red glow nibbling away at the butt clasped between shaking fingers, and looked away.

James shoved past her into the hallway and mounted the stairs. "Daddy's coming, sweetheart."

Holly stubbed out her smoke and buried her face in her hands. Vivid red and purple circles plumed and unfurled inside her eyelids. She swiped away angry tears, doubly furious he'd made her feel like a heartless cow, even though she knew she was right.

She stared at the bundle of papers before her. The deeds to the house. Their house. But not anymore. He'd signed it over to J.T. Whitworth & Sons, behind her back. What a respectable name for a loan shark, she thought as she bitterly scanned the letter that had arrived that morning, ordering them leave the home she'd thought was theirs, bought and paid for.

"It's not the monsters under the bed we need to be scared of."

***

James opened Penny's door with a reassuring smile painted on his face. He'd failed as a husband, but he'd be damned if he was going to let down his daughter.

"It's all right, Princess," he cooed in a voice almost betraying the tears catching at the back of his throat. "So, where is this bad old monster this time?"

"It's here, Daddy," came the whimper from the bed. "I heard it get out from under the bed. It's here somewhere. Make it go away."

Light flooded at the flick of a switch. Its warm glow glinted off butterflies painted on Penny's headboard and the sequins on the purple dreamcatcher hanging above it. James looked around. No scaly black imp lurked in the corner. There wasn't even the slightest whiff of brimstone in the air.

Penny gasped and recoiled beneath the covers as he reached out to pat her shoulder.

"Silly thing, it's just me," he said, pulling down the counterpane to reveal his daughter's pallid, wide-eyed face. "No one here but your Daddy Bear." He reached out and gave her nose a gentle tweak before bending and kissing her forehead. "You must have been having one of those nasty dreams again. There's nothing here that's going to hurt you. We all love you. Me, Mummy, even Perkins."

Father and daughter looked up as the door creaked and opened a few inches, only to gush with relieved laughter as a calico cat with a ragged ear slinked in and blinked up at them.

"See? Even Perkins says there's nothing to be frightened of, and he's scared of the plastic bags and the vacuum cleaner!"

Holly giggled and held her hand out to the cat, which strolled over, sniffed her fingertips, and sat like a fat, furry sentry on the floor next to her bed.

Feeling his daughter starting to relax, James stood. Waggling his eyebrows and holding his finger to his lips in a theatrical shushing gesture, he yanked the curtains open to reveal … nothing except a wall in need of a fresh coat of paint and a few stray dust bunnies. Penny giggled and settled against the headboard to enjoy the show.

James repeated his pantomime, creeping up on the wardrobe in the corner of the room and pulling open the door with a flourish. The most terrifying thing inside was Bernie, the battered old velveteen dog with one eye missing and one leg hanging on by just a few threads.

"Don't forget under the bed, Daddy!" Penny had now forgotten her fears and was enjoying the game.

James got down on his hands and knees and made a great show of checking the space beneath the bed, then clambered back to his feet and looked down at Penny. "Nope, nothing. I think your monsters are the biggest scaredy-cats of all," he laughed. "Now, you lie back down and start thinking of rainbows and flower fairies to make sure you have some sweet dreams."

"I'm not a baby!"

"Yes, you are." The relieved father smiled. "You're my baby, and I'm never going to let anything bad happen to you. But first, you have to snuggle down and go back to sleep."

Penny shuffled down the bed, turned on her side, and looked up. "Can I have a drink of water? And tell Mummy to give me one of her special sweet dreams kisses."

***

Holly looked up as James entered the kitchen. "Is she okay?"

"Yeah, but she wants some water. And she wants you too," he answered with a reproachful look that made her squirm. "She must have heard us fighting and got upset. You know what kids are like. Let's go up together, all sweetness and smiles, for her sake. Okay?" He reached for Penny's favorite glass— one with a Princess and a small, friendly dragon painted on the side.

Holly took it and opened the tap to let the water run cold. She filled the glass, then splashed her face and patted it dry with a hand towel. "Okay, let's do this."

***

Perkins shot out of the little girl's bedroom as the couple reached the landing. They were too busy carefully composing fake marital harmony on their faces before going in.

The bed was empty. No dark curls peeked out from under the covers. No bump in the comforter betrayed her hiding place. Nothing was hiding behind the curtains or under the bed. But the wardrobe door was ajar, and Bernie the Beagle had tumbled out onto the floor.

"Come out, come out, wherever you are," sing-sang James as he pulled the door wide. The cupboard was bare but for a few shoes and party dresses hanging from the rail above.

***

The Richards searched the house from top to bottom five times, and the garden twice, before calling the police. No clue hinted at an intruder or how a six-year-old could have disappeared into the January night.

No clue was ever found.

***

There's no home our kind hasn't visited. No sleep we haven't shattered with a spasm of fear and panic. No locked doors or barred windows that can keep us out.

We gather your fears, take sustenance from them, use them to build our dark subterranean kingdoms.

We are the Dreamcatchers.

AJ Millen

AJ Millen has been telling stories all her life. During the 1980s, she worked as a newspaper reporter in England. In 1989, she left for what was meant to be a six-month semester in Greece. That was the plan—until a brown-eyed boy from Samos persuaded her to stay. He is now her husband and father to their twenty-year-old son.

She lives in Athens and works in Corporate Communications. To date, AJ has participated in two collaborative novel writing projects (with another in the pipeline) and has stories published in six anthologies. Read more of her words at:

http://shemeanswellbut.blogspot.com

Slayer
by Kevin Grover

The moon was red when the Black Knight came to my village. People took a red moon as a bad omen, but way I sees it, ain't nothing but a beginning. Least, that was my beginning when I was a girl of thirteen. Remembered him well as he rode in on a horse black as his armor. People just seemed to know to get out of his way. All us villagers gathered, 'course, as strangers weren't really common in Dragon's Spit.

Well, there we were, watching this giant of a man in black armor ride in from south across the Wilds. Pa was the first one to approach, asking him all sorts of questions that the knight seemed to take exception to, 'coz he jumped down from that big old horse and grabbed Pa around the throat. Ma screamed as Pa landed lifeless right by my feet. I knelt down and shook him, telling him to get himself up and tell the bad man to go away. Ma burst into tears, and I ain't never seen that before. Then the Black Knight swung his sword around, cutting people down as he walked calmly through the village. Seemed like a hundred more knights came riding in then, with flaming torches held high. They threw those torches about and set fire to homes. The smell was sickening, and the heat burned my face. I pulled Ma's hand to try to get her moving, but she just stayed right there by Pa's side, her head buried in his chest as she sobbed.

"We've got to go, Ma!" I cried, desperately pulling on her hand. Finally, she looked up and wiped her tears. She stood, and we hurried through the smoke and screams. I didn't know where we were going, but I kept my eyes fixed on the red moon whenever there was a break in the smoke. That was, until the Black Knight rose into view above me. He didn't even glance at me as his sword slashed out. Suddenly, Ma's hand went limp in mine, and she fell on top of me. The Black Knight was already stepping over Ma's lifeless body, and I watched his booted feet kick up dust as he hunted down the last of the villagers.

Closing my eyes, I lay very still, pretending I was dead like Ma. I cried silently, screwing my eyes shut and trying to ignore the screaming. Eventually, things went real quiet, apart from the crackling of fires as they burned long into the night. When I dared to open my eyes, the red moon had gone, along with the Black Knight and his army. With a little effort, I pulled myself from under Ma and stood in the early dawn light, surveying the carnage.

There were piles of bodies everywhere. Stunned, I stumbled through my dead village. I hurried down the hill towards the forest where I had played the day before. What the Dark Lord had wanted with my village, I had no idea. We never had a cross word with anyone. I wandered the forest, barefoot and cold for most of the day. Was really numb by the time I came across the little wooden hut. Must've walked for miles and miles 'coz I remember the shadows were falling around me and the sun was sinking real low. A man was chopping wood by the hut, bare-chested, sweat glistening off his muscled torso. He swung the axe high, then sent it straight through blocks of wood, splitting them without effort. Dunno how long I watched him, too scared to speak, too scared to leave. Finally, he noticed me.

"Late to be wandering the woods," he said, wiping sweat from his brow with the back of his hand. "Where you from?"

I pointed behind me. The old man's eyes narrowed as he looked over me, and he nodded. Looking back, I saw black smoke rising above the trees, and I knew the old man had seen death in that. He took me into his hut and wrapped me in a warm blanket as he made a fire. He gave me water and fed me hot soup, which I forced myself to eat.

"You got a name?"

I stared at my empty bowl and felt pretty much the same. Red moon had been the end of my life and any name I once had. "Ain't got no name, Sir," I muttered, averting my eyes from his curious gaze.

"I'm no sir," he said gruffly. "People know me as Cleaver. Least, they used to know me as that." He gave a half smile.

"Pa used to speak about Cleaver the Legend," I said brightly, but I was suddenly filled with grief that Pa wouldn't be telling me no more of his stories. Cleaver let me cry, made a weak attempt to comfort me. I wasn't sure when I stopped crying, because next thing I remember is waking up with bright sunshine streaming through the window and the smell of roasting meat.

"You're just in time for breakfast," Cleaver said, pushing a plate into my hands. But I wasn't much hungry. My mind traveled back to the night of the red moon, and I found myself unable to work out how long it had been. I forced myself to eat while Cleaver busied himself around his hut, avoiding talk with me. It was obvious Cleaver was only used to his own company, and I had invaded his world.

"Are you really the Cleaver my Pa told stories about?"

"He tell you the story of how Cleaver fought the King one on one and beat him?"

"That's my favorite. Is that you?"

"Aye, though I suspect the story is bigger than the truth."

"Then what are you doing here?"

Cleaver grunted. "Retiring. Legends eventually fade into old men who yearn for past glories. My name will live longer than me, told by drunk men in taverns who envy the man I was." He sounded sad yet content. It reminded me of how Ma would talk about meeting Pa for the first time and I saw that distant look as she would go inside herself. Before grief took me again, I thought about my name. It was fading from memory—a meaningless thing now the ones who had given it to me were gone. "What name would you give *me*?"

Cleaver stared at me intently. "Depends what you want to do in life."

Without thinking, I said, "I want to face the Black Knight who killed my parents."

"A black knight? That's a dangerous path to take. You'll need a mighty name."

"So name me."

Cleaver tugged at his grey moustache. "Slayer."

It sounded good. Felt like my name was a weapon. "Will you teach me to fight?"

Cleaver got to his feet and turned his back to me. For a long time, he was silent, staring out the window into the woods. After a while, he turned to me and knelt. "You are choosing the path of the warrior, Little Slayer. It is filled with death and destruction."

"If my past is filled with death and destruction, then so must my future. Train me or send me on my way."

Cleaver nodded. "First, we must break your body and your mind before building you stronger." He opened the door and went out, beckoning me to follow. "Run around this clearing as fast as you can until your legs collapse. When you recover, run some more."

Screwing my face up, I asked, "How will that make me a warrior?"

Cleaver grunted. "It won't, but 'tis a necessary first step to train your body. Tomorrow, you will be running with a log on your back."

That was how I found myself running around his clearing until my lungs were burning and my legs gave way. But I found a rage within that gave me the strength to get to my feet. By the time dusk came, I was limping into the hut, my entire body on fire. The next day was the same, but this time I carried a heavy log upon my shoulders. By the time it was noon, my legs had given way and I limped back to the hut where I lay, unable to move. Cleaver was not sympathetic. He made me food, brought me water, but told me that I was to get back outside and continue training.

The weeks went by and became months. By the third month, I was running around the clearing with a log on my shoulders for the entire day. My legs had grown in size, and a new power was there. Without the log, my running speed was immense and my endurance like nothing I had ever experienced. But Cleaver wouldn't let me hold a weapon or train me in its use.

"You have speed, but now you need strength," he said. I knew not to question.

There was a tree with a low-hanging branch he made me use to pull myself up. I struggled with one, but by the end of the month, I was pulling myself up thirty times in a row, my arms bulging with newfound muscles.

"When the body is strong, the mind follows," he told me as I worked out one day.

I slumped down against the tree, exhausted. "I want to learn how to kill," I said. "I'm ready."

Cleaver shook his head, his face hard as a rock. "No, Little Slayer. You have just started."

***

Training with Cleaver was real hard, but I reckoned it would be worth it. It was months until he let me hold my first sword. I couldn't hide my smile. By now, I must've had my fourteenth birthday, but who was really counting? Instead of years, Cleaver measured muscle size, speed, and strength. The old man was a gruff sort to the point he seemed unloving and cold. But I caught the look of pride in his eyes when I made unexpected progress, and that was enough for me. Way I sees it, he avoided actually feeling stuff, and I learned to do the same.

"Have you ever loved someone?" I asked Cleaver as my arm shook with the weight of the sword. The challenge for that day was to hold the sword for as long as I could, and after a while, I was getting bored, desperately wanting to slice it through the air.

Cleaver sat on a tree stump, his eyes fixed on me, ready to punish if my sword lowered. "Aye."

I stared at him. "Who did you love?"

Cleaver took a deep breath. "The only thing you need to love now is your sword. Keep it that way, and you'll never break, never waiver, and always win."

My arm cramped, and I felt the weight of the broadsword increase. Sweat ran down my face, and I took deep breaths, bringing my mind to focus on the task. "Is that why you don't love?"

"Mmm?"

"Because you broke once and lost?" I smiled cruelly, enjoying the look of uncertainty on my master's face. But my mind had wandered, and the sword lowered. Before I knew what was happening, Cleaver was on me, sweeping my leg away and knocking the sword from my hand. Landing heavily on my back, I lay gasping when the air was forced out of me, looking up into Cleaver's red face of rage.

"You broke," he said, pulling me up. We looked at each other for a few moments until I could no longer hold his stare. Without needing to be told, I picked up the sword and held it in my sore arms, deepening my stance and clearing my mind. When the sun came down, I never wanted to hold a sword again.

Only next day, Cleaver had me up at dawn, holding out the sword until I could no longer. The muscles in my arms screamed at me, and I wanted to scream back, but I kept my gaze ahead and focused. The sword was my arm, I told myself. It was part of me, and I was part of it. I could not lose the sword in the same way I could not lose my arm.

These days went on until I could stand holding the sword without a single shake in my arm from dawn to dusk.

"Now you are ready to fight," Cleaver said, taking the sword from me. "Tomorrow." He disappeared into the hut and left me in the forest with the shadows darkening around me. I tensed my arm, muscles bulging. *Finally.* When I went to bed later that night, I dreamt of my Ma and Pa for the first time in ages. Waking, I found myself crying but unable to recall what the dream was about. When Cleaver came into my room, I quickly wiped the tears and pretended to sleep.

"Come, Little Slayer. Now it's time you learned how to fight."

For months, Cleaver taught me how to use my sword to block various basic attacks. "We repeat these moves until you can do them without thinking," Cleaver told me. It was boring, but as time went by, the moves became as natural as breathing. Between this, Cleaver had me doing more running and lifting work, turning my body into a deadly machine. Slash, block, slash, block. The clang of metal on metal became music, growing faster and faster, and the months sped by. When I reckoned I must have been fifteen, we changed my training to attack. My sword flew through the air to be parried by Cleaver. We danced this metal dance through the day, swapping from attack to defense. Cleaver shouted to keep my stance strong or hold my sword tighter. Once, I slipped through his defense and cut his arm. He told me to ignore it and continue. But my eyes were fixed on the blood trickling down his arm, and I remembered my Ma bleeding to death on top of me. I threw the sword down and walked away.

"Where are you going?" Cleaver called.

I ignored him and hurried through the forest, my mind filled with images of Dragon's Spit. Was it really two years ago that I wandered lost and barefoot through this forest? I don't know how I found my way after all this time, but I came out right by the river running through the village. The sun was bright, shining through the ruined remains, and a gentle breeze blew overgrown weeds. It seemed a twisted version of how things were. As I wandered between the ruined remains, I noticed there were no bodies.

"I buried them," Cleaver said from behind. "The night you came to me. I worked until dawn."

I turned to him. "This is just a memory," I said. "It's not my home." I looked around, noticing the mounds where bodies had been buried. "I wonder where you buried my Ma and Pa?"

Cleaver shrugged. "Didn't know anyone from here."

"Why did they kill everyone?"

"Maybe one day you'll have your answer." He avoided my eyes, and I wondered if there was more he wanted to tell me. The sun began to sink, and shadows spread across the land. That was the last time I saw my village. Cleaver was my only family now.

***

I hacked and slashed at the old oak out back of Cleaver's hut. My breath came out in sharp bursts as I swung each strike, imagining a towering opponent before me. Across the clearing, Cleaver sat skinning a rabbit. He looked up from time to time at my progress. Years had passed, and I reckoned I must be over eighteen now. The years had shaped my body into a powerful thing, yet the maturity of womanhood fought against me. My breasts had grown, filling out my top and making swordplay that much harder. Cleaver avoided looking at them, and it made me smile to think I had this womanly power.

Sometimes, I found myself looking hungrily at Cleaver as he trained himself, his bulging muscles glistening with sweat. The warrior was ancient but fitter than any man I had ever seen. But there had been no men to see since my time in exile with Cleaver, and I was unsure of the new desires I found awakening within. Sometimes when he slept, I would watch the gentle rise and fall of his chest and found myself longing to climb into bed with him, to be naked and free together. When that desire hit me, I ran and ran through the forest until I dropped.

There was a wall between us, but I reckoned it was Cleaver who had built it. Never had he uttered a word of affection towards me or held me in a warm embrace. There was a cold center to Cleaver, one not even I could warm. Suddenly, I realized I was staring at him, and I blushed, turning back to the tree and my swordplay. As I took chunks from the tree, I realized I loved the old man but doubted he was capable of the same feeling.

"I think that's enough training today, Little Slayer," Cleaver said in his gruff voice.

Panting, I turned to face him. "Do you love me?" Didn't know where those words came from, but they were out, and I reckoned I deserved an answer.

Cleaver's face grew red, his eyes falling away from me. "This is not the talk of a warrior."

I took a step closer to him, looked him right in the eyes now we were the same height. "Why did you look after me? I love you more than anything in the world, yet you pull away from me. Have you not noticed I am a woman now? I've seen the way you take secret glances at me."

Cleaver locked his eyes with mine. "Such love will make you weaker, Little Slayer. I once had a wife and a family, but all things die. Even you."

For a moment, I caught a glint of a tear in his eye, but it was gone, and the hardness returned in his old face. Then I understood him after all these years, but never did I reckon he had a family of his own. "You're scared to love, aren't you? Reckon you'll lose me one day?"

Cleaver turned from me. "Everyone leaves. Everyone dies. 'Tis life."

"But what's the point to death if you've never lived?" I went to him, placed a hand on his cheek, and raised my lips to his. We kissed, and I weakened in his embrace as he kissed me back. Then he pulled away. "What's wrong?" I panted, my hands traveling down his body.

Cleaver sighed, pushed me away. "This can never be," he whispered.

Staring at him, I urged him, "It can happen. You want me, I can tell." I started to slip my top down, but Cleaver's hand caught mine and stopped me. He pulled my top up over my shoulder again. "I want to give myself to you!" The anger made my voice shake. "Everything I have is yours! For what you did for me."

Cleaver shook his head. "If you do indeed love me, you'll understand why this can't be."

I pulled away from him, hanging my head in shame as my head cleared of desire. "I'm sorry."

Cleaver stroked my hair back from my face and lifted my chin. "You are ready to leave, yet you linger here, tied to this old man. You were ready to fight a long time ago."

I smiled. "You are my world."

Cleaver nodded. "Aye, but there are more worlds out there for you to explore." He wandered away, once more becoming that emotionless rock I knew and … I guessed I loved. But there would never be a return of the love I sought. 'Course, I knew the old fool would never allow himself to love. Instead of following him, I sheathed my sword and walked the opposite way, cooling my desires in the breeze. Walking through the forest, I thought upon Cleaver's rejection of me. Somewhere, I reckoned, there was a loving man. He had buried that person deep down, hiding it from daylight. His tale had ended a long time ago; now he was just legend.

Cleaver the Legend. What was his real name? Knew I would never learn the answer to that, and my own name was now a distant memory. Today, I had almost brought Cleaver back to life and had felt something between us. A river crossed my path. I crouched and splashed water on my face, enjoying the coolness as it put out my fire. It hadn't been my intention to embarrass the old man, but I had. In truth, I was feeling the beginning of guilt and shame. Biting my lip, I remembered his kiss and felt a flush across my face.

As I walked back through the forest, I thought about Cleaver's words. Was I lingering longer than I needed to? Training hard every day, I was pushed on by the thought of standing face to face with the man who had killed my Ma and Pa. Now I was more than ready, yet here I was. My love for Cleaver held me back. Tonight, we would talk about me leaving. Maybe Cleaver could come with me to the nearest city and face the world again. How long had he been hiding in the forest by himself?

When I returned to the clearing, my eyes locked on a man standing at the center, a broadsword pushed into the ground before him. Tall and proud, the warrior stood with his bulging arms across a firm chest. When I took a step closer, the man pulled the sword from the ground and held it out before him. "Today we will fight and see what kind of warrior you have become," Cleaver said, his eyes narrowing. "And you will finally face the truth about this Black Knight."

"Truth?" I asked, taking a cautious step towards him. There was steel in his eyes, rock in his stance. "He destroyed my village. That is the truth."

"No, Little Slayer. You know there was no Knight, just death." Suddenly, he lunged towards me, swiping down his sword in an overhead blow I narrowly missed with a quick sidestep, losing my balance. When I righted myself, Cleaver's sword slashed out, and I jumped back to a safe distance, drawing my own sword.

"What are you doing?" When he spun into another attack, I deflected the blow aside without much effort, knocking him off balance. "I don't want this."

Cleaver smiled coldly. "You *need* this. We will fight until you face the truth of what really happened."

Crouching into a defensive stance, I swung my sword around and held it up. Locking eyes with Cleaver, I could tell he was not playing. Reckon it was like the sound of thunder when our swords struck. Ain't never been one for fancy words, but I could see beauty in our deadly dance. Metal has a sound that sings shrilly through the nights and days. To my ears, it is the most harmonious thing I ever heard. As I stared through the sweat and effort at Cleaver, I saw he was lost in the music just like me.

"Come on, Little Slayer," Cleaver teased. "I know you have more to give than this."

With a sudden ferocity, I came at him with strike upon strike. Each attack was deflected with ease, and I felt his entire strength behind his sword. Falling back, I regained my breath, frustrated I could see no way through his flashing blade. It was like the man had two swords. "I don't want to hurt you," I panted.

Cleaver grunted, then rushed me with a slashing cut to my throat, which I brushed aside, pushing Cleaver off balance. He spun round before I could get my final strike in and blocked. "One of us dies here this day," he said breathlessly.

Taking three large steps back, I gave myself some room to breathe and study his defense. There was a glint of death in his eyes. With a sudden sprint, he sliced out. This time, I was too slow, and his blade cut my arm deep enough to know he was serious. Anger now urged me on as the pain sharpened my senses. I feinted an attack to his right, then came in to his left. His sword deflected my attack, but I had drawn blood from a deep cut to his side.

"Can we stop this now?" I was really scared— fear like back when I was a child who had lost her parents.

Wincing with pain, Cleaver shook his head. "Not until you face the truth."

I deepened my stance, ready to snap into my next attack. "The Black Knight came and—"

Cleaver's sword cut through the air, and I dodged it, jumping back. "There was no knight!"

There was a sudden flash of memory. It wasn't Cleaver before me, wasn't the present. The Black Knight towered above me as my village burned. But this time I could fight. I threw attack after attack at him. The knight became Cleaver again, and I was back in the woods. He was tiring. The old man was skilled, but he lacked the stamina my youth gave me. If I could not cut him down, I would wear him down.

"A plague swept the land," Cleaver said, clutching the bloody wound at his side. "Entire villages were burnt to prevent the spread. They called it the Black Blight."

Cleaver's words dug into me, sharper than his sword had. "The Black Knight—"

"You made him up!" He attacked again, feinting a head attack then striking at my legs. Jumping back, I lost my footing and stumbled. "It was a plague that spread through your village bringing death, no knight. I helped burn it down!"

Angry, I went into another frenzy of hacks and slashes. Cleaver's arms shook as he held his sword to my blows, but he was soon on his knees. With a final blow, I knocked the old man's sword from his hands. "You burned my village?"

He looked into my eyes as I held my sword to his throat. "There was nothing but plague-ridden bodies. I thought you were all dead. I didn't see the little girl hiding among the bodies, didn't know anyone could survive the Blight."

Holding my voice as steady as I could, I asked, "Why did you let me believe it was a Black Knight all these years?"

He sighed. "You needed something to believe in, to grow strong and focus your rage at. Now it's gone, Little Slayer. There is just us." He dropped his eyes from me. "And now one of us must die."

I brought my sword up high, ready to cut my master down. The last of the sun's rays washed over me, and I felt the warmth of the day fading fast. Slowly, I brought my sword down. My mind went back to that distant day at Dragon's Spit as I saw my parents sick and dying. Unable to help them, I lay down next to my Ma as flames spread through the village. My eyes tightly closed, I imagined a dark figure hunting everyone down. Wasn't quite sure what was happening to me as I stood with Cleaver's life in my hands; reckoned I was dying, 'coz I fell to the ground and everything went black.

"Come back, Little Slayer," Cleaver whispered.

I opened my eyes and stared up into his rough old face. "Did I die?"

"Aye, but now you get to live again."

I sat up, throwing my arms around Cleaver. I kissed him, expecting he would pull back again. Only he didn't. Finally, I pulled away, gasping but happy. "So you *do* love me?"

He smiled for the first time in … forever. "Aye," he whispered, pulling me to my feet. No other words were needed.

"Was all that training for nothing?" My head was spinning. "There is no Black Knight to face?"

Cleaver shook his head. "There are always Black Knights to face and people to be protected from them. I have given you the tools, shaped your body and mind. You are ready to go out into the world and live."

Suddenly, I saw many paths before me that had been hidden before. Cleaver's clearing seemed like a small place, and I struggled to breathe there. He was right, I realized; it was time to move on and explore the land. Even though a Blight killed my Ma and Pa, I would still find and fight any evil I came across. From the smallest village to the largest kingdom, there were the weak who needed to be protected. There were lost girls like I had been.

"Come with me," I said to Cleaver.

Cleaver shook his head. "No, my story was done a long time ago. Let me fade to legend while you write a new one."

I kissed Cleaver. "Your legend shall live on through me." As the sun faded, we went to his hut and closed a chapter on my life. And when I emerged, I was a woman at last, blinking at the light of a new dawn.

Kevin Grover

Kevin Grover lives in Kent, England. His passion is writing horror stories, and he strives to get your heart racing at any given opportunity. Kevin's short stories have been published in collaborative horror collections and in 2012 placed runner-up in Writing

Magazine's annual ghost story competition. His debut novel, Father's Song, is available now through Amazon. Monsters Mostly Come Out At Night is his second novel. www.kevingrover.co.uk

Unicorn Music
by A.E. Stueve

Eric wanted a divorce. His wife, Hannah, sleeping in the passenger seat of their red Caravan, was unaware. Behind them, their eight-year-old twins, Tom and Tonya, snored, oblivious of their father's plans. SpongeBob Squarepants sang about campfires on the headrest screen hanging in front of them. Eric grimaced and hit cruise control. He had been driving northeast on Highway 275 toward Omaha for a little over an hour, and his eyes drooped. The caffeine in the thirty-two-ounce Mountain Dew Hannah had forced him to buy when they were leaving Oakview wasn't helping.

Neither was the air conditioning. After the

day's festivities in the scorching July heat, nothing could alleviate his exhaustion. His entire extended family had congregated at his grandma's acreage for her ninetieth birthday on the edge of Oakview, Nebraska. It had been a crowded mess of screaming children, chattering women, and laughing men. Now, at 7:00 p.m., Eric knew this relative silence was only a break before another loud mess at home. He would tuck in the twins, listen to them whine about bellyaches and fears, and deal with his daughter's incessant inability to fall asleep.

He took a deep breath and used the switch on his steering wheel to turn off the television and turn on the radio. An AM preacher's obnoxious voice screamed about hellfire and brimstone, coming from the speakers just softly enough to bother him but not disturb his family. He hit SCAN. That preacher's flaming accusations might have helped keep him awake, but he thought he would rather fall asleep and die in a horrible, fiery wreck than listen to it.

He kind of liked the bitter, ironic flavor of that thought.

In Southeastern Nebraska, there were an unheard-of number of radio stations. Anyone, it seemed, could own a transmitter and find a home on these airwaves. Unfortunately, they were all either 1990s pop-country purveyors or conservative evangelical Christian lunatics. After a few minutes, the radio picked up a weatherman talking about low pressure systems and an approaching storm.

If that happened, if the thunder and lightning ran rampant through the sky the way Eric suspected it would, Tonya would join Hannah and him in bed. Later, after Tonya finally drifted off into dreamland, Eric would carry his daughter to her bedroom and pray she didn't wake up. Then he would return to his room, where he would be Hannah's sounding board. She would run a gamut of praise to gossip about his extended family at the party earlier. He would sit on the bed, agreeing with the drone of her words until he dozed off. The next morning, there would be work, where his approximately seven thousand bosses would tell him to do approximately seventy thousand jobs that all contradicted one another.

Noise. Just noise.

Hit repeat. For the rest of his life.

Is it any wonder I want to leave all this? Eric thought.

The weatherman's voice faded as Eric slurped the soda he didn't like and watched the road zooming by in black, grey, and yellow lines. He hit SCAN again. In the white noise, he daydreamed of his divorce, his plans for a new job and a new home, and the freedom it would entail. He was happily pondering his upcoming solitude when the radio gave a buzzing lurch before sputtering into silence. He tapped SCAN again; nothing happened. Time passed, and the sun sank, turning the sky into a masterpiece of splashed colors. But in the distance, there was a blackness that made Eric uneasy. The road, surrounded by the bright greens of the Midwest summer, had become inexplicably empty, their van the only sign of life. Eric thought that from above, it must have looked as though God had slammed a blade into the green. The road was the cut and Eric's van the first droplet of blood springing forth.

Hannah stirred. Eric kept cruising down the highway at sixty-three miles per hour, but an odd sensation forced itself up from the depths of his mind, making him feel like prey—a blind rabbit in some fox's keen eyes. He couldn't explain it. Perhaps it was God standing somewhere in the clouds in silent awe and slight anger at the gash in his greenery. But no. It was something more physical, more present … more *real*. He found himself searching from one side of the road to the other.

"Something's out there," he muttered. The sound of his voice was eerie in the quiet.

The radio sparked back to life, and the sudden noise almost made him scream. It was playing one of his dad's favorite songs—"It's the End of the World as We Know It (And I Feel Fine)" by R.E.M—not too loud, not too soft.

No one else stirred at the sound.

Eric nodded, showing his appreciation for whatever universal oddity had caused this and whispered, "Perfect," bobbing his head, trying to remember the lyrics, and letting his unease fade. He was hearing his dad singing on stage at Lemon's Bar in Council Bluffs, Iowa, with his mom standing next to him, slapping the tambourine on her hip. He smelled the stale smoke and the spilled beer. He tasted the peanuts and felt their shells break below his Converse. He heard the raucous laughter and felt at home. He thought about his childhood, his parents' friends who would come over to their house behind the bar and jam. This was the kind of life he loved. This was the kind of life he missed. He was smiling a real, true smile—the kind of smile Hannah had fallen in love with fifteen years earlier at Lemon's Bar—when a unicorn trotted out of the woods to the west and paused in the middle of the highway, about seventy yards ahead of their van.

It gave off a white light that burned before the sky's purple, red, orange, and blue. Eric slammed the brakes, crying out. The unicorn shot off eastward toward a patch of trees that couldn't quite be called a forest. Hannah and the twins woke with a collective start.

"Dear God," Eric muttered. He didn't notice his wife's slender fingers reach for him. He didn't feel her gentle touch on his shoulder.

He didn't hear her curious voice ask, "What's wrong?"

Eric's body shook. His mouth dried. *This is shock,* he thought.

"Honey," Hannah said more loudly as Eric turned off the van and stumbled from it, "are you all right?"

All Eric heard was Michael Stipe's voice as it

was cut off at the word "feel." He took massive strides toward the woods, tears streaming unbidden from his face like rivulets of regret.

"Eric!" Hannah's voice was laced with fear as she shouted after him.

Once he reached the forest, Eric heard only silence, smelled only the fresh scent of trees, dirt, nature. He paid no heed to the branches scratching his face as he pushed them aside. He slowed down and crept, taking light steps, breathing only when he needed to, and searching with not just his eyes but his heart for what he *knew* he had seen. It had to have been real, he reasoned. Beauty such as that could not have been conjured by the human brain, especially his miserable, depressed, tired excuse for one. His chest tightened; he smelled the electricity in the air. The storm clouds were closer than he thought. Maybe the unicorn had brought them.

A unicorn. It was impossible, and yet, there it had been. Its body was horse-like, as the storybooks from his youth had implored him to believe. But there was something more to it, something he could only describe as magic. Only, it wasn't magic as he had understood it. It was different than anything he had been privy to in his scant thirty-seven years. It was special in an indescribable, wholly new way.

It was as though the creature had emerged from a perfect place where beauty reigned supreme, where happiness was a touch away, where his father was perpetually singing a song he loved, and where there was no doubt or regret. It was a world that wasn't one big ball of screaming children, nagging wife, idiot bosses, and imminent death.

In the distance, he heard Hannah calling. He thought he heard his son crying too but couldn't be sure; his attention was drawn elsewhere, pulled from them like a child caught in a river's current.

The small patch of trees grew larger as if by the beast's magic. Eric clawed through, knowing the unicorn was near. He couldn't say how long he walked or how the sprinkling of trees had become a nearly impenetrable forest. He couldn't say when the sun finally sat and let a silent, dark coolness slip into its place. He couldn't say when the wind picked up and made him shiver.

Eric could, however, say what it felt like when he saw the unicorn again, standing in a clearing. A break in the clouds cast the moon's pale blue glow around it like nature's spotlight. Seeing it felt good and bad. It felt perfect and wrong. It felt like he had been sucked into an impossible paradox. His stomach churned. He belched and tasted a mix of the Mountain Dew he had barely touched and the sweets and barbecue he had been eating all day at his grandma's. He felt a raindrop.

The unicorn stared at him, charcoal eyes blazing holes through his soul. They were a deep contrast to the virginal white of its coat, horn, and hooves. They reminded Eric of the storm clouds above. The dirt beneath the beast shimmered as if some of its magic had fallen to the ground. When it neighed, Eric's heart stopped.

Eric fell to his knees and retched. "Hello," he stuttered, wiping his mouth. There was a small part of him—growing larger by the second—that believed he shouldn't be doing this, that believed he wasn't worthy of communicating with this beast.

The unicorn chewed on a few strands of grass hanging from its mouth, defying Eric to say it wasn't the most beautiful thing he had ever seen.

"Do you…" Eric began as he stood on shaky legs and took a nervous step into the clearing. "Do you *want* something?"

The unicorn made no noise but shook its head. Its mane danced through sparkling dander; its horn shimmered in the pre-storm drizzle. Thunder broke the silence, and Eric jumped. Somewhere in the distance, he heard his children cry out. Hannah said something he couldn't understand.

The unicorn whinnied. The sound was like music. It was his wife's voice whispering his name mixed with Tom and Tonya's first laughs and his father singing. It was the words, "I love you," on his mother's lips. It was his dog Blue's bark he had heard every day he returned home from school from his sixth birthday until just after his seventeenth. It was the sound of the school bell at 3:00 p.m. and his first car's engine revving in his driveway on a winter morning. It was his favorite business professor's lecture. It was bottles clanging together at Lemon's

Bar. It was Van Morrison playing "Crazy Love" at his wedding. It was the sound of his life. It was overwhelming and brought Eric back to his knees in the chilly dirt. The wind howled through the branches around them.

"Why are you here?" he asked through tears and raindrops.

The unicorn's mouth worked the grass. The silence was punctuated by increasingly heavy rainfall.

"Why are—" He was cut off by a stirring behind him. He looked back to see his son emerge into the clearing like a wrecking crew, followed closely by his wife and daughter.

The unicorn darted away.

"Eric?" Hannah's voice shook with nerves.

Eric turned around and marched toward the van without a word.

He didn't hear Tonya utter, "Daddy?" as he trudged through the trees.

His family followed him quietly, shocked. Their faces wore fear like masks. Rain fell hard now, wind roared. Eric's back was rigid; there were bloody, burning scratches where branches had cut through his grey t-shirt. His hands were splayed out like claws; they tore their way out of the woods.

Hannah reached for him again. Her hand brushed over his shoulder. "Honey…" She hesitated. "Are you okay?"

"I don't know," Eric stuttered. He shook his head. "Get in the car."

Hannah raised an eyebrow; her arms were wrapped around Tom and Tonya's shoulders. Her lips shook, and her mascara ran with the rain. "I think I better drive now," she said through chattering teeth.

A different type of silence followed the family the rest of the way to Omaha. It was nervous, eerie, and interrupted by crashes of thunder. Hannah offered Eric sidelong glances but kept her words to herself and her hands on the steering wheel. Tonya gasped every time the thunder boomed. She had her head down and a book unfolded on her lap, but it was too dark to read.

Tom stared at his hands, gently crying to himself.

Eric studied the trees as they passed, dark and watery. The sounds he had heard when the unicorn whinnied echoed through his mind. Noises he thought were making him miserable danced with happier memories. It was as though they were partners, working together to create music Eric felt was almost too miraculous to be real. But that was exactly what they were, and perhaps that was the miracle. He cried to himself, his eyes on the trees as they blurred by.

***

Hannah shut their bedroom door. "So," she began, her voice quivering as water dried on her skin while she tried to find a proper way to express her fear, "what happened out there?" She stood inches from the bed where Eric sat. The children were asleep; Tonya had done so quickly, despite the howling storm.

Eric shrugged. He turned and studied his own pale reflection in the mirror on the wall. He was haggard, his ripped shirt scratched and dirty. Compared to the unicorn, he was monstrous. He looked at the beige blanket on the bed in their grey bedroom. He rested his head on the headboard, eyes still on the mirror. "I thought I saw something is all."

"What?" the word came out like a whip-snap and surprised them both.

"Something."

Her cheeks reddened. "I'm not an idiot, Eric." She jerked the back of her hand across her cheeks. "You didn't just *see something*…"

He reached for her.

"Don't touch me!" She slapped his hand away and turned from him.

"Hannah…"

"You've been acting strange lately, Eric. Sad…" She sighed, looking at the carpet before raising her head to him. "Fine. What did you see?" Her voice was steady and cold. In the mirror, Eric could see her own eyes blazing with anger and hurt.

He studied her reflection. A trick of depth perception made it look as if she stood next to him. She was beautiful, even in her sadness and rage. "You're crying," he said, leaning over and touching the mirror.

She nodded and sniffled. "Why wouldn't I be?" Her arms were crossed over her chest. Her shirt was still wet from the rain that had soaked her when they unpacked the car.

"Look." He turned to face her. "I'm sorry. You're right. I have been... depressed lately. I've been... It's just..."

"What?"

"I don't..."

She placed her hands on her hips. "Eric, what is it? What happened out there?" She let her hands fall to her sides. The tears dried and the anger died while concern grew. "What is going on with you?"

He shook his head. "You wouldn't believe me."

"Try me."

He swung his legs off the side of the bed so his back faced her. He ran his hands through his hair. It was still wet too. "There was something in the road, something... something I've never seen."

"What?" She sat next to him and curled her legs underneath her. "Talk to me, Eric. Please." There was a pleading tinge to her voice that hurt him.

He took a deep breath and took her hands. "A unicorn," he said through a sigh.

Silence padded into the room and sat between the couple as Hannah digested this. "A unicorn?" Her voice was soft. "Eric... I don't... What?" She leaned toward him, trying to find her husband's eyes with her own.

Eric turned away and began to cry. "It was so *perfect*, Hannah." His body convulsed. "And I'm not," he said. "There is so much going on and... I don't know... I've been thinking about... Then I saw this *thing,* and it was so amazing... and then what I heard... it was magic... and I don't know what's wrong with me."

"What are you saying?" she asked.

"I don't know what I want anymore."

"Yes you do," Tom's voice sounded from the hallway. "Unicorn music does that."

Eric and Hannah stood as one and followed the sound. Tom was fixed in the light from the bathroom door always left half-open for the children. His dark bangs hung in front of eyes like his mother's. "The sound made me cry too," he continued. "It's okay to miss stuff, Dad. It's okay to be sad about things, even angry." Tom reached up, and Eric took him in his arms.

"What are you talking about, son?" Eric asked. "You saw it? How?"

"My mind was open to it. The unicorn makes you think of... It makes you think of the past... it makes you..."

"Regret?" Hannah asked, placing a hand on her son's cheek.

"Yeah," Tom said.

"Regret what?"

Tom squished up his face in a look of deep concentration. "I don't know. Growing up?"

"Why did I see it?" Eric asked.

Tom shrugged. "Your mind was open to it too. Unicorns also make you realize what you have, what you don't regret along with what you do. It's in the music. How it all works together, the good and the bad. It's what being alive is. It's all a miracle. Everything. You were already thinking of the bad. The unicorn reminds you of the good."

Eric sat down with Tom in the hallway and the boy hugged him tight.

"How do you know all that?" Eric asked.

Tom grinned. "It's okay, Dad. We all regret stuff. The unicorn told me a man without regrets is a liar." Then he stood up and walked back to his room, rubbing his eyes all the way. "I don't know what that means but I thought you'd like to hear it."

Hannah knelt, wrapped one arm around Eric's chest, and rested her head on his shoulder. "So what *don't* you regret?" she asked.

Thunder boomed.

Tonya cried out, "Daddy!"

Eric stood. "I don't regret this," he said. He squeezed his wife's hand and helped her to her feet. Together, they walked down the hall toward their daughter's bedroom.

AE Stueve

AE Stueve writes and teaches in Omaha, NE. He

holds an MFA from the University of Nebraska, where he was the recipient of the Wendy Fort Foundation Prize for Exemplary Work in Fiction. His work has appeared in such journals and collections as *The Journal of Compressed Creative Arts*, *Dark Moon Presents: Zombies!*, *HVZA*, *Dark Fairy Tales Revisited*, *Picaroon Poetry,* and *MidAmerican Fiction and Photography.* The first three parts of his graphic novel hybrid series, *The ABCs of Dinkology,* as well as his sci-fi, dystopian, horror novel *Former*, are available wherever good books are sold.

The Fairy Door
by Kelly Matsuura

"I really hate it here." Rayyan threw a fist-sized rock into the muddy creek and watched it sink with a scowl. "I want to go back to Penang. To my friends."

Dhia slapped his bare arm. "I'm your friend, aren't I?" Rayyan's words stung. She understood it was a big change, to move from a beachside tourist city where something was always happening to the little fishing community in northern Malaysia. But Dhia's family had moved there two years ago, and she had adjusted fine. And when Rayyan's family decided to move too, she had been over the moon. So it hurt that he didn't immediately feel the same way. Perhaps he just needed more time.

Rayyan put an arm around her shoulder. "Of course, you're my *best* friend. But I miss everyone else. It's only our families here, and it's boring. I hate the smell too." He sniffed the air with another scowl.

"It's not so bad." Dhia didn't want to admit how much she liked the jungle. All the pretty birds, butterflies, and little animals scurrying around allowed her to believe she was in a fairytale world. There was something magical about this part of the jungle, she thought, but a boy wouldn't believe it, so she never told Rayyan her feelings. She didn't want him to call her a baby; just because he was a year older than her didn't make him smarter in any way.

Rayyan grunted, picked up another rock, and tossed it to the other side of the narrow creek. The leaves of the low bushes rustled, and an animal squawked, startling the birds in the nearby trees.

"Look!" Dhia pointed excitedly to the mouse deer that bolted from its hiding place. The little mammal dashed through a clearing, the white markings on its rear disappearing into the greenery. "Come on, let's follow it!" She leaped into the shallow creek, not caring about her sandals getting muddy. She heard Rayyan running behind, and she followed the pathway where the mouse deer had headed.

The path turned sharply, and Dhia tripped on an exposed tree root. Rayyan caught her just in time. "Watch out," he said, righting her on her feet again. Both kids were out of breath.

"Oh no, we lost it!" Dhia was disappointed, though she didn't know what she had expected to happen.

Rayyan smiled and pressed a finger to his lips. "Sshh. It's right there."

Dhia turned her gaze to where Rayyan pointed and broke into a wide grin.

The little mouse deer was nibbling on the long grass by a fallen tree only a few meters away.

"Aw. It's so cute."

Rayyan peered closer. "I thought it was a baby, but it looks like a full-grown kancil."

"Do you think so?" Dhia asked softly. "Is it a boy or girl?"

"Can't tell," Rayyan replied, still watching the small creature.

The kancil looked up then, as if it understood they were discussing it.

Dhia took two cautious steps towards the animal. She didn't believe it would let her close, but she wanted to see it more clearly before it ran away.

"Hey, what's that over there?" Rayyan asked, nudging Dhia's waist. "It's glowing inside."

"Inside what?" It took Dhia a second to find what he meant, but then she saw it. A large banyan tree, a little farther behind where the mouse deer fed, glowed a soft green light inside its hollow trunk. Dhia had never seen anything like it in the real world, only in her picture books. "It's some kind of magic!" she squealed, her voice startling the mouse deer, who leaped over the fallen log and disappeared again.

"It's not magic, silly. It could be glowworms or tree fungus or something cool like that." Rayyan walked towards the glimmering tree. There was no clear pathway, so he had to step over the various low growing plants and clumps of grass. Dhia followed more cautiously behind. Rayyan reached the tree first and looked back at Dhia. "I think I can fit inside."

"Hmm, maybe you shouldn't do that…" Dhia warned, but Rayyan had already bent forward to stick his head inside the hollow space. "Rayyan?" she called, still a few steps away.

Rayyan didn't reply, and then his whole body vanished into the glowing space, as if he had been sucked in by an unseen force.

"No!" Dhia shouted. She stopped moving forward though, afraid that the tree would suck her in too. She wanted to be brave, but tears welled quickly and poured down her cheeks. Rayyan was gone, taken who knew where, and she was now alone in the jungle. Because they'd chased the mouse deer, she had no real sense of where she was now or how to get home again.

As she stared at the tree, the green light disappeared and was replaced by a small, carved wooden door.

"He shouldn't have gone in there," a female voice scolded. Dhia spun around, surprised to find she was not alone after all. But it was the little mouse deer she saw, no one else.

"Did you…" She felt silly asking, but she had clearly heard a voice behind her. "Did you say something?" Her cheeks burned with embarrassment at talking to an animal.

The kancil lifted its head. "Yes, it was me. I'm not supposed to talk to humans, but children rarely come this far into the jungle, and I can see you need help."

"I…" Dhia twisted the hem of her skirt in both hands, nervous as to what to ask the mysterious animal. "Where did Rayyan go? What is that… that place?"

"Your friend fell through the gateway to the fairy world. I didn't know humans could see it, but I understand why he was curious and went too close. Don't worry about him. He won't be harmed there."

"Rayyan's in the fairy world? It's real?" Dhia wanted to believe that he was all right and that the fairies would take care of him, but a moment of doubt clouded her thoughts. The kancil had been nothing but friendly, but Dhia knew from her picture books that they were cunning animals and told wild stories when it suited them. "Wait, you're a trickster, aren't you? Books always say so." How did she know the kancil wasn't lying to get her to leave the jungle without Rayyan? What if he was somewhere really terrible and needed to be rescued?

The mouse deer laughed at her concerns. "Little girl, I have no reason to trick you! You aren't a crocodile or a hunter wanting to eat me. I only want to help. Truthfully, your friend is in no danger. I promise."

Dhia sighed with relief. "Will he ever come back?"

"He will," the kancil replied, nodding its head gently. "Well, he'll return, but he won't be the boy you remember."

Dhia didn't understand what the kancil meant, but she only cared about seeing Rayyan again. "When? How long until he comes back?"

The kancil picked up its front legs and shifted its stance. "You can wait for him. He'll be back before too long, I imagine. Why don't you sit on that log there, and I'll bring you some fruit to eat?"

Dhia sniffed. "Okay." Now that her fear of losing Rayyan and being lost in the jungle had calmed, she realized she was hungry.

The kancil brought several pieces of fruit, delivered one by one. "Thank you for your kindness," Dhia said, noticing how comfortable she felt talking to the animal now.

"My pleasure," the kancil told her. "But I'm afraid I can't wait with you. I have young ones to check on at home. You take care now."

Dhia nodded. "I will. Thank you again." She wondered where the small animal lived and would have liked to see its babies, but she had to be there at the tree when Rayyan returned. He would never leave without her if their situations were reversed. "Bye." She waved to the kancil as it took off into the denser jungle, then sighed. She wasn't scared to sit there alone, but she was anxious to see Rayyan and learn where he had been taken. What had the kancil meant about him being different?

While Dhia waited, she thought about her best friend. She lifted her right foot and crossed it over her left knee so she could reach the blue silk friendship band she wore around her ankle. Rayyan had made it for her when she had left Penang, and he wore a matching one around his wrist.

When she had shown it to her parents, her mother had winked to her father. "One day he'll give her a ring, perhaps?"

Dhia had blushed and stuck out her tongue at the suggestion, but she had secretly agreed. Rayyan had never said anything so serious, but Dhia had dreamed his family would follow hers north too, and it had come true. She believed in destiny and caught glimpses of her future in her nightly dreams. She didn't always remember them, but they left her with a strong awareness of time beyond the understanding of a typical child her age. Her grandmother had the same dream-sight and had taught Dhia to trust that such messages had meaning.

The shadows grew longer and the birds in the jungle louder, signaling the coming end of the day. Dhia stood and stretched, her heartbeat increasing as she pondered whether to keep waiting or to try to make her way home alone before dark. The kancil had promised Rayyan would return soon, but Dhia's doubts began to rise again.

"Oh, Rayyan! Please come back soon!" she called towards the door, following her words with a loud sigh. She refused to cry.

Not long after, she noticed the door gradually opening. Rays of green and gold peeked through the opening, lighting up the clearing in the jungle and silencing the birds.

To Dhia's surprise, a small boy stepped out from the doorway. He stared at Dhia, then quickly turned back to the door. "Papa! Hurry up!" the toddler yelled.

A tall woman exited next, fair-skinned with long raven hair and adorable pointed ears. She took the boy's hand and smiled as she glanced around at their new surroundings.

Before anyone spoke, a man stepped through the magic door. He smiled at the fairy woman and patted her shoulder, then walked straight towards Dhia. "Dhi-Dhi, how can you still be here?" he asked softly, kneeling to meet her at eye level.

Dhia could only stare at the faded blue strap wound tight on his wrist. Shivers rippled all over her skin. His voice was deeper, older, but unforgettable, even if she hadn't recognized his face straight away.

He had grown up without her. In another place and time. She had questions, a million questions, but all Dhia could do was cover her face to hide the tears she could no longer contain.

"Oh, no. Come here," Rayyan called, and she

rushed into his arms. It felt good to be held, like when her father hugged her goodnight. And he smelled like a farm. Not the stinky animals, but sun-warmed grass and wild flowers.

"Is she all right?" the fairy woman asked.

Dhia snuck a peek over Rayyan's shoulder to inspect the newcomers once more. A feeling of déjà vu washed over her when she looked at the little boy again. He looked so much like Rayyan at the same age. She had seen him in one of her dreams, without the pointed ears, but she was sure it was the same child. There was a daughter too in Dhia's vision, her features a perfect blend of Rayyan's and her own.

"I'm so sorry, Dhia," Rayyan whispered. "I didn't know that time—"

"It was supposed to be me," Dhia cut in, sobbing harder against the grown man's shirt.

"There, there," Rayyan soothed. "The fairy world is wonderful, but there are no videogames or movies. You'd have missed Earth a lot more than I did." He stroked her hair and gave her plait a gentle tug before releasing her.

"Sure," Dhia agreed, but her heart broke into tiny pieces. She had meant she was supposed to be his wife, not the enchanting fairy behind him, holding hands with his son. *Their* son. It was all wrong.

Dhia was only nine years old, but she felt destiny shift under her feet, turning her away from all she knew and changing the trajectory of her entire adulthood.

Kelly Matsuura

Kelly Matsuura grew up in Victoria, Australia, but always dreamed she would live abroad. She has lived in northern China and Michigan in the US and over ten years in Nagoya, Japan, where she now lives permanently.

Kelly has published numerous short stories online, in group anthologies, and in several self-published anthologies. Her stories have been published by Visibility Fiction, Crushing Hearts & Black Butterfly Publishing, A Murder of Storytellers, and Ink and Locket Press.

She is the creator and editor for *The Insignia Series*: a blog and anthology series dedicated to promoting Asian fantasy stories, books, and authors.

Facebook: Kelly Matsuura/Kelly Noro Author

Honor
by Jennifer Della'Zanna

The area was usually deserted, but Lyra's ingrained habits would not allow her to let her guard down without a full reconnaissance. Only when she'd thoroughly assessed the beach did she allow herself to relax, remove her helm, and approach the water. She kneeled in the waves lapping at low tide. Her red cloak settled as she put both hands on the hilt of her sword and lowered her head. A ruby button on the tip of the pommel winked in the sunlight. Red—the color of blood—was one more way for her to remember.

Lyra came here every year to honor the day her life had changed forever. The day she'd been Chosen. The day she made the pledge she now waited to complete. Her cloak rippled as a breeze brushed by, but the wind didn't last long enough to give any relief from the relentless late-summer heat. The water wouldn't be much cooler either, but she must wade in to feel closer to her promise.

Eight years ago today had been glorious. Lyra had become a woman that day. The memory of wedding Romano came close to prying loose the armor now guarding a stone-cold heart—an armor even harder than that on her warrior's body. She unbuckled boots and greaves, feeling almost free as she waded into the warm water and allowed her mind to wander as she did only on this day every year. Any more would have driven her insane.

Perhaps she should be happy things worked out this way. Her body was hard, muscular. She'd discovered things about herself in these past years she never would have if she'd been allowed to pursue her life as a cottager's wife and mother to the horde of children they both had wanted. Now a master at sword and bow, unbeaten by man or woman at the academy for three years, she enjoyed her work teaching swordsmanship to the newly Chosen. But every year, she remembered. Every year, she renewed her pledge. She never felt any less regret for the woman she could have been—even in light of the decorated knight she'd become. She'd promised to defend this land from its enemies. Now only Final Confirmation stood between her and her fate.

Nobody ever knew when Final Confirmation

would come. There would be a sign. Her Chosen sign had come on this very beach that day so long ago. A knight, all in black and riding a black horse, had appeared at the edge of the trees. He'd ridden toward the couple and stopped. When Romano had approached the stranger to ask his business, her beloved was struck down without a word. He had lain still, already dead, by the time Lyra reached him. Ignoring her terror-stricken cries, the knight had only pointed to a woman standing in the trees from where he'd approached. He rode away without a word and threw something on the ground by Romano's head.

The woman had approached Lyra and taken her away, assuring her that Romano's body would be cared for. Lyra couldn't fight the woman's magic that had compelled her to leave her husband and new life behind. She'd learned her duties as a Chosen empire warrior with a numb heart in the beginning but, with time, had gained a sense of purpose and excelled in her work. Final Confirmation would come when those in power felt her ready to carry out those promises to the empire. She had done all she could to prove her worth and loyalty.

As she prepared to leave the water and return to her duties, Lyra felt something hard underfoot. She picked it up, wiped away the caked sand, and froze when she realized what was in her hands. From the pocket of her vest, she pulled an identical amulet— the one the knight had thrown when he killed Romano.

At the edge of the trees he stood. The black knight. Her Confirmation was upon her.

The man did not move, so Lyra rebuckled her boots, put on her helm, and picked up her sword, all without ever taking her gaze from the knight. He remained still.

Lyra walked with a purposeful, warrior's ground-eating stride toward the inky spot against the brilliant white and green of birch trees. As she approached, he called to her. "Lyra, Knight of the Empire, are you ready to fulfill the promise seen in you when Chosen?"

"Yes, Sir Knight, I am ready to keep the pledge I made on this day eight years ago."

"Come closer, then, Lyra. Your time has come."

Lyra walked a sword's length away from the knight. She remembered what the woman had told her when Lyra asked why the knight had slain Romano. "He would be a hindrance. You belong to the empire now. Nobody else."

A hindrance. The resentment for having her life ripped away and all her choices ground to dust choked her, as it always did. A haze descended over her vision.

"Raise your sword." The knight's voice cut through her memories again.

Without a sound, she raised her sword and stopped level with his heart. She met his steely gaze with equal determination and smiled, just a little. This was it. This was the moment she'd planned. It had to be the same knight. Except in cases where the knight who Chose you died, the same person Confirmed you. She hadn't seen him at all during her eight years of training. She would have known him. His visage burned itself into her memory on that day. She'd prayed daily that he hadn't lost his life, because she wasn't sure she could go through with her oath if it were not he delivering her Confirmation.

She'd done everything ordered of her. She'd fulfilled the promise those who'd Chosen her foretold. The waiting was over.

With all her might, she thrust her sword past the point of respectful salute to the point of murder. Of revenge.

The alarm in his eyes was gratifying. As he slid to the ground, she thrust again into his heart, and he died amid a wash of blood not unlike Romano's.

Lyra turned away, sword still in hand, chest heaving with every attempt to draw breath into her lungs beyond her pounding heart. In all her planning, she'd never considered what to do next. Was it because she didn't think she would succeed, or because she didn't care what became of her afterward? She considered walking into the ocean and leaving this world in hopes of finding peace in the afterlife. But that was the coward's way out, and Lyra was no coward.

She glanced once more at the water she'd probably never see again, said a prayer for Romano, and walked toward the fallen knight's horse. There would be supplies and money in his bags—enough for a start. Lyra leaped into the saddle of the black horse and headed toward the trees. She would be in exile, but she would choose her own path from this day forward.

Jennifer Della Zanna

As a freelance writer, Jennifer has had articles published in more than thirty print and online magazines, as well as six articles for the *Encyclopedia of Sex, Love and Courtship in the Medieval World.* She works as a medical writer, online instructor, and public speaker in the allied health field while working on her fiction career. She writes historical fantasy and mythic fiction and is represented by Eric Ruben at The Ruben Agency. She looks forward to the sale of her first novel, with many more to follow. You can contact her at:

www.facebook.com/JenDellaZanna

Eye of the Keidan
by Michael R. Baker

"So, this is the place?" Mury Tarnoak shivered uncomfortably. "That was a hellish ride." She looked around, tucking her fur robes around her for warmth.

Her uncle Stephen Tarnoak looked on, frowning. It had indeed been hard—days of rough traveling to reach their path. The meeting chamber of the Keidan welcomed them, an unknown entity. Was he doing the right thing?

"Aye. Not one I want to do again." Mury's brother Adane scowled as he shook his head vigorously. Droplets of rainwater went everywhere, his black locks sleek and dripping wet. He pulled at his peeling boots with a grimace. "Finest horse leather, too. Cost me two hundred Penns," he grumbled. "All for this shitstain on the earth."

"Hold your tongue. Remember where we are," Stephen retorted, glaring at his nephew. Adane scowled, removed his travelling cloak, and threw it to his sister, who shivered as she wrapped it around herself. She was a sweet thing, Stephen thought, so unlike her older brother. Adane was prickly and proud to a fault. *What was our Banemort thinking, bringing him with us?* It brought a bitter taste to his mouth—what he had come here to do.

Adane shook his head and stalked away, far from the rest of their party. Stephen took a deep breath to calm his nerves. He wished he could take a swig from his wineskin, but he needed his wits about him. It had been a long and treacherous journey traveling with his family members, and he couldn't wait to get it over with. He took his surroundings with distaste, shuddering at the sight.

So, this is where the pacts with evil are performed. The foyer was wide and unwelcoming, the walls made of smooth, unrelenting stone. He noticed the pillars too—great structures of obsidian, simple in their construction. There was something beautiful about them, the way they shimmered, the chamber illuminated by ghostly chandeliers hanging from the ceiling. *We shouldn't be here.* This was the stronghold of the Keidan, the unspoken fortress of cruelty and blood. Even in the far north back in his holdfast, Stephen had heard many dark tales of their history and what happened inside their forbidding walls. But Banemort had promised they could help. *They can help our Bale become king. That's what he said.*

Banemort Augustin was their saviour, and Stephen trusted him with his life. They were here to help put Bale Mornmont on the throne, at any price. *Any price.* That sent a shiver down his spine. He wasn't certain he could do what was needed. But Stephen was a man of duty, and men of duty always obeyed.

Adane stood with the escort guard—a gift from his father. Stephen heard the captain mutter something, and both burst out laughing. Their mirth echoed back in the shadows, leaving only their breath.

"We're here on a very important mission for our king, Adane," Stephen called to them coldly. "Your arrogance will not be tolerated here."

Adane's sharp little eyes flashed at the cruelty of his uncle's rebuke, but to Stephen's amusement, he didn't remark at it. "I'm not being arrogant. Only a jest with Randy, here." He shrugged. "Just saying I believe we wasted time walking all this way. We should have taken my father's advice and taken a boat to Kanzie, then ridden here." His mouth curled into a sneer as he looked at Stephen. "We would have made it in half the time. But no, my adoring uncle decides we ride the whole way." He shook his head as he turned away from him, laughing. His mirth echoed off the walls.

Stephen glared at him. *Don't bring up your idiot of a father.* "Yes, which would have cost almost three times as much. You know these are harsh times at it is, with the war." How many times did he have to point that out? It always came to his elder brother—the lackwit who Adane looked up to with such pride. *Dalguir, you keep planting incompetent seeds into your woman's cunt.* His brother's wife Lanane was amiable enough and pretty, but her spawn were idiots. Mury was the only half-decent stock to come from his brother's brood, and even she was weak-minded at times. Robin was a little toe-rag, constantly demanding cakes and sweets in his annoying, high-pitched wail, while her eldest were both incredibly dim-witted or arrogant—Adane and the slut Ami, who had been found rutting in the barracks with five guardsmen. The young king needed better friends for the trials ahead.

The chill in the chambers bit into his flesh. Rubbing his hands, Stephen glanced to where their guard huddled at the doorway. They were a dozen in number and a surly bunch. Even so, Stephen had grown fond of them. They hadn't complained once and made for decent company during their ride. Randy Oudin, Adane's right-hand man, at the very least had all the patience and caution Adane lacked.

Adane was complaining again. "The Undines can rot for all I fucking care. So can the pretenders. What should we care for who controls the kingdom, or what's left of it? They should leave our holds in peace and deal with themselves." He quailed under Stephen's gaze. His ugly cheeks, pockmarked with the scars from the pox, reddened.

"You know why we are here. Take that as a warning, nephew." Turning heel, he strode away from the pair and walked across the chamber. His boots squeaked against the polished stone before he reached Randy, who grimaced at him.

"He giving you trouble?"

Stephen scowled and made no reply.

Randy let the ghost of a smile slip through his thin moustache. He was a slender, short man of slight build and a stern face, but there was always a sparkle of life in his eyes. "Apologies, my lord. He's been in a black rage for days." He tittered along with the other men under his command. The escort was small. It made for faster travel, and the Keidan would have taken to a larger party poorly.

"Many thanks for bringing us here," Stephen told him. "It means a lot."

Randy bowed his head. "No need for thanks, my friend. My men are here to serve you as well as your nephew." But there was something else stirring underneath his smile. "My men are scared." He turned away curtly.

He's tired. Stephen felt a pang of sympathy for him. Randy was only there under Adane's orders, and they had ridden with little comfort. He would reward him well, once they returned to the safety of the Hordlands.

Stephen looked around once more, frustration mounting. The letter from the Keidan had told him to come into the main hall and await someone to take them for their meeting, but this wait was wearing on him. *Where are they?* he thought feverishly, rubbing his hands for warmth. His calloused skin was prickled with goose flesh. He opened his mouth to speak when a voice behind him made him jump.

"You are here. Welcome to our domain."

Adane whirled around sharply, his hand darting to the hilt of his broadsword as he searched for the source of the noise. A boy walked towards them, clad in a thin grey robe which fell past his knees and a white hood over his face. Stephen judged him to be no older than ten—the same age as his youngest son. *Children serve in this host?* A cold trickle prickled the hairs on his neck. Stephen could bear the silence no longer.

"I am here to see the one you call the Trader." His voice wavered slightly, and he berated himself. *Stop being a coward, Tarnoak. You have a duty to perform.* "Take us to him," he commanded. His fingers brushed the sword he kept concealed inside his cloak to remember he still had it. No weapons were allowed in open sight in the Keidan, but Stephen wasn't fool enough to wander into their arms unguarded.

The boy smiled thinly and spread his arms wide. "That is me. You are Stephen Tarnoak, I take? I am what you name the Trader."

Stephen took a step back. There was no way this scrawny child could be behind the cruelty in that scroll. He could still feel the cold sweat drenching his clothes when he'd read the reply from the Trader, ordering him to travel to their stronghold to negotiate a contract. '*If you are prepared to pay the price of the contract and the service you seek,*' the words warned, the black ink smeared against the parchment, '*come to our domain. I await your reply.*' He only hoped the price was worth it. Shooting a glance to where his nephews stood, he couldn't deny he felt doubt gnaw at him now. *This is wrong,* he thought suddenly. *I can't do this.*

Adane was the first to recover. "Really?" He pointed at the Trader, his face contorted with mirth. "You're a little boy! I've shat more threatening things than this one!"

Damn you, nephew. "Adane, keep silent," Stephen snarled. Nobody else laughed. The Trader, fortunately, paid no attention.

"Follow me, Stephen, and we shall begin." With that, he stalked away.

Stephen exchanged a glance with Adane, who merely shrugged sheepishly. *You're lucky, fool.* They were in dangerous hands. He beckoned to his party, and they followed them out of the chamber.

Adane sidled up beside him, the laughter long dead on his lips. "Can we trust them, Stephen?" The arrogance lacing his voice had vanished. He looked younger—like the boy he was.

He's just a young jackal, dying to make his impact on the world. Stephen suddenly felt a stab of anger for his nephew. *He's going to get us all killed.* "They are the Keidan, nephew," he said slowly, picking his words. "If they can't be trusted to kill, we can trust nobody." They needed this. Their king needed it.

They had been overheard, for the Trader in front of them spoke, his tone soothing. "You have come to the right place, child of Undine. There is nothing to fear. Not far now. Keep silent as you pass the shrine. It is punishable by death to speak in the presence of the Lady during their prayers. This is sacred ground you walk on." He said it as casually as though he offered them some wine. Stephen gulped. Adane shuddered and said nothing.

If he scoffs at any point, we are done for. Fortunately, Adane kept silent. There came a solemn chanting from within one of the closed gates. The words passed over Stephen in a language he didn't know, but there was a beauty to their prayer.

The group followed down the corridors, the stone unyielding. They were deep underground now, and the chill inside the passageway was biting even through their thick wolf furs. He felt sympathy for Mury, who was still swaddled in his traveling cloak. Then again, it was her own fault for packing so lightly for the journey. He jerked his head in irritation. He was surrounded by fools, the lot of them. The singing grew louder, and Stephen was captivated by it. *What are they speaking?* It wasn't the common voice, that was for certain. He remembered the markings etched upon the archway where they'd entered the Keidan—the symbols of ancient Valia. It could have been Valian—the old, magical race now long gone. Its only survivors were in the Pharos Order—a backward religious sect, corrupt and broken.

After what seemed hours, going deeper and deeper underground in the winding labyrinth, they finally came to a halt as the Trader brought them into a small hall. It was cramped and freezing, the air in the room choking before a golden light illuminating the walls. The circular room was pitch black, the only other light coming from the hung torches on the stone walls of the archway, silhouetting their movements. It was barren of distractions, with only a stone table in front of them and stone slabs on which they all would sit. The Trader sat down opposite them, lowering his hood. His hair was thin and frayed at the ends, bleached white. His cheeks were hollow, with dark circles underneath his eyes, but his face still held the youth of his child-like features. Stephen felt himself shudder as he stared into the boy's eyes. *This is no ordinary child, that's for certain.* His eyes sparkled a dangerous yellow glow.

"Allow me to introduce myself. My name is Soul, and I am the Keeper of the Lady herself. You're on sacred ground. Remember that at your peril."

It was spoken softly without any hint of

malice, but the warning rang through their ears. Nobody spoke; Adane looked fit to gag. *It is for the greater good,* Stephen thought. He waited for his next move.

"I apologize for the lack of comfort," the boy continued. "We don't need such trivial things. It is something you will have to endure." He leaned forward, looking Stephen in the eye. "Now, tell me. You are a Marshall from the Hordlands, yes?" It was not a question.

"Aye," Stephen replied uncertainly.

"It is rare for somebody within the Undines to contact the Keidan like this. There are many within your borders who can fulfil your needs, yet you come to us. Why is this?"

Now was the moment. Stephen chanced a glance nervously at Adane. His hands were clasped together in front of him, twisting together as they always did. *'Rare for somebody within the Undines,'* he had said. That could wait for the moment. "We require services, yes. There is a war growing in our borders—"

"Growing? It has done for the past six years, child. The King is long dead, his people fighting like vultures over a carcass," Soul interrupted, his voice snapping like a whip. He smiled and leaned farther forward. "Now answer my question. *Why* do you come to this domain?"

"Because such a task cannot be trusted with people alone." Stephen had spent a long time marshalling his thoughts. Everything in the past year had led up to this moment. "We need the new king of the Undines dead before it is too late."

"The new Undine they call Yarwick the Butcher, yes?" Soul turned his eyes upon Stephen, then Adane and Mury in turn. His smile curdled into something more sombre—mature. "The price is high, especially for a king. You serve what some call the chosen of the Octane."

Stephen reeled. How could he know? He glared at the boy, beads of sweat on his cheeks.

"The Keidan sees many, and there are many in the world who seek our interests. You want that boy to come to the throne."

Stephen said nothing. His mentor and friend Banemort had rallied his banners for him, to his shock. Banemort Augustin was formidable, one of the greatest military commanders in the Undines. For years after young Talismane died, barons had fought each other and the Undine government, either trying to gain independence or take the Undine's throne for themselves. Brutal, intelligent, and fierce, Banemort was also one of the most cautious men Stephen had ever known, not stirring from his fortress in the early years of the war. However, when his nephew Bale recovered from the same fever which took the young boy King Talismane, Banemort rallied his entire house to support his cause. The grace fever should have killed him. How could a disease, this pestilence against the Gods, kill a royal child and cast his kingdom into ruin, yet leave the soul of a mere baron's son intact? It had to be fate.

"Bale should have died that day," he said cautiously. "The grace fever is fatal to all those who suffer it. Even our boy king Talismane succumbed to the plague, and he was blessed with the treaty of the Octane itself."

"A poor argument. The Gods have no mercy for royal blood. The Messeahs take who they want, regardless of who they are," Soul said coldly. "Nobody on this earth is free from the void. We're destined to rejoin its depths."

"That's true," Stephen admitted, but inside, his blood boiled. *I'm not here to debate the concept of Gods.* He had to tread carefully. Any wrong movement, and he'd plunge through rotten ice into the abyss of which this Soul spoke.

"The boy was clinging onto life. I was there when our healers tried to leech him, gave him every medicine known to man. I even called for a faith healer from Klassos to work his art, yet he failed. Banemort had him executed for his failure. We accepted his son would die. However, he recovered, and told us it was the Octane themselves who came to him in his dreams, granting him the purpose to live. It's a message from the Gods themselves. That boy is the salvation of our hopes."

"The hope to take the Undines for himself." Soul stood, his focus turning to Adane. He had remained silent this whole time, his fists clenched and still in his lap. "Is that right?"

"Yes," Adane whispered suddenly. He was shaking. "We need them dead. Every one. The new king, though, is our goal. Without him, the loyalists' cause is lost, and we'll have the opening we need. Bale is the key to our greatness."

And you said the wars are no concern of yours, nephew? Stephen thought coolly, but his nephew's outburst was typical of him, fickle to a fault. *No matter what he says, he's still loyal to our boy king.*

"Yarwick the Butcher? You pick a dangerous enemy to fight." Soul placed his hands upon the table, his slender fingers like white spiders. "A costly target. This new king will be hardened from long years of war. He won't take risks."

He knows. "Bale needs Yarwick dead in order to have any claim at all," Stephen said. "The throne is his."

"But he has little blood right," Soul replied, his voice cold with amusement. "Therefore, the throne cannot be his, truly? Another twenty have already claimed that right."

And swords can put him on the throne far easier than such meaningless debates on the right of blood. Banemort's household was wealthy and could muster the largest host of all the barons. They had been fighting each other as long as they'd been fighting the Undine royalists. According to the last news they'd heard as they made south to the Keidan, the ancient Pharos Order had pledged their wealth to his cause, but the skilled Kanid Kanae marched north to confront Banemort's host with twelve thousand men. *If they could put their differences aside and join forces...* Stephen focused his attention on the markings on the table—two carvings of twisted serpents entwined, rearing to strike. They looked oddly real.

"That is true. Others have a greater claim than our Bale," he said finally, the truth coming out of him in a snarl. Banemort's family was rich and once closely linked to the Undine royalty; his own grandfather Olxick had been married into the old kings. But now, the Undine royalty barely gave them a second thought, and the child Bale had even less recognition. It had always rankled deep inside him. Stephen wanted the best for the boy. But since the civil war began, many vassals had declared their claim. "We can put him there by force if need be."

"You did not come here to tell me your strategy," Soul stated. "For all you know, I could be acting against you. Maybe others have turned to us to get rid of you." The way he smirked spoke otherwise; he was fooling them. "Of course, even if I did, I wouldn't be telling you. Lesson one, never reveal your game to anybody."

Stephen fell silent, seething. *He thinks this is nothing more than a game of words.* He willed himself to stay calm. Soul infuriated him, but he couldn't do anything about it. He kept silent, resisting the urge to bite back. He would take any abuse from this child if it meant the Keidan would grant him his wish. He was almost there.

"So," Soul began. "To the task at hand. Listen closely, Stephen, because I will only ask you this once. When I wrote to you, I asked if you were prepared to pay the price." His eyes flicked between Adane and Mury, back and forth. Stephen watched their faces carefully for signs of recognition, but to his relief, none came. *They still don't know.* His doubts now screamed in his ear. "Now is the small matter of payment."

Stephen hesitated for a moment. *They're my family, whatever they are. I owe it to my brother at least.*

You owe Banemort and your king more, another voice argued. But before he could reply, Adane stood.

"As you wish. Men." He nodded, reaching into his robes.

What is he doing? Stephen wondered as Randy and their guards followed suit. Bags of gold, leathers, and skins were placed upon the table, Adane removing his golden rings and throwing them onto the pile with some distaste. Soul looked on, his expression one of polite disinterest.

"There," Mury said breathlessly. "We offer the payment. It is yours."

There was an unpleasant silence, and Stephen saw Adane's furrow deepen. *You fools,* Stephen wanted to shout. *Are they really that stupid to believe the Keidan can be bought with cheap trinkets?* He made his decision then.

"Is there a problem?" he asked.

Soul surveyed the materials with discontent. There were some valuable items in that pile, Stephen recognised. He knew Mury's boar-skin shawl was a rare trade, worth a considerable amount in the Undines. *Of course. The Keidan don't pay for deeds in coin.*

"What are these useless materials?" Soul asked softly. "This is not what I asked." He cast Stephen and his party an ugly glare. "Oh, this will not do at all."

"What do you mean?" Adane looked up sharply.

"These mean nothing to us." Soul swept a cold hand over the items. "These garments. What use are they?"

"They are rare materials!" Adane took a step backwards, his round, youthful face reddening. "My ring alone sells for more than a thousand Penns!"

"Pointless," Soul whispered. "The Keidan is wealthy enough. This is *not* what I asked for."

"Gold is never pointless."

"It is to the servants of the Lady." Soul sat back down, taking some of the Penns in his fingers, the dull metal glinting in the candlelight. "We have no need of gold, child. The Keidan's wealth matches that of the rest of Harloph. What could we need with dirty, unclean payment such as this?" He snorted, throwing the coin upon the ground.

"You procure services, I give you gold. Isn't that the point?" Adane shot back.

Stephen saw the danger, but it was too late. *'The Keidan believe it is an act against their God to demand gold for their services,'* Banemort had warned him. *'Are you sure, you are willing to pay the price they will demand?'* It had been a particularly cold night the evening he left. He would never forget the chilling parting words Banemort had left him with before he wheeled his horse and left the keep to begin the journey south. *'I hope you know what you are doing,'* Banemort had warned. *'Bale is our lifeblood, and he is our king.'*

I won't fail you, Stephen thought. *Adane is a fool.* Banemort had the right of it. He was ready to pay the price for his king.

Soul closed his eyes, and for a moment, Stephen swore a cold wind blew through the chamber. Finally, the Trader's eyes opened—or what was left of them. Stephen reeled as he stared into empty eye sockets, two wounds gaping into the air. He saw Adane stumble backwards in shock, his hand reaching for his blade. *He's ruined it.* However, when Soul spoke, his tone was light, friendly.

"Life is a greater gift to us than anything the illusion of wealth can ever do. It is *blood* we seek, Adane, not your meaningless promises of gold. Only blood can pay for the life you want us to take.

Stephen understood this. You can too."

Adane glared at him, and Stephen could feel the weight of his gaze—accusatory. *No point looking at me, nephew,* Stephen wanted to say but kept silent. After a moment, the arrogant man shrugged, drawing a dagger from his undergarments.

"Fine. If it's blood you want, it's blood you get!" His teeth were gritted and his pupils dilated. The blade was jagged, the serrated edge sliding against his thumb. Soul looked on, silent, as Adane pulled back his sleeve, bearing his olive, tanned skin.

"Brother!" Mury reached for him but turned her head away quickly as Adane slashed his arm with the dagger. He gritted his teeth harder, grinding his jaw as his eyes shut tightly with pain. Blood ran from the deep cut in his arm, seeping through his robes.

"There!" he spat. "Blood! That's what you wanted, wasn't it?" He was panting, twitching his fingers. He let out a soft moan as he slumped onto his seat, and Randy rushed to his aid.

He cut deeper than he intended, Stephen realized. He smiled grimly. *Oh, nephew, how little you know.* He and Soul exchanged a meaningful look. This was not left unnoticed by Mury, who knelt over her brother.

"What was that?" she demanded. Her eyes were unusually bright, her chest heaving. Stephen said nothing. "What have you done, so that my brother believes he has to cut himself open?" She glared at the Trader. "I want us to leave. *Now!*"

Stephen made no reply, his eyes upon his younger, gentler niece. *I'm going to miss her.* "That's not possible, I'm afraid," he said softly. Tears of lingering remorse welled, but he brushed them aside. He turned to face the guards, men who had followed them all this way. He felt some sadness for them. *They did not ask for this, but it has to be done.*

"What is the meaning of this?" Adane coughed, his face pale. He let out a gasp. "What?" He choked. Randy turned around and grabbed for his sword. Hooded figures had appeared in the chamber with them.

How did they get here so fast? Stephen wondered. He hadn't heard them enter—not a whisper. *The Keidan are nothing if not efficient.*

"Well, Stephen," Soul said, and Stephen felt as though an invisible force pulled his gaze to the ancient boy. "You consent to the price?" His hands were clasped together, the fingers pointing upwards.

'Choose who you want and let them pay the price for our goals.' Banemort's rough words echoed in Stephen's ears. He slipped his hand into his robes. Mury and Adane were the two who had sprung into his mind first. Incompetent and hot-headed Adane— the boy who had proven to be little more than a nuisance. And soft-minded Mury, who spent more time spreading her thighs for anybody who spoiled her. His thoughts twisted in his head as he thought of the task, now so close to being complete. He imagined the cruel, fat lips upon his nephew, Adane

screaming with lust as he rutted with a tavern wench, as Stephen had once caught him. Then his thoughts turned to Mury, the wallflower who kept borrowing gold off him and not paying it back. On and on his memories twisted, until nothing remained. *They deserve this,* Stephen thought grimly. He smiled at them, feeling his cheeks stretch.

"Uncle?" Mury's voice reached him, wavering. She forced herself to her feet, glancing around at the band of shadowed men who blocked the doorway. "What do they mean?"

Stephen closed his eyes. *Forgive me, but you are expendable.* "This is for our king. The young Bale will take his rights." His tone surprised even him. It was cold and without any hint of the nerves which clung to him like sweat. "I consent, Soul. Take them. They are yours."

"*What*?" Randy pointed his sword at Stephen as Mury screamed. "You sold your own—you traitor!"

Traitor. A cold trickle filtered down his neck, but Stephen ignored it. *I did this for you, Bale.* He had done Banemort proud.

Soul's eyes returned to their sockets, now bleeding red. "Very well. Servants, begin the sacrifice," he commanded. Adane lurched heavily to his feet, his clothing stained with his blood. His eyes were glassy, two orbs staring at something he couldn't see. His movements were slow and impaired; the cuts he gave himself had bitten too deeply. Alhmir rushed to support him, his shouts for help barely reaching Stephen's ears.

The men of the Keidan closed in.

"Like hell." Randy wheeled his blade—a two-handed greatsword—around himself in a huge arc, his aim at Stephen. Stephen reeled as he lurched backwards, stunned by the assault. A furious glare flooded Randy's eyes, his cheeks red with rage. He made no sound, but Stephen could read his lips.

He's trying to kill me, he realized. His hand reached for his own sword, but it felt useless—a mere toothpick against Randy's steel. He would be overpowered in moments. Seconds later, Randy was joined by several of his guard, who had drawn their weapons and advanced upon Stephen the turncloak. *I'm going to die here, alone,* was his first thought. Then he thought of Banemort and the boy king. *No,* he remembered, seizing the memory like draining water in his palm. *I'm not alone.* He began to laugh.

Even as he threw himself out of the way, a howling sound froze him on the spot. The air had frozen, the chill putrid. It clung to his nostrils, smothering him. It smelled like death. Randy's eyes widened as his sword fell from his numb grip, clattering onto the ground with an echo ringing through the walls of the chamber. Something had stunned him. He opened his mouth, but no sound came.

"Commander?" One of the men managed to choke out, just in time to see Randy fall to the ground, blood trickling from the gaping hole in his stomach. A small, sharpened stake protruded from it, and the smell made Stephen clamp his hands to his nose, retching. A sudden burst of pain in his head made him scream out; it was like fire—white-hot needles piercing his skin over and over again. The agony forced him to close his eyes.

A pitiful whimpering made him open them again, and a sudden savage pleasure willed him to force himself onto his feet. Adane was on his knees, pressed up against his chair—that uncomfortable slab of stone about which he had complained so much. Blood trickled from his mouth and nose, mingling with the mucus and tears. On the ground lay the bodies of Randy and his recruits, their mouths open. Alhmir lay on the ground next to Randy, his body so viciously stabbed he would have been unrecognizable were it not for the distinctive scorpion tattoo imprinted on his arm. The chamber was deserted again except for Soul, whose appearance had changed. He was now completely black, his skin scorched by unseen flames. Only his face remained— two terrifying, hating eyes.

"Please." Adane licked his lips, and Stephen was pleased to see that he had evacuated his bowels, staining his fancy clothes with piss and shit. The commotion had cracked the stone table in two, and their gifts had slumped onto the ground, discarded and forgotten.

"Mercy!" Adane sobbed as Mury lay by his

side, her eyes vacant.

My, she looks no different, Stephen noticed, and Adane's screams slowly ebbed away. Smiling wider, Stephen suddenly lurched forward, vomiting upon the ground as the horror of the scene finally reached him; the expulsion was not of disgust but of triumph. He had performed his task.

'Of course we will come with you!' Mury had said excitedly on the dawn of their departure. *'Bale is our king, and we will do anything to ensure that.'* Her brother, the idiot Adane, was no less devoted but had been more condescending. It was such a pity; their devotion to their cause would cost them their lives. But blood must be bought in blood. That was the price of the Keidan. Stephen threw his head back and roared, the mirth spread across his lips. *And what a cheap price it turned out to be.*

Michael R. Baker

Michael R. Baker is twenty-six years old and lives in the United Kingdom. An avid fan of history and fantasy, he graduated from the University of Sunderland with a Bachelor's Degree in History and Politics, and he has always found the history of world cultures fascinating.

Writing, however, has always been an interest to him, especially fantasy. He has been building his own fantasy world of 'Rengar' for most of his life. The first novel in his Counterbalance trilogy will be released this year:

https://www.patreon.com/anduril38

Aomedus Fell
by Kathrin Hutson

The pedestal of a goddess wasn't what it used to be. She only had to think, and a golden goblet formed in her hands, filled with the sweet, cool wine of the heavens. The drink went to her lips, but the luxury had been used and decreasingly enjoyed for thousands of years. And her love of the immortal world was waning.

Aomedus—goddess of independent thought and strength. She was only a replacement deity, having been created just a handful of centuries before. The Olympian gods had returned to their Mount long ago, when the fall of Greece had become an imminent tragedy. And in turn, they had created a volley of tiny entities to take over until the time came to gift themselves to the open world once more. Aomedus herself had been formed from the right hand of Athena, to preside over a seemingly small portion of the gods' responsibilities. But that did not mean she had been inactive and unimportant. She had been the cause of all the strength and wit of men who had fought in countless wars over the centuries. That was where they needed her the most—there and in the strength of a man's heart.

Thinking of these things, as she always did, she reached out her slender, ivory-pale fingers to the sky around her, and through the clouds shot a flashing streak of swiftness. It stopped abruptly as she closed her fingers around it, snatching it out of the air with skill and indifference. Nothing surprised her here; she knew everything that had and ever would happen in the land of the gods. And she had everything she wanted, which bored her to no end.

She rubbed her thumb over the smooth hilt of the spear now clutched in her hand, the cool, steel spearhead glinting at her against the sun. A war spear—the vision of her existence and all the work she had accomplished. No matter the outcome, her work was always an accomplishment. Sometimes, she helped a man's strength in the most critical of movements; other times, she dulled his wits. It all had a purpose. After all, there always had to be a victor in war, and there remained always to be the defeated man. And it had been her responsibility, for so long, to discern between the two.

Aomedus pulled the spear into an embrace and looked down into the glinting steel. A heavenly reflection stared back at her—shimmering, wavering skin covered in the white robes made from the very clouds around her; a head cascading with fiery red curls; and the blue orbs of eyes that reflected for ages her entire existence. And though it was a sight to strike men dead in their tracks—and had done so—it was something Aomedus had grown tired of seeing. It had become a sight in which she no longer found any pride. She had always been this way, and it had never changed.

The spearhead shone in the sun, and she forced her spirit into it, withdrawing the visions of the things she had done. The steel tip reflected all the wars over which she had presided, and among these major battles—these fights for a struggling future—she saw every single one of them. There she saw the men of thousands of years, those who remained nameless to her but whom she knew inside and out. She had forced her spirit into them countless times, had given them strength in all their trials, mind to fight for their lives, their rights of manhood. If it had not been for Aomedus, as only duty had allowed, man would not have made it this far. She had seen the world almost destroy itself, had watched as hope disappeared over and over like a fleeting and scattered memory. But she had always given it back to them. And they had not yet completely failed.

She stared into the reflections of her spear and looked again into the faces of the men. Their eyes that always hardened over the years. Their tried, life-filled bodies, made of muscle and bone and blood. Aomedus knew their strength lay in their blood—a thing wholly sacred among mortals and a thing she longed to feel.

A sudden fiery desire flashed through the goddess, shimmering about her wavering skin and brightening her eyes. She had been here in the heavens, harboring the burdens of the gods, for longer than most of the world could remember. And she was finished enjoying it. The Olympian gods had had their fun with the world—had put themselves onto the earth to play a part with mortality. That must have been what had kept the gods occupied, if not sane—until they had retreated. And she was a goddess, was she not, small and unnoticed as she was? Why could she not do the same?

Anxious excitement filled her, alighting on her passionate discovery. She *could* do the same. More than anything now, she wished to be in the world of men, to be among those whom she had watched for centuries, to feel what they felt. If the other gods had done so before, there was nothing to stop her now.

She wouldn't tell the others. There was a certain precious fragility in the fact that this was her want, her choice, and her act alone. Aomedus wouldn't be missed for long; she didn't plan to spend more than a few days upon the earth. That would be more than enough time to explore, at least at first.

It may have been a hasty, anxious decision, but the goddess paid no heed to her remnants of a conscience. Her own expectations wholly consumed her, and there would be no stopping her. Gazing into her spearhead, she searched among the world for a man—any man at all. She found one in the modern world who may have stood out to her. He may have been nothing more than ordinary at all. But it did not matter as she felt all her power surging toward the life of that man who would soon become hers.

***

A small, glowing something flitted over her in a slow, lazy rhythm, and she heard the tick of metal tapping against metal. She felt her eyes heavy and real as they never had been before, and she slowly opened them. Looking around, Aomedus found herself in a large, square room, white walls surrounding her on all sides. To her right sat a window over which hung a thin metal shade. The shades tapped against the open window, spilling that glowing light onto her body. The wind coming in from outside blew the shades back and forth.

Slowly, she realized she was lying down, and therefore brought herself to sit up. Her hands supported her weight, and she felt the reality of a soft bed beneath her body—one she knew would not vanish with her thoughts. The mattress fell slightly under her weight, and the sheets were soft and still warm from her body. The experience of these new sensations intrigued her; her own form had never released its own physical heat. She'd never felt any weight of her existence. These were mortal things.

The room around her was white and blank as she examined it, decorated with nothing but the mattress covered in a blue and red plaid comforter. But she knew there was more. She felt the muscles in her new body tighten as she stood from the bed, and a wonderfully tingling sensation shuddered over her as the air from the open window brushed her skin.

Bare toes slid against the smooth hardwood floor beneath her, and it took her more seconds to gain her balance. Surely, she made her way through the bedroom, opening the door and loving the way the cool brass knob fit into her clutching fingers. She exited through the door, and her proud mortal legs carried her into a narrow hallway. As she passed, a shadow of something else moved to her left. Tensing, aware, she retraced her steps in the absolute silence of the house to find herself facing a crystal-clear, body-length mirror hanging in the hallway.

She was caught up immediately in the vision of herself—or the body of the man she now occupied. She stood completely naked, taking in the glorious sight of a male body that had been well tended. The legs were hardened and trained, the chest and stomach rippled in chiseled perfection, and it gave her a fiery excitement to feel the power that simply studying the male body seemed to give her. Gods, of course, lacked such reproductive organs, and glancing at the one she borrowed now made her understand exactly why men were so protective of them.

The thing that caught her most, that reminded her of the fact that this could never be permanent, was the man's face. It was hard and strong, with smooth skin that must have been shaved just recently, lying beneath a close crop of dark hair. But above all these things, the bright, ice-blue eyes of the goddess stared forth—her eyes, and the tie to herself. She would always have her own eyes.

She spent many long minutes staring contentedly at the new body until she decided to move on. Coming through the hallway, she found herself in a large, clean kitchen. It was bare to look at but suited its purpose. Here, too, could she test the reality of her presence in this man. She called for wine, just as she had done countless times in the heavens. She called for it with more intent than she ever had, and this time, nothing came. No golden goblet materialized before her, no swirl of clouds and taste of sweetness on her lips. Aomedus had never been so satisfied and excited in all her existence. She knew now that she was no longer a goddess of the heavens with the gifts of her solitary powers. No— now, she was a man.

A gurgling sound filled the room, and it took her a while to realize it was her human stomach growling in hunger. Smiling at these urges, she took herself to the white refrigerator in the kitchen and found a carton of milk, from which she took an incredibly long draught. The smooth, sweet taste of it lingered on her lips, and she sighed. In this, she could take real pleasure.

A sudden thought occurred to her as she relished in her surroundings. There was so much more to this world than simply these few rooms. She should go outside, explore the world on foot and through the eyes of man. A sudden anxiety to leave the building filled her, and she made her way through the rooms, trying to find a door that looked as though it led outside.

She came into another room laden with couches and chairs and a large door with many locks, and she knew she had found the right place. A pair of blue jeans hung over the couch, and she was reminded of the human need to be clothed and covered. It was a pity, she thought, for she rather enjoyed the air and freedom of bare skin. But she wanted to experience all this as someone who fit in, not one who drew attention. She slowly brought her legs into the pants, spending minutes on figuring out how to fasten the button and zipper. Pants were enough to wear for now, and she opened the large door and headed out.

Aomedus stepped out onto a platform of three stairs leading right down to a narrow sidewalk. The air was clean but warm with the morning, and as she looked across the street, a row of apartments just like the ones from which she had emerged stared back at her. A small, frail tree grew from a grate in the sidewalk, and Aomedus heard a bird singing in its branches. She had never before imagined anything like this. All was silent for a moment, save for the bird and the wind, before a car moved slowly down the side of the street. She watched it drive on tirelessly, the sun glinting off the shining paint and the window, and then it was gone.

Standing there longer still, she took in the sights and smells around her with the senses of the man's body. She told herself she would stay as long as she could, to experience all that was possible in a matter of days. That would be enough for the first time.

The most exciting thing she could think of was to interact with other humans on this earth. She had watched them all for centuries, but to actually be seen—to be talked to and touched—was something for which she had always yearned. And then, almost as though Fate had heard her wishes, a figure appeared from around the corner on the sidewalk, sauntering at a fair pace in her direction.

The figure wore a dark jacket that looked hot for the sunny morning, and Aomedus could tell it was another man. Invigorated, she decided to approach the figure. Perhaps she would start a conversation with him about the weather or who he was. But she knew the human wish to hide emotion, so she walked as though she had other business elsewhere.

As they approached each other, Aomedus noted the other man glancing about the street and at the doors of the apartment buildings, nervous and on edge. She wondered why, but that only stirred her eagerness to talk to him.

They moved closer and closer still, slowly, and she could not keep herself from smiling. Surely this would be a memorable experience—her first with a human. The man stopped quickly before her, and a gruffly strained voice came forth from his mouth.

"Stop!" he yelled at her, and Aomedus obeyed. They were only a few feet from each other, and she realized how heavily the man breathed and with much apparent anxiety. He very obviously glanced down at the right-hand pocket of his heavy jacket, under which something pointedly protruded. Aomedus couldn't tell what it was, but she seemed to have appeased the man's wishes with her glances at the object, for he looked up at her again.

"Give me your wallet. Give me everything you have!" the man commanded, struggling fiercely to keep his voice down and still anxiously glancing all about them.

Aomedus found herself smiling at this. The man had in fact started their conversation and interaction, and she found him fascinating. The way he moved and judged his surroundings, how he believed her to be nothing more than another man on the street, filled her with awe at an encounter as close as this. She met his eyes briefly, before he anxiously looked away, and gave as wide a smile as her borrowed body would allow.

"Now!" the man hollered once more and violently shook whatever it was in his coat pocket.

The humanized goddess only smiled more. Now that she no longer sat above everything in her domain, governing the thoughts of those who inhabited this world, she wanted to see what humans were capable of when left to their own devices. She had seen the deeds of man and had every faith in their abilities in this age, after everything they had been through as a race.

"I said now!" the man yelled again, angry at her lack of response. "Give me everything now!"

Aomedus reached out her hand, taking a step toward the man and speaking. "Why don't you—"

Her words were immediately interrupted as a loud bang cracked through the air, shattering her sentence with a gasp. She glanced, dumbfounded, at the man's hand, now holding a pistol from which swirled a single stream of smoke.

The shock of the noise subsided, and she felt a most remarkably unpleasant sensation in her body. She realized it was pain—a human pain of flesh that had been torn and completely destroyed. The hands belonging to the man she had become were clasped upon his bare stomach, wet and sticky with a warm red that spilled and clung to the skin. She looked back in surprise at the man who had shot her, who now glanced around nervously before finding his own means with which to flee.

Aomedus found the body failing as she came to her knees, then fell onto her back. A pang of regret flooded through her. She had ravaged this man's body, without him ever having had a choice or having known. Her experiences as a human had been cut incredibly short.

The body had difficulty breathing now, and she found herself staring up at the clear blue, early-morning sky. It was the worst of experiences, but she, unlike the man whose body was ending, would come again as a goddess in her true form. She would continue her duties.

Her hands were warm and sticky with flowing life, and she noted the irony. As always, through her fingers flowed the blood of men.

Kathrin Hutson

Kathrin Hutson lives in Grass Valley, California with her husband, daughter, and their two dogs. She works full-time through her company KLH CreateWorks as an author, Fiction Editor, and Alternative Medicine Copywriter. She attended the University of Colorado at Boulder for a Bachelors in Creative Writing Fiction, and her writing focuses in Fantasy, Sci-Fi, and some Literary Fiction. The first two books in her Dark Fantasy series, Daughter of the Drackan and

Mother of the Drackan, are available wherever books are sold. She also serves as Chief Editor for CWC (Collaborative Writing Challenge) and CWPH (Collaborative Writing Publishing House).

When she's not passionately consumed by everything writing, Kathrin spends her time hiking and exploring the beautiful mountains of northern California, maintaining her twenty-year love affair with classical piano, singing, and songwriting, and of course curling up with a great book at the end of the day.

www.kathrinhutsonfiction.com

The Vigil
by Phoebe Darqueling

They waited, breathless.

The old man's heart finally stopped beating, his mouth closing for the last time. His spirit had clung to life like fungus, its tendrils somehow sucking nourishment out of the husk of his body, until it had finally left to join the others. It was selfish, really, to hold onto this life when he knew from the moment he'd been chosen that he would never truly die.

If you only looked at their clothes, the people standing around his corpse would appear to be mourners. Then your gaze would stray to the hunger in their eyes, revealing a far more sinister intent. They dared not push or scrape at each other in its presence, as if the magic would punish them for impatience, but they could not help but lean in ever so slightly to see if the family legend was true.

They had been careful to respect the other parts of the story. They'd lit the incense, even though it made the air in the darkened room almost unbreathable. Perhaps this part of the ritual was to make their eyes sting, so the dying man might believe they were crying over his death rather than praying for an end to the interminable wait.

Even as the old man had lain insensate in the great canopy bed, no one dared to remove it from his body. They knew that as long as he still had breath, it would be impossible. That hadn't kept them from approaching his deathbed and placing a kiss on the black stone. As their lips brushed the ring, somehow warm despite the clamminess of the wearer, they whispered entreaties.

Choose me.

I am worthy.

Now the vigil was over, and their fates would be sealed within a few heartbeats. Everything hung on that thin band of silver and what it would do next. With its wearer still, the ring was free to roam.

The facets of the black stone began to vibrate. The edges, once sharp enough to cut glass, softened, the planes undulating as the gem melted. The blackness spread over the silver and swirled into every pore before being absorbed into the band. An opalescent shimmer erupted across the surface of the metal, and the ring glowed, a miniscule homage to the smiling face of the full moon outside. As the blaze faded, the ring turned to quicksilver and flowed away from the old man's finger and onto the polished floor.

The keen eyes of his children and grandchildren followed the movement of the molten puddle. Even in the shuttered room, light seemed to glint off the liquid surface as it trickled in one direction, then another, seeking its new host. The older generation stood back; their chance had come and gone in this very room a long time ago. The magic occasionally skipped a generation, but it never repeated.

There was only one person in the room whose eyes did not follow the play of light and shadow. The mousy girl, all but drowning in the billows of her sister's hand-me-down gown, approached the dead man. No one had bothered to shut the heavy brocade curtains in their covetousness or close his eyes. Though the eyelids drooped, Nia could still make out the stormy blue of the irises and the milky sheen of cataracts.

She took another tentative step forward, wincing as the swish of her skirts broke the utter silence of those assembled. The widow glared at her least favorite granddaughter for a moment before turning her haughty stare back to the selection process, but no one else tore their rapt attention away; the magic of the ring had ignored her branch of the family far too long for her to matter. Nia carefully gathered her skirt in one hand to keep it from whispering across the floorboards and took another step.

She had never met the old man until the family was ordered to assemble at the vigil, and he had been unconscious when they arrived. Though her siblings had been thrilled to be summoned away from the farm and into the great manse, her curiosity was piqued by more than the estate or chance to be chosen. What sent her heart fluttering was knowing that she would come face to face with death again.

The first time it happened, she was five years old. Her brother Vladi was out in the fields learning the secrets of planting and harvesting with their father, and Nia's mother had left her behind when she and Nia's sister Deya went to town. Mother had tried to find her free-spirited child, but with the countryside as her playground, there was no sense trying to find Nia if she didn't want to be found. So it was that Nia returned to the yellow house set into the hill to find it as empty as her little stomach. She crawled up onto the sturdy wooden table in search of bread when a sudden sound at the window almost made her fall. When she went outside to investigate, she found a bird lying on its back under the window. Its wings were spread wide, the white of the coverts standing out against the grayness of the flight feathers. The black legs twitched as the eyes blinked slowly from a head lying at an unnatural angle. She'd taken the slight body in her hands (how could a living thing weigh so very little?) and felt the panicked breathing slow, then stop.

The last death she witnessed was human. For months, she had watched her mother's belly swell, seen her cooing to the life growing inside her. When the time came, she told Nia not to be afraid, that her body knew what to do. As was their way, the menfolk were made to leave the house, and the women of the village arrived. They sang and chanted and braided Nia's hair while they waited. But when the time came, their incantations were no match for the call of Grandfather Death. After more than a day of labor, her mother gave a final, exhausted push, and the blue-tinged body slid from her. The cord that had fed and nurtured Nia's little brother while he had listened to her mother's prayers was now a noose around his tiny neck.

Nia could not shake her desire to understand the moment of transition, fullness to emptiness, and the strange old family tradition had given her another opportunity for further study. She stood beside the body, taking in the changes it had undergone in the past minute. It would have been best if she could have taken notes, but she knew not to seem too eager in her pursuit of this knowledge lest she be marked as strange, and strangeness was enough to be branded a witch.

The huge and stately bed was tall enough that the dead man's body was at chest height on a girl the age of twelve. Her grandfather was so heaped with blankets that only his face, and of course the hand with the strange family heirloom, was exposed. Nia was on the other side, wishing that his other hand was exposed so she could touch it. As curious as she was, she dared not touch the dead man's face, which only a minute after death still appeared very much alive. The muscles had only barely slackened; the color of ash had not yet infiltrated his complexion.

On the other side of the bed where the eager family stood waiting, there was a sudden, collective gasp. Nia assumed that meant the ring had chosen its next host, and soon they would all be escorted out and she would see no more. Then the gasp turned into a series of confused whispers, and when she looked up, she saw her cousins and their parents stooping and pointing at something under the bed.

Without warning, she felt a searing pain in her foot. She shrieked and tried to jump back, but it felt like a nail had been driven through her arch and pinned her to the spot. Nia clawed desperately at her skirts to see what had bitten her and sent this poison through her body, but when she exposed her foot, all she could see was a pearly sheen creeping up her shin. She screamed again and looked around her for help, but she was only met with faces full of rage and confusion.

The shimmer seeped into her skin and out of sight, but she felt the power of the ring moving through her body, burning like acid. After what felt like a lifetime, the sensation reached her shoulder, then her elbow, her hand. Here the pain stopped, and the prismatic gleam resurfaced and congealed on her middle finger. A glistening band emerged from her flesh—a swirl of gold, silver, and black—as it decided what its new shape should be.

The ring had made its choice, and against all the odds, it had chosen her.

Phoebe Darqueling

Phoebe Darqueling is a storytelling vagabond who can be found blogging at SteampunkJournal.org, coordinating at the CWC, and posting excerpts and drabbles at PhoebeDarqueling.com. She quit working in the real world a few years ago after a "quarter-life crisis", but writing and making art is helping her make a full recovery. Visit her author page (https://phoebedarqueling.com/) to find out more about her upcoming series, Mistress of None, and all of Phoebe's shenanigans at Steampunk conventions.

www.ingramcontent.com/pod-product-compliance
Lightning Source LLC
Chambersburg PA
CBHW020906200626
46814CB00001BA/195